John Patterson Lundy

The Saranac Exiles

A winter's Tale of the Adirondacks.

John Patterson Lundy

The Saranac Exiles
A winter's Tale of the Adirondacks.

ISBN/EAN: 9783743357228

Manufactured in Europe, USA, Canada, Australia, Japa

Cover: Foto ©Andreas Hilbeck / pixelio.de

Manufactured and distributed by brebook publishing software (www.brebook.com)

John Patterson Lundy

The Saranac Exiles

THE

SARANAC EXILES:

A Winter's Tale of the Adirondacks.

NOT BY

W. SHAKESPEARE.

"Pray that your flight be not in the winter."

THE AUTHOR'S UNPUBLISHED EDITION,
FOR PRIVATE DISTRIBUTION.

Philadelphia.
1880.

ADVERTISEMENT.

SPECIMEN frostwork of the Adirondacks—Of recent production—Frozen as compactly and fantastically as six consecutive winter months could do it—Easily scratched—More easily dissolved—Quite ephemeral—Hazy observations and floating recollections of a dozen years; thin, vapory films of fancy; cloudy experiences, cumulated opinions, and dark lowering denunciations—all here condensed and crystallized. No critics are invited or hired to inspect the work. Patient invalids may derive some useful information from it, or a little diversion. Commended to the loyal students and lovers of Nature. Written especially for all Saranac Exiles, past, present and future, whose winter experience is sure to be, Reader, not *As You Like It:*

> Blow, blow, thou winter wind,
> Thou art not so unkind
> As man's ingratitude.

CONTENTS.

THE SARANAC EXILES.

I.

INCEPTION.

OUR Saranac exile began in storm and earthquake.
None of us were going to be married, and the bad
weather did not alarm our fears, nor did the earthquake disjoint our spirits. We were a set of jolly
invalids bent on having as good a time as possible,
and minding our autocratic doctors as much as we
pleased. Some of us were in the habit of philoso-
phizing a little after the manner of David Hume,
and the antecedent cause of all this hubbub in earth
and sky was not hard to find. The loons had been
piteously wailing night and day before the storm
burst; therefore, the loons had caused the storm.
Lunatic scribblers of funny magazine articles pre-
ceded the earthquake; therefore, these lunatics had
caused the earthquake. *Non sequitur*, do you say?
But does not every cause go before its effect?
Yes; but every effect must have an adequate cause.
True; but—read this initial chapter carefully and
impartially, and then decide the matter of adequate
cause.

2

That fair and " fancy-free " maiden of journalism, significantly styling itself *Atlantica Menstrua*, had been trying with all its feminine might and main to verify the Adirondacks from the horsey encomiums of ex-parson Murray. Month after month did this ocean maid pour forth her humorous effusions in vindication of the Adirondacks and in smiling derision of the bombastic and incredulous account given of them by this poor, bankrupt, clerical horse-jockey. To be sure, the wit was not very sparkling or pungent, and the humor was the gentlest and thinnest compound possible. But the author had gained an entrance into the charmed circle of the immortal *Cabiri* of Boston, and that was all-sufficient. Kings rule in church and state, why not in the realms of literature and science? Kings are out of date; and republics are again coming into fashion to be ruled and ruined by partisan oligarchs as of old. The republic of letters is scarcely an exception to the rule. The great literary gods nod their august heads on the heights of Charlestown and Bunker Hill, and lo! publishers and people gather round in eager expectancy; one for the large profits of trade, the other for momentary gratification. The foremost scholar of the time in the literature of Dante and his age gains no favor here, because he happens to be a modest and unknown denizen of the Quaker City on the Delaware. Homer is not half so witty as Holmes, and Plato's philosophy is

superseded by Fiske's. Boston is Athens and
Pergamos and Alexandria rolled into one, with the
insignificant modern additions of Oxford, Cam-
bridge and the German universities. Lettered and
artistic culture has here reached the very zenith of
all possible attainment to find in suicide, murder
and Ben. Butler, the chief end of man. Prof.
Webster, the artist Hunt, and Butler's large following, give point and illustration to the superior
culture and intellectuality of Boston. Butler trod
religion in the mud during the war, in the person of
her representative, Chaplain Hudson, the gentle
and accomplished Shakesperian scholar; is it any
wonder that Boston follows him with votes and
plaudits? Her scholars must ignore religion
altogether; and some of them have already appointed a committee of investigation of the cruel
ways of God to men, whose report is to be read at
the great and final judgment, and the Almighty
Himself to be put upon trial. As yet, this is an
open secret only bruited at literary dinner-parties.

It is as plain, therefore, as the nose on a man's
face that the *Cabiri*, of Boston, have taken the
affairs of the whole universe in charge, and that the
old gods of the Oriental Pantheon are wholly de-
throned and gone into permanent exile. The march
of empire has been westward, and Boston is its seat.
Let us be grateful. Let us pray. If any one
wishes to know who these old *Cabiri* are, let him

read Lord Byron's favorite book on the subject, published many years since by that rare and accomplished scholar, George Stanley Faber.

Inasmuch as the Adirondacks constitute the oldest part of the Western Continent, if not the very oldest portion of the habitable earth, it was surely a very characteristic and proper thing to do thus to investigate their claims to this remote antiquity; and, if possible, verify their blue blood descent and genealogy. Blue blood is very dear to the heart of Boston; and it would be not only a singular gratification but a proud confirmation of her rightful supremacy over this region, to find that the blue magnetic iron and steel here abounding in such vast quantities as to be practically inexhaustible, were veritable elements of the aristocratic current throbbing in her own veins. Common iron is brown and gives color to the blood of the world's very ordinary people. The blue iron of the Adirondacks is exceptional and much sought after to make the blue blood and hard steel of the arrogant aristocracy of wealth and lordly presumption. The new member of the *Cabiri* ring was despatched on the momentous errand of investigation. Much was expected from the mission. A whole summer was diligently occupied in the verification of the Adirondacks. Among other things, it was discovered that these blue-blood mountains had not escaped the universal curse of the *benefit of clergy*. "A

minister of some sort of everlasting gospel, with
a smooth-shaven face," who might once have been
a gentleman, was actually detected in pursuit of a
deer swimming in the water to escape from the dogs,
and yet was unable to kill it with a thin shingle
of a paddle, passing it over to his guide to cut its
throat, and eating of the fresh venison at supper.
Emphasis is laid upon the strange fact that this
smooth-shaven minister of some sort of everlasting
gospel " *was* a gentleman," as though it might justly
be a matter of grave doubt that others of the cloth
were gentlemen, or leaving it to be inferred that
they were gentlemen of this questionable type.
The covert sneer and the omission of the capital G
in Gospel, betray the animus of the writer, and
leave the impression that his gentle humor is the
soft cat's paw that can scratch and tear the mean,
contemptible, mousing clergy at least, grown fat on
the cheese of some sort of everlasting gospel, and
on venison brutally killed out of season. Perhaps
though, he was only playing with Parson Murray,
and putting him to torture and death.

The whole dribble of *Atlantica Menstrua* in its
vindication and verification of the Adirondacks
was to this effect, viz.: that the needless slaughter
of a poor wood-chuck was magnified into the kill-
ing of a great black bear; that Nature was pitiless,
stoical and brutal because, without a guide, this
city green-horn wandered into the woods and lost

2*

himself for a few hours; that he actually caught a
trout nearly a pound in weight that threatened his
very life, so savagely did it fight and tear around;
that, Jaques-like, he pitied a poor old doe chased to
death by dogs and forever separated from her
fawn; that he really found one man in this wilderness who read the *New York Tribune*, and had become a philosopher and a poet; and above all and
finally, that he had once tried the experiment of
camping out with ladies and got wet. Could investigation go further? Is not the verification
complete? Mr. Colvin may step aside, and his
scientific survey of the Adirondack region may
cease. The New York Legislature need pass
no more laws for the better preservation of the
Adirondack Forest for sapient governors like Rob-
inson to veto, since a Warner comes to make us
smile and be happy in the possession and perusal of
his inimitable verification.

Good old John Cheney was not very compli-
mentary in his criticism of Parson Headley's book
on the Adirondacks, simply because of its exag-
gerations and fancy touches; Murray's book created
a furore for a time, and misled many a poor invalid
to his death, and lured many a tourist and sportsman to utter vexation and disappointment by its
wild assertions and fictitious episodes; and thus
far, among the matter-of-fact guides and people of
this region, Warner's verification of the Adiron-

dacks falls short of the mark. It has produced no
impression; it is almost unknown. When I took
it out one day to read to the boys in camp, nobody
smiled but myself; and one of them, more blunt
and bold than the rest, slapped his thighs and exclaimed: "more trash and lies about the Adirondacks." If the literature of the Adirondacks is
ever to produce any good results, such as the inde-
fatigable and accomplished Colvin has for several
years been attempting by his scientific exploration
and survey of the region, it must rise above the
mere buffoonery of the "modern Babes in the
Woods," Stoddard's hand-book of "The Adirondacks Illustrated," and even such an obvious
travesty of Murray's performances, as Warner's
contributions to *The Atlantic Monthly.* All of
them and others like them are utterly unworthy of
the subject. Perhaps this attempt of a Saranac
exile will succeed no better. So be it. The diversion of many a weary and painful hour in the preparation of the work must be its own reward.

Nero fiddled while Rome was burning up. Fun
is extracted from the Adirondack forest, more
rapidly disappearing before axe and fire than is
commonly thought or admitted. Let the great
pines go down, and miles of aromatic balsams disappear in roaring flames and pitchy smoke, what
matters it so long as profitable fun gladdens the
face and fills the pockets of our popular publishers?

Right earnest, plain, manly **work done for the** preservation of this **and other** American **forests** from the devilish spirit of wantonness **and greed,** is not in the line of our pictorial popular **maga-** zines, and may **go** begging like a tramp. Bagpiper **&** Brothers, Spitzenberg **&** Co., the *Atlantica Menstrua*, and others like them, disdain **the manu-** script with smiles and thanks. The **title is not** taking; **the** subject is trite ; the style is heavy; and the author **is not well enough known.** Even **little** Beer and **Breeches** turn up their noses **at it ; and** the great millionaire **Puckerbed,** finding no money in it, catches up his **old hat and trots off to have it** ironed, **leaving you to some new speculations on** the subject **of economy and the acquisition of** wealth. **Aldus printed model books from love of** good literature ; **Pickering was his bankrupt** En- glish disciple ; but Puckerbed, the American **Aldus,** will run no risks. So far as Aldus **is** concerned, **it is** a name given to **a** profitable hotel **in** which Puckerbed is deeply interested ; and he **is annoyed** if any body hints that he has gone into the hotel business **on** the reputation of **the old Roman** Aldus. This encouragement **of** native American literature is having a most happy effect. It enforces Darwin's doctrine of "the survival of the fittest," and gives us the immortal works of the Boston *Cabiri.*

On an early Sunday morning, November 4th,

1877, just after the materials of the " Adirondacks verified " had been carefully and laboriously collected together, an earthquake shook the whole region to its deepest foundations. The shock was felt in Canada and along the Hudson River below Albany. Hume's philosophy of antecedent and consequence never had a better illustration. Seldom or never, within the memory of living inhabitants, had such a thing been known before. No tradition of anything like it among the little surviving remnant of the St. Regis and Saranac Indian tribes is known to exist. Early explorers and lumbermen of the region recall nothing of the kind. No such effect had ever been produced by Headley or Murray. Even John Burroughs, when he explored the Adirondacks for new specimens of birds and to feel the pulse of nature to ascertain how much vigor was yet left in her veins, never once felt such an earthquake-throb as this. Had he been looking for ancient aristocratic blue blood, it might have been different. The blue blood would doubtless have asserted its vigor in grand style. But being nothing more than a careful naturalist and a pleasant writer on the special subject of ornithology, and having no prominent place among the blue blood immortals of the exclusive *Cabiri* junto, of course dear old mother Nature could not be expected to give any special extraordinary intimation of her long genealogy from the King of Kings to such a poor plebeian as this, even though he might be one of her most loving and loyal sons. The secrets of Nature are only for the favorites of the family. The elder sons inherit the title-deeds and family records. When, therefore, a Warner comes on a mission of verification from the great intellectual Chiefs of Boston, what could be expected but an earthquake?

Still-hunters have gone through this peaceful wilderness for years slaying their three and four score deer every season, each; amateur sportsmen have followed in their train with breech-loading rifles and double-barrelled shot-guns, to indulge a sharp practice at targets, empty cans and whisky-bottles, or expedite the flight of some solitary crow, hawk, or "shite-poke," in the absence of better game; the woods ring every summer with the obscene songs and genteel blasphemies and nightly orgies of young *blasé* city swells or old used-up *roués;* roguish guides play their tricks and crack their stale coarse jokes, gamble and carouse, after the hard day's work of two or three hours at the oars, or are sleeping in the woods with the hounds chained to their belts while you are watching for deer during six or eight long weary hours; trout fishermen, with costly split bamboo rods and ponderous fly-books, go forth with guides and gaiety to the "best fishing-grounds in northern New York," and return with scores of

frogs and bull-pouts; havoc and desolation mark
the track of the iron master, the lumberman and
the squatter; railroads and steamboats have invaded the region, and threaten its peaceful life and
beneficent influences; large fashionable hotels are
growing up, with more to come in the near future;
swarms of tourists and invalids resort here for
pleasure and health; sporting is doomed, and in
many places already well nigh dead; the doctors
and fashionable women are doing their worst to
make this wilderness otherwise more attractive;
artists and authors are striving to make it better
known; and yet for all this, no shock or commotion was ever felt here until the blue blood verification was complete. Then, and not until then, did
these mountains skip like rams, and the hills like
young sheep. Old Whiteface shook with envy and
indignation at Mt. Marcy lest the monument of
our Boston Mercury should be placed on the loftier
summit, mounted like the prophet Balaam on an
ass, lifting one hand to the constellation of the
Great Bear, and the other to the constellation of
the Fishes, in proud and perpetual reminder of the
grand achievements here consummated over bear
and fish, and so worthy of immortal record in
bright silvery characters on one of the pages of the
illuminated blue book of Heaven.

Material cause, efficient cause, formal cause, and
final cause, as old Aristotle has them, are here em-

braced in Hume's invariable antecedent; for is it
not a fact of almost daily experience that the whole
North American continent shakes at every after-
dinner manifestation of Boston wit and wisdom?
No wonder Dr. McCosh spent one whole summer
in the Adirondacks diligently studying the subject
of Teleology anew. The whole design of the ex-
alted blue-veined Adirondack region he might find
to be nothing more or less than a summer paradise
for the development of the rare humor of our sweet
Boston innocents, with special reference to the
transfusion of more blue blood into the delicate
veins of the maid, *Atlantica Menstrua.*

Mighty winds may be indications of earthquake,
but are they the invariable antecedents? Heralds
and attendants they may be, but are they efficient
causes? Such a tremendous vacuum was created
by the departure of the great *Atlantic* humorist
from the Adirondack region that it is easy to account for the high winds that blew for two whole
weeks just preceding the earthquake. A dark, unbroken, leaden canopy of clouds hung low and
sullen over the entire wilderness. Drenching rain-
fall, fierce gusts of sleet and snow alternately swept
by, with little or no sunshine to relieve the gloom.
The great forest roared like the sea in storm or like
Niagara. All the springs, and rills, and ponds, and
lakes innumerable of this elevated region were now
filling up to supply the wants of man and beast in

the distant plains and valleys below. It is just
possible that this Adirondack region may have been
designed to serve the purpose of a water-supply for
the sustenance of animal and human life, like the
Alps and Appenines in Europe, or the Caucasus and
Himalaya ranges in Asia, or the Mountains of the
Moon in Africa, or the Rockies and Cordilleras in
America. Possibly, were we not confronted by the
fact that Boston wisdom recognizes no such designs. Water is too thin and insipid for Boston
deglutition; it must have blue blood. Ogre-like,
its fierce grim spirit stalks all abroad, with squint-
eyes in a "fine frenzy rolling," terrifying the
children by its hoarse iteration. " Fee, fi, fo, fum,
I smell the blood of an Englishman; dead or alive,
I will have some; just for the sake of a little fun."
The numerous mountain-peaks, clad in snowy vesture, trembled at the sight of this man-eating
monster, as the startled sheep do in Höfner's picture at the sight of a jack-rabbit mounted on a
rock. The rabbit looks as if he enjoyed the fun of
so terrifying a whole flock of sheep grouped behind the great ram for protection. So Marcy stood
lifting high his head in utter amazement at the apparition, with the whole Adirondack flock behind
him waiting for the charge. Thump, thunder and
crash it did, as the great head went down in the
rushing onset of that swift stormy earthquake.
The ogre nimbly slipped into the first convenient

3

hole, sickly laughing on the other side of his mouth
as the rock received the shock.

Encamped on the shore of that little limpid lake
called the " Tear of the Clouds," 4,000 feet up the
sides of Mt. Marcy, one might have divined the
meaning of this storm and earthquake. It had a
voice of majesty and power proclaiming the very
inception of this whole mountain and lake region in
far distant and more terrible convulsions of nature,
the purpose of which seems to have been that which
an old Hebrew poet and philosopher designates,
when he speaks of the wisdom and forethought of
the Creator—He layeth up the deep as in a treasure
house : the waters go up as high as the hills, and
down to the valleys beneath : He sendeth the
springs into the rivers which run among the hills :
all the beasts of the field drink thereof, and the
wild asses quench their thirst ; beside them shall
the fowls of the air have their habitation, and sing
among the branches. He watereth the hills from
above ; the earth is filled with the fruit of His
works, — grass for the cattle, green herb for the service of man—food, wine and oil. And all these
dependent upon the pure fresh water of every
mountain range in the world, clad with the thick
green verdure of pine, spruce and balsam, on purpose to collect, preserve and regularly distribute
the life-giving supply. The quick puffs and blasts
of wind in the pines overhead seemed to be dis-

tinct voices proclaiming the great law of forest-
preservation as a necessity for the preservation of
human and animal life ; and they said emphatically
to the idle and thoughtless campers, " if you cut,
burn and destroy this forest more, you shall be cast
out to starvation and death."

" Ha! ha! you're only blowing," answers the
camp, " blow on and burst your bellows ; we're here
to enjoy ourselves in our own way, and shall play
the very devil in the woods if we choose. There's
no better place than this to let the Old Boy loose.
Pile up the camp-fire, and make the kettle boil for
the whisky punch. If the forest kindles and makes
a roaring conflagration, you winds are responsible
for the mischief. We shall drink, fiddle, dance
and sing."

This is one of the ways and means by which
great tracts of this beautiful and beneficent forest
have been destroyed, as the frequent fire-slashes
attest, some of them miles in extent ; but any popular humorist who should venture to call attention
to the matter in booklet or magazine article would
only get his fingers burned when he burns his rejected manuscript. Publishers and their laughing
patrons are thus in full accord with gay and festive
campers over the increasing destruction of this
magnificent Adirondack forest. Game laws are
here a mere laughing stock ; nobody regards them,
for the reason that they are seldom or never en-

forced ; and because the poor natives here depend
on game for all the fresh meat they ever eat, all the
year round. Sportsmen and campers must take
fish, partridge and deer during their summer vaca-
tions, or live on salt pork and canned meats ; and
one of the most notorious violators of the game
laws of the state of New York is the present Super-
intendent of her Prisons, Pilsbury, a greedy angler
who took from the spawning beds of Big Clear
Pond, during September, 1879, a barrel of large
trout which he salted down for the winter's use.
He enforces the punishment of other violated laws
and escapes merited punishment himself.

But the violated laws of Nature carry with them
their own punishment. Forest-destruction uniformly brings with it drought, famine, desolation
and death. It makes deserts and pestilential wastes
where no man can live, and from which all game
disappears. No fish can live in warm, depleted
water-courses ; no deer can remain in settled districts or forests disturbed by fire and the woodman's
axe. In all the cleared districts of the Adirondack
region and around all the hotels, fishing and hunting are almost at an end, by the inexorable law of
forest-destruction and disturbance ; and if this region is to retain any of its game in the future, its
forest must be most rigidly kept from further destruction.

And then again, as a health-resort this natural

evergreen garden ought to be preserved. Every
body knows, or ought to know, that trees are necessary to the purity and salubrity of the atmosphere, as absorbents of noxious gases. How much
impaired health has already been restored, and how
many valuable lives have been saved by the pure
air of the Adirondacks, it would not be easy to
compute; but the experience of some of us Saranac exiles, extending now over a period of a dozen
years of consecutive sojourn, enables one of their
number to assert that, of the hundreds of delicate
persons who have been sent here by their physicians
for health, rest, and recuperation, at least three-
fourths have found benefit and length of days in
consequence. I write knowingly and feelingly
here, because within the circle of my own dear
family two of its beloved members have derived
incalculable good from the summer, autumn and
winter sojourn in this elevated mountain and lake
region. Three eminent physicians and one chemical
scientist of great ability and original research, whom
I have long known, have personally tested the
healthful qualities of this Adirondack atmosphere,
and have arrived at the same conclusion respecting it.

Dr. Albert R. Leeds, of the Stevens Institute, of
Hoboken, New Jersey, in a pamphlet on the
" Recent Progress in Sanitary Science," says of
ozone tests : " As an instance, I may cite some un

3*

published observations during the past summer
(1876), upon the atmosphere of the Adirondacks,
where the indications of ozone were of the most
decided character, and at times of atmospheric disturbance, intense. In this pure mountain air, the
invalid, prostrated with malarial poison or catarrhal
affection, rapidly regained mental vigor and bodily
strength. Similar ozone tests, exposed during the
same season in Hoboken, where catarrhs are rife,
and where the badly drained marshes, if they do
not actually produce ague, are at least very un-
favorable to recovery from it, showed a great defi-
ciency in the amount of ozone."

In "The Medical Record," of New York, for
April and May, 1879, Drs. Loomis and Trudeau
speak of the perfect purity of the Adirondack
atmosphere as necessary for the healing of diseased
lungs, and attribute this healing quality to the
presence of ozone. The purity of the atmosphere
and the presence of ozone are attributed to the
elevation of the region, its sandy soil, its broken,
undulating surface which ensures perfect drainage,
and the absence of dense population. The forest
and the lakes also have their due share of healthful influence. "That the atmosphere of such a
region, especially when set in motion, should, by
its contact with myriads of tree-tops and pine
sheaves, become heavily laden with ozone is a
natural sequence. Whatever other properties this

gas may hereafter be found to possess, we know
that it is a powerful disinfectant, and Nature's
choice agent for counteracting atmospheric impurities. This process, which, during the summer
months is carried on by all varieties of trees,
during the winter months is maintained by the
evergreens, while the deciduous trees are deprived
of their foliage. Pine, balsam, spruce and hemlock
trees abound, and the air is heavily laden with the
resinous odors which they exhale. An agent,
which it is universally admitted, exerts a most
beneficial influence on diseased mucous membranes
is thus brought in contact with the air-passages,
while balsamics, which are also disinfectants, purify
the atmosphere, which is constantly impregnated
with them. Besides this, the air of the wilderness
is optically pure, noticeably free from dust or visible particles of any kind. The invalid, therefore,
is here surrounded by a zone of pure air, which
separates him, as it were, from the germ-pervaded
world, and his diseased lungs are supplied with a
specially vitalized atmosphere, free from germs
and impurities of any kind, and laden with the
resinous exhalations of myriads of evergreens."

This concurrent scientific testimony, seems to
reveal another design of this Adirondack region
and forest, which is that of a health resort in a
pure atmosphere ; but a design altogether unrecog-
nized by our *Atlantic* humorist in his gentle and

lamb-like verification. Is it worth while to go on
with our plea for forest-preservation, so conducive
to atmospheric purity and human welfare, when it
is not even deemed worthy of mention by the sagacious Charles Dudley? Shall our cause here and
now be final? Shall the dear old Adirondacks be
dismissed from further consideration by a foolish
grin or a covert sneer? Heaven help our infirmities in protesting against the prostitution of this
paradise to mere frolic and fun. We conceive our
cause to be good enough for the best investigation
we can give it; and we shall not write *finis* until
our story is all told. The debt of gratitude we
owe to this restful health-giving region is too deep
for silence or for trifling.

LITTLE TUPPER LAKE.

There is a lull in the storm and it looks like
clearing. The reader is invited to join a little
hunting expedition during these latter days of
October and·beginning of November. The air is
crisp and fresh; the hounds are keen and eager;
the guides are unusually confident, and full of
promises of good sport. We shall go to the famous
region of Little Tupper and try our luck. Jack
Stout ingratiates himself into our confidence, by
his smooth, fluent tongue and affable manners, as
our chief guide. Pliny Robin's fat boy is a slow
apology for another guide; and young Moody,

best of all, will join the expedition when we reach
his father's house on the Raquette River. The
Sweeny carry or portage is closed, or is too muddy
to cross, and we shall go round by Corey's. Mrs.
Corey's venison steaks and nice coffee are worth
the additional time and trouble. It is a long and
tedious ride down the Raquette to Sim Moody's.
This river was once the sparkling joy of the
angler's paradise; it is now the noxious sewer of a
malarial desolation, so doomed and dammed by the
Legislature of New York for the accommodation
of a few Potsdam mill owners. Twenty-seven
miles of the most beautiful valley in the world have
been utterly ruined by the great dam at Setting-
Pole rapids, of which iniquity Mr. George Dawson
thus feelingly speaks in his book on the " Pleasures
of Angling:" " It has caused the overflow of tens
of thousands of acres. * * * The receding
waters in midsummer must leave this whole region
a reeking mass of decaying vegetation, filling the
air with fever-exciting miasma, and making a sojourn in the midst of it exceedingly hazardous.
Its effects are already seen in the thousands of
dead trees which mar the beauty of the river's
banks, and the coming August will demonstrate its
pernicious influence upon the comfort and health
of visitors, and the scattered residents upon its
borders. If the effects apprehended are realized,
the dam will be abated as a nuisance, by lawful

process or otherwise—unless indeed the threatened
suits for damages by parties aggrieved, shall induce
its owners to rid themselves of troublesome litiga-
gation by destroying the dam themselves" (p. 217).

Since this was written and published, a commission has been appointed by the New York Legislature to investigate the matter and report ; and that
commission has now completed its investigation,
and say in advance of their official report that the
condition of the Raquette, from Johnson's to
Setting-Pole Rapids is so horrible that, if it had
been anticipated, no Legislature would have given
permission to build the dam at all, and that it must
come down. Even so, it will take many years for
a new growth of forest trees and the restoration of
this hideous desolation to anything like its original
beauty and attractiveness.

It is an hour or two after sundown before we
reach Sim Moody's, chilled to the bone. A blueish-
gray wall of clouds was rising along the westerly
horizon, slowly and portentously. The warm welcome, fire, and supper of the neat, trim farm-house,
with a good sleep, restore our spirits and energies.
But the morning is not very promising ; the sky is
completely overcast, and a stiff cold breeze is blowing. No matter, time is precious; hope is bright
and warm. We enter our boats, and soon find ourselves tossing and pitching on Big Tupper Lake.
Rain begins to fall copiously, and our hands nearly

freeze in bailing the boats. We reach Cronk's
about noon, after the hardest pulling and experience against wind and water of all our lives. The
down-pour that afternoon was tremendous, and the
night brought snow. Sunshine, wind and scudding
clouds came in the morning, and we push on up
the Bog River towards Little Tupper, which we
reach before sunset. Two fat deer hang near the
landing by way of welcome and good cheer, at
Pliny Robin's hostelry.

After a late supper we retire for the night under
the roaring and swaying pines around the house,
only to be rocked and tossed, and terrified far more
than we had been in our boats for two days on
stormy waters. One great bang or thud put an end
to sound sleep instantly, and I quickly start up in
bed to look through the window to see what had
happened. I thought that the pine grove around
the house had been knocked down by a cyclone, as
it has since been by one. But the tall, slender
pines were all standing motionless. Then a terrific
thunder-clap was suggested, only that the roar was
not so sharp and distinct, being more of the nature
of an underground explosion. The shock or motion was instantaneous and appalling, as though the
mountains had fallen down or the solid ground was
giving way. The strange and sudden concussion
made the stovepipe rattle and the unwashed supper
dishes dance on the bare pine table; the bed and

the log cabin heaved for an instant, and then all
was still again.

Not knowing what better to do than await some
further developments, and then take to my heels
like Launcelot Gobbo, I was somewhat startled by
the appearance of a pale and trembling apparition
gliding up to my bed with a dim tallow candle in
one hand, and, as I now conjecture, with an old
broom or a Winchester rifle in the other. Here was
a new and startling development, indeed. The apparition was in human shape; and Shakespeare had
taught me that a man might take up arms against
a sea of troubles, and by opposing end them; but
was it also possible thus to deal with this tremendous midnight marauder of an earthquake? Was it
Warner reappearing upon the scene at the crisis of
his verification? Or was it Diogenes looking still
for his honest man in this remote wilderness?
Warning was now too late, and the cynic philosopher would here search in vain. Honest men never
came to these woods except to be corrupted. At
last a low husky voice, breaking loose from the
jaws of the apparition, timidly ventured the question, " Doctor, are you all right ? "

It was a great relief, and I breathed freely enough
to say, " Is it you, John? what's the matter?"

This was a question somewhat confusing and
irritating to the nervous guide, and pitching his
voice on a higher key, he exclaimed, " Matter!

Great heavens, sir, didn't you feel and hear that earthquake which has just gone by? That's matter enough, I should say."

As this was my first experience of an earthquake, and John seemed to be so well informed about it, as indeed he was on every subject, if one might judge from his glib talk and great confidence in himself, my reply was, " Certainly, John, I felt and heard something strange and unaccountable; but how do you know it was an earthquake!"

" Because it couldn't have been anything else; for nothing else in these woods could have waked me up so quick out of a sound sleep. I thought I was a goner. It wasn't wind, and it wasn't thunder. It shook me like the devil, and scared me nearly to death. Nothing but an earthquake or the day of judgment could do that."

Intuition was here right for once. Investigation was impossible, and experience in his case there was none, just as in mine. Curious to know the meaning of the broom or rifle in John's hand, I asked him to explain it. " Well," said he, " that unlikely story of a bear hunt which you read us last night must have been running in my head faster than Warner was running through the raspberry patch; and if I seized my gun and came in here on the double-quick, I hope to be excused for taking to my heels with a big earthquake after me.

3

The story was uncommonly absurd, and I laughed myself to sleep over it."

" For that purpose only was it written, to raise a laugh," I replied; "and I state the simple truth when I say that there was no bear at all, but only a poor harmless woodchuck."

Although Jack Stout was somewhat better educated than the most of Adirondack guides, he was still a strict literalist and tolerated no play of the imagination in the narration of incidents and adventures of Adirondack life. Striving to the utter most to be popular as a guide himself, he would not allow it to be right in a poor author to make his magazine articles popular at the expense of bald, literal truth. All creative fancies and captivating embellishments were lies in his estimation so far as Adirondack literature is concerned, while at the same time his own seductive and misleading stories about good fishing and hunting, his depreciation of other guides, and his constant iteration and reiteration of his own superior qualities, betrayed the usual inconsistency of poor human nature. A poor sickly guide who could talk intelligently about Homer and Virgil, as John could, might be excused for a little brag and self-laudation in the struggle after popularity and existence. His lies were no worse than Headley's, Murray's, and Warner's; nor were his struggles after popularity and a livelihood any more reprehensible. While a

student, his health had broken down, and he came
to the Adirondacks for recuperation. Becoming
enamored of the life here and finding it necessary
to remain in order to live at all, he was compelled
to resort to guiding, fishing, hunting, and trapping
for subsistence.

"Well, well," he exclaimed, "if that's the way to
gain popularity and a living in literature and professional life, I'm satisfied to have lost my health
and to be a poor hard-working guide, sometimes
earning enough in summer to keep me through our
long hard winter, and sometimes not."

Hard as a guide's life here now must needs be by
reason of the scarcity of game and the failure of
lumbering, and knowing from long experience the
precarious nature of professional life, I could not
help admiring the pluck and the wisdom of John's
choice. His young dream of ambition in law and
letters had all faded out; and he was now content
with the shelter of a little slab hut, a little coarse
food, whisky and tobacco. To such a low and
sorry pass as this may ill-health and poverty com-
pel the loftiest ambition to descend, just as the
eagle here stoops from his highest flight to catch a
fish or a hare.

Believing, as I do, with Plato and St. Paul, that
nature is a living organism and not a mere mechan-
icism, instinct in every part with a Divine spiritual
life, and not with a blind, aimless, wild, and ungov-

ernable force merely ; and curious to know John's
opinion of the earthquake, I said to him; " Science
is searching for facts in order to ascertain the law
or modal cause of earthquakes, whether it be chemical, volcanic, or due to the mere cooling and shrink-
ing of the earth's crust ; what do you think it is ?"

Adirondack guides have decided opinions on
every subject under heaven and beyond it ; their
knowledge is as vast and deep as their conceit and
presumption. John was no exception, even with
the smattering of knowledge gained in a Vermont
labor academy ; if anything he was even more oracular and self-conceited than his fellow guides ; for
him and his precarious occupation a little learning
was a dangerous thing, inasmuch as when this Sir
Oracle went into the woods on a hunt no dog was
ever known to bark ; and therefore I was all the
more curious to ascertain his opinion on the subject
of earthquakes. Looking at his candle and snuffing
it with his finger and thumb, as if to gain some additional light on the difficult question, the oracle
gave forth this profound response : " You must
know that the earth is full of caves and holes, and
that these caves and holes have rivers and lakes in
them ; when this water has worn away the foundations of the hills and mountains, and some of them
slip down, there is a great thump and shaking far
and near, or an earthquake."

My reply was that I had already heard something

like this idea of earthquakes expressed before by
an eminent geologist, and that John must have
picked it up in his intercourse with some scientific
gentleman in his exploration of the Adirondack
region, adding that the objection to this and all other
theories of earthquakes so far advanced was that
none of them fully accounted for the facts. Mountains or strata that slip down into big holes are
somehow just as high as ever; earthquakes occur
independently of volcanic eruptions, and volcanic
eruptions occur without producing earthquakes;
chemical agencies and explosions deep down in the
earth are beyond all human examination and experience, and are therefore matters of mere conjecture; so that the whole subject of earthquakes was
still an open question. Assenting to all this, I
next directed John's attention to Hume's theory of
causation, and asked him whether the antecedent
Warner was not the cause of the earthquake:
whether, in fact, the presence of man on the earth
had not always occasioned these and other like
commotions, since no knowledge of them exists
except within the human and historic period.
Ideas and concepts being the only basis of knowledge, of course the cause of an earthquake must be
according to our best conception of it. No other
cause is at all possible. Our knowledge and experience must determine all existences and limit all
possibilities. Beyond this knowledge and experi-

3*

ence there is nothing. Therefore, since the best
mechanical theories of earthquakes are at fault, we
are perfectly free to fall back upon Hume's philosophy of experience and invariable antecedent cause,
and account for this special Adirondack earthquake
by the theory of the special presence and interposition of our Atlantic Warner.

This muddle of metaphysics acted as a stimulus
to John's tobacco mill, causing him to eject from
the orifice of his thin straw-colored moustaches a
stream of the richest and clearest juice ever made
for the nicotine coloration of white floors or meer-
schaum pipes. " It was all darned nonsense," he
maintained ; man might be in some sense the lord
of creation, but he could't make earthquakes to
order, nor could all his boasted knowledge and experience predict when or where or how they might
come. Nature had been so uniform here for ages
in her quiet ways that the last thing to be thought
of or expected was an earthquake. It was therefore something like a miracle—a prodigious departure from the ordinary course of Nature, yet within
her domain, the result of some occult law or force
of Nature as yet but little known. John had
abandoned his slippery theory, and I had helped
him in the formulation of his present statement.
He could not consent to the proposition that the
hero of the bear story and the savage trout, and

the chase of the poor old doe had anything whatever to do with this Adirondack earthquake.

Bidding him good night, I slept soundly far into
a bright, still Sunday morning. Nature seemed to
be exhausted. And although it is always Sunday
in a vast forest solitude like this, except in storm
and earthquake, it now seemed all the more quiet
and serene by the recent contrast of our own hard
experience. Here the church doors are always
open; the grand cathedral aisles are full of light
and beauty so soft and entrancing as to fill the soul
with child-like delight, leading up as they do along
the mighty columns of evergreen life to the vast
blue apse of heaven, where clouds of incense are
rolling away in rainbow hues, and where the bright
windows are gleaming with the smiling faces of our
dear departed ones in the blessed company of the
Lord and His countless host of celestial and earthly
worthies. The organ here for the most part dis-
courses the soft pathetic minor music of Lent,
reserving its thunder and trumpet tones for the
Easter resurrection of Nature, and the tumultuous
joy and plenitude of her summer life; and on a
Sunday morning like this, the very bridal of heaven
and earth, one might hear as Elijah did after the
storm and earthquake which shook his forest
retreat, the still, small voice of the Eternal, ming-
ling with the bird calls, and whispering peace and
love. An æolian harp is in every tree; and a peace-

ful benediction stills the tumult and soothes the
pain of life. The soul rests in reverent attitude
and devout contemplation as a conscious and appreciative partaker of all this Divine Nature, breathing
out its recollections and aspirations for the eternal
home whence it came, and giving vent to its instinctive joy of worship. It was in the forests of
the primitive world that the recognition of the
Divine in nature was first made and worship first
began ; it is here that the sad and tempted soul of
man still comes for peace and strength to be for
awhile alone with God. Moses and Elijah, and a
far greater than both of these, retired into the wilderness to think and pray. Of course the devil
appeared to dissuade them from their holy pursuits
and purposes, but the opposition and trial only
strengthened their good resolves. Boston makes a
huge outcry against the slaughter of deer in our
Adirondack forest, but has nothing to say about
its preservation as a grand natural temple for restful meditation and worship, which, after all, is its
main design.

Before the consideration of this important matter
in the next chapter, it may be well to conclude this
with a brief statement of our experience of Little
Tupper as a hunting and fishing region. Years
ago, when Mr. George Dawson found so much
pleasure in angling along the Raquette River
and elsewhere in the Adirondacks, his remark

about "Little Tupper as a great resort for deer,"
is undoubtedly true, and sportsmen were well paid
in going there for them ; but the region has of late
years been hunted to death on account of its traditional fame, and our own experience for two consecutive autumnal hunting seasons was not encouraging. Early November may not be the best time
for hunting because it is apt to be too stormy ; but
when six men and as many dogs spend two weeks
in capturing six deer only, something else than
stormy weather must be the matter. Either men
and dogs do not understand their business, or deer
are scarce. During our stay at Little Tupper in
November, 1877, my kinsman and companion, Mr.
C., saw no other deer than the two dead ones
already hanging at Pliny Robins's shanty on our
arrival there, although we hunted as often as the
cold windy and snowy weather permitted. As for
myself, I saw but two deer alive, one of which I
shot. The guides captured all the rest ; and they
made us believe that we had come too late in the
season for good hunting. The next year we resolved
to go earlier by a month, and the October of 1878
gave us the perfection of weather. We had other
and better guides as well as dogs ; we were near
Little Tupper for two weeks ; we hunted every day
but Sunday ; and our party of five men and four
dogs killed just four deer. Three or four other
hunting parties in the same neighborhood fared no

better than we did, not even Corey himself, who
led one of the parties, and is considered one of the
very best hunters in the woods. From all which I
draw the conclusion that deer are not so plenty
now in the Little Tupper district as they once
were, and that the sportsman had better go elsewhere for the pleasures of the chase.

In speaking of the trout fishing at Little Tupper,
Mr. Dawson says that there is something in the
water of the lake and its outlet that causes a great
deterioration in the fish, which he describes as
" lean and of poor flavor—not in winter and early
spring alone, for the trout of all waters are infested
with unpalatable and unseemly parasites until they
pass into the rapids in the spring—but at all
seasons. This positive statement may 'turn the
stomachs' of some of my friends who like to visit
this lake because its trout are sometimes large and
always abundant. But I can't help it. Truth is
truth, and unclean trout should not be eaten."

Questioning the guides about this matter, I was
informed that trout were sometimes taken here that
had worms along the inner sides of the spine, but
that they knew nothing of external parasites or
lice. Determining to find out for myself the truth
or falsity of Mr. Dawson's accusation, I went out
one dark breezy afternoon early in November with
my fly-rod to catch a trout or two for examination.
A large, well-known spawning-bed was in the first

bend of the outlet of Little Tupper near the lake; and
the familiar tamarack lamming-pole lay across a fallen
tree, projecting into the water far enough to reach
the bed, and here the trapper caught his bait during
the autumn and early winter months for his numerous traps set far and near for mink, otter, muskrat,
etc. In the elegant vernacular of the woods, this
outlet is called " The Slang." It is a sluggish
stream full of stiff grass and water lilies. I threw
my flies on the ripples of the spawning-bed, and the
response was almost instantaneous on the part of
two of the most disgusting, miserable-looking creatures in the shape and appearance of trout I had
ever seen. Poor, lean, slimy, and thin as shingles,
with the spawn dropping from them egg by egg, I
refused them entrance into the boat, and turned
them back into the water from the landing-net after
a momentary inspection. They were large enough,
and would probably have weighed two or three
pounds each at their best. Another cast brought
two others of about the same size and condition to
the net, which were likewise returned to their maternal duties. But a male trout, badly hooked and
hurt beyond recovery, upon which I had broken a
joint of my rod in striking him too near the boat,
was secured for microscopical examination and
mink bait. His gills were a mass of parasites, of a
whitish color, double, and corrugated like the lobes
of the brain. I had in mind in such examination

of the gills what Sir H. Davy says in the second edition of his *Salmonia*, p. 272, about the hucho of some of the streams of Upper Austria : "The hucho preys with great violence, and pursues his object as a foxhound or a greyhound does. I have seen them in repose : they lie like pikes, perfectly still, and I have watched one for many minutes, that never moved at all. In this respect their habits resemble those of most carnivorous and predatory animals. It is probably in consequence of these habits that they are so much infested by lice or leeches, which I have seen so numerous in spring as almost to fill their gills, and interfere with their respiration, in which case they seek the most rapid and turbulent streams to free themselves from these enemies." Izaac Walton speaks to the same purpose when he says of the trout in English waters : " You shall in winter find him to have a big head, and then to be lank, and thin, and lean ; at which time many of them have sticking on them sugs or trout-lice, which is a kind of worm, in shape like a clove or pin, with a big head, and sticks close to him and sucks his moisture ; these, I think, the trout breeds himself, and never thrives till he frees himself of them, which is when warm weather comes, and he gets from the dead still water into the sharp streams and gravel, and there rubs off these worms or lice."

Commending these statements to the special

consideration of such as fish for trout through the
ice of the Adirondack lakes and ponds during the
winter, I go on to remark that our large and abundant Little Tupper trout have no rocky, rapid,
gravelly streams to run in to free themselves from
these lice; and as a consequence they are, as Mr.
Dawson says, lean, lousy, and poor of flavor at all
seasons of the year. "The Slang" is their chief
resort outside of the lake, and slangey trout they
must always be, unfit for the refined taste of the
true angler, scholar, and gentleman.

From such an inception as all this the reader will
be disposed to infer a gloomy and tragic end of our
winter's tale. But let him or her read on and learn
that "all's well that ends well." Nature's storms
and earthquakes were not half so destructive or
hard to bear as the storms and commotions of
human passion and folly which distracted and
upheaved our little Saranac community during the
long and dreary winter of 1877–78, at which we
now smile in the vigorous reaction of restored
health and renewed cheerfulness of spirit. Our
experience convinced us that the Adirondack wilderness, while a most gloomy and inconvenient
place to pass a winter of six months in duration, is
better for health than the crowded and exciting
resorts of Southern Europe or America, even
though the cost of living may be a little greater.
The preservation of its magnificent forest as a

4

prime necessity, was the chief lesson impressed
upon us. When man had destroyed his first Paradise, the one remaining Tree of Life was guarded
by Kerubin and a flaming sword, so that the earth
might not become a complete desolation and a
silent charnel-house. From the records and papers
which contributed to the amusement of some our
long winter evenings, the following homely verses
bearing upon the subject of forest-preservation, are
selected for transcription :

ADIRONDACK GUARDIANS.

Flaming on the mountain tops,
   Standing on their slopes,
Jewel'd with the Iris drops,
   Gleaming in bright hopes,
See the mighty Kerubin,
   Guardians at the gate
Of an Eden made by sin,
   A ruined lost estate :

     Adirondacks wall it round,
     It is still a holy ground ;
     For the Tree of Life is here,
     And the crystal waters clear.

Garden of the Living God,
   Where His footsteps fall ;
By the sick and weary trod,
   At His loving call ;

Who dare cut and burn it down,
  In a madness fell ?
Making it like sultry town.
  Or a dismal hell !

    Adirondacks, guard your trust,
    From all human greed and lust—
    Health and plenty, life's pure air,
    From the hosts of grim Despair !

Flaming on the mountain tops,
  Moving on their slopes,
Jewel'd with the Iris drops,
  Gleaming in bright hopes,
Come the trooping clouds amain,
  Riding on the blast.
Pouring down relieving rain,
Routing drought and fast.

    Adirondacks, from your store,
    Send it out forevermore
    On the valley and the plain,
    For the grass and golden grain.

II

FORESTRY.

It is obvious from the nature of things and from the oldest human records that the whole land portion of our world was clothed with vegetation to make it a fit habitation for the human race; and that the human race, whether Adamic or prehistoric, first lived in forests in common with those animals which were necessary for food and clothing. Human life, therefore, had its inception in the woods, and the woods have ever been necessary to its continuance and welfare. Mountain ranges, clad in pine forest and perpetual snow, are the water-sheds for the arable plains and valleys where man has usually lived and developed his progress and civilization. The forest is below the snow line to serve the purpose of protection and regular distribution of the waters to the lowlands. Otherwise, avalanches and floods would rush down to make ruin and desolation. The Adirondack wilderness is such a water-shed, and its forest must be preserved for the welfare of the larger portion of the State of New York.

The scientific survey of this elevated portion of northern New York, by Mr. Colvin, estimates its extent at from three to five thousand square miles, diagonally traversed by the Adirondack range of mountains, some of whose peaks are over five thousand feet in height; and that the plateau itself is at an altitude of from two thousand to five thousand feet above the sea level, giving some portions of it the climate of the barren region north of the Saguenay River, in Canada. Moreover, the survey claims this region to be the wonder and glory of New York—a vast natural park or Persian paradise—one immense and silent forest, curiously and beautifully broken by the gleaming waters of a myriad of lakes, between which rugged mountain ranges rise like a sea of granite billows; and the special portion around Mount Marcy containing the sources of the Hudson River, a region of wonderful beauty and picturesqueness, and having the highest mountains in the State, which ought to be preserved from ruthless desolation by fire, as a park and pleasure resort.

This survey also, most pointedly calls attention to the purpose of the forest as far more valuable in its growth as a shelter for the snow and as a modifier of evaporation, than as cut down for lumber and as fuel for charcoal iron furnaces, now that other coal is so cheap and abundant. It insists upon the practical importance of preserving the forest of this elevated region, because of the necessities of inland commerce, as well as the necessities

4*

of health and agriculture. The continuance of
the State canals, or their enlargement for shipping
purposes, whether it be the Erie, the Champlain or
the Black River, depends in the future, as it does
almost entirely at present, on the numerous rivers
of the wilderness; and there is not a builder or a
farmer throughout the State but is interested in
preserving from fire and destruction this vast forest
which alone is capable of supplying cheap lumber
and pure water. For all time to come this vast
wilderness will remain as now the only source
within the State borders from which an unfailing
supply of water can be obtained for all the purposes of human existence. Here the water is
absolutely pure, and it is beyond all possibility of
poison or contamination, because the country does
not admit of extensive settlement. It is not possible to protect from defilement those rivers which
run through a settled country, such as the Croton
and the Schuylkill, supplying New York and Philadelphia with an impure and distasteful compound
called water. The Schuylkill water is worse than
the Croton, because it contains the slops and filth
of more towns and settlements, and chiefly because
of the percolations and washings of the vast ceme-
teries on its banks near Philadelphia. In summer,
when the river is low and sluggish, the fluid is both
scarce and disgusting, having a bilge-water odor.
After every heavy rain, and more especially in the

spring, the water is thick and muddy, like that of
the yellow Tiber at Rome. The uncertain flow of
all such rivers as now supply our large cities, together with the defilement of their waters by the
refuse of settled districts and towns along their
banks, will in time make it necessary to draw a
better and more certain supply from fresh-water
lakes, as Chicago has done. Philadelphia may
have to go to Lake Erie, and New York, Brooklyn
and the large towns on the Hudson River, may
have to go to the Adirondacks.

Mr. Colvin's survey informs us that since the
first settlement of New York, there have been constant endeavors made to clear and cultivate the
Adirondack wilderness; and crumbling buildings
here and there upon its margin and along the road-
sides far into its depths, are the records of wasted
effort, squandered capital, and ruin. These unfortunate attempts at settlement originated in wild
and false statements made by land speculators as to
the richness and fertility of the region, supported
by the specious argument that it must be fertile
and valuable because the lands on the St. Lawrence
River, further north, even in Canada, were fruitful
and productive. All this trouble, all this wasted
labor and confusion, can be directly traced to the
low state of the physical sciences in those days,
and the absolute ignorance which then existed and
has continued up to a recent period, of the science

of the atmosphere and climatology. The people of
those days did not know, and many of them do
not even yet know that, practically in agriculture,
every thousand feet of elevation is equivalent to
one or two degrees of north latitude; so that this
whole region must have a peculiar climate much
more severe than that of the lowlands of the same
latitude nearer the sea level. The elevation of
some portions of this region is equal to four degrees
of north latitude, so that agriculture is exceedingly
precarious, and for some products impossible. The
soil is sandy and rocky; there is frost every month
in the year; potato vines, buckwheat, oats and
hops are often killed early in August; the winter
begins in November and lasts usually until May;
the snow is six or seven feet deep, and the mercury
often freezes and bursts the bulb of the thermome-
ters, marking 40° below zero; so that the poor
natives consider it a good fortune to obtain food
and provender enough for their bare subsistence
and that of their cattle and horses. Sometimes
the cattle starve to death, and families have been
found in a starving condition, or at best, reduced
to a scanty subsistence on potatoes and salt.

It is plain, therefore, that this region was never
designed for agriculture, and that it can never be
extensively settled. The Hon. George P. Marsh
well states the design of the Adirondacks, in his
" Man and Nature," when he thus speaks : " Nature

threw up these mountains and clothed them with
lofty woods, that they might serve as a reservoir to
supply with perennial waters the thousand rills and
rivers that are fed by the rains and snows of the
Adirondacks, and as a screen for the fertile plains
of the central counties of New York against the
chilly blasts of the North wind, which meet no
other barrier in their sweep from the Arctic Pole.
The climate of northern New York even now
presents greater extremes of temperature than that
of Southern France. The long continued cold of
winter is far more intense, the heats of summer not
less fierce than in Provence; and hence the preservation of every influence that tends to maintain an
equilibrium of temperature and humidity is of car-
dinal importance. The felling of the Adirondack
woods would ultimately involve for Northern
and Central New York consequences similar to
those which have resulted in the laying bare of
the eastern and western declivities of the French
Alps, and the spurs, ridges, and detached peaks in
front of them," which results have been so disastrous
as to cause alarm, and create in France special
schools for the study of climatology and forestry,
as well as special enactments of government for
forest care and preservation. The same is the case
in Germany.

Mr. Marsh also points out the importance of preserving the Adirondack wilderness and retaining it,

or a portion of it, as a park by the State of New York
to be a natural museum for the instruction of the
student, a garden for the lover of nature, an asylum
for the poor worn-out invalid, and a home for the in-
digenous tree and shade-loving plant, as well as for
fish, fowl, bird and beast, for the enjoyment of life and
for its perpetuity, which park, museum, garden,
asylum and home all combined in one if well-
preserved and well-managed, and kept full of game,
fish, bird and animal would yield a revenue in timber,
iron ore, in fishing and hunting taxes, larger than the
whole cost of purchase and preserving. Old Adirondack anglers now go to Canada for the better
fishing of its preserved streams, and do not hesitate
to pay a high tax for the privilege ; can there be any
doubt about a state revenue being equally possible
in New York, if the waters and sporting grounds of
the Adirondacks were carefully preserved and made
more attractive with abundance of fish and game?
The present neglect, lawlessness, scarcity of game,
and increasing inroads upon the secluded portions
of the wilderness, are anything but attractive and
encouraging. Distant Colorado and British Canada, and even Maine, are attracting scores and
hundreds of sportsmen, many of whom had a preference for the Adirondack woods twenty or thirty
years ago when deer and trout were everywhere
plenty ; and thus the money that might be secured to this region which is in so much need of

it, goes elsewhere, with the near prospect of reaching the vanishing-point, so far as the poor guides and their suffering families are concerned. And the State of New York loses a portion of what might be a considerable revenue, were the region carefully preserved.

But the most important part of this subject of Forestry is that equilibrium of nature in earth and sky, attracting so much attention in France and Germany as well as in some of the States and Territories of this Republic, upon which the welfare of civilized society depends. When that equilibrium is disturbed or destroyed the consequences are most disastrous. The definite conclusions thus far reached by the science of forestry at home and abroad are these : That forests preserve the equilibrium of the atmosphere, making it pure and healthy for all animal and human life; that they preserve the equilibrium of moisture and the rainfall; that they preserve the equilibrium of heat and cold or temperature; that they regulate the flow and distribution of water, making it more equal and constant, or in other words, preventing droughts and floods; and that evergreen forests serve these functions at all seasons of the year and in all places, in some of which deciduous trees act less vigorously, where they have not disappeared altogether. Observations made during the last six years in the neighborhood of Nancy, France, by the students

of the School of Forestry in that city, under the
direction of M. Mathieu, sub-director of the School,
give these results: The temperature of the forest
is more equal than in the open country, although a
little lower; it is warmer in winter and cooler in
summer; forests increase the precipitation of the
atmospheric moisture, and favor the growth of
springs and underground reservoirs and passages
of water; forest regions receive more water under
cover of the trees than the open country; and
forests diminish in large measure the evaporation
of water received by the ground in which they
grow, thus maintaining the moisture and regulating
the flow of water sources. Another French observer, M. Fautrat, for four years sub-inspector of
forests at Senlis, arrived at similar conclusions by
a different method, to the effect that forests preserve the equilibrium of temperature and moisture,
in these respects: 1. It rains more abundantly
over forests than over a cleared country, under the
same circumstances, and it rains most copiously
over a green forest than over a dry one; 2. The
moisture of the air is greater over forests than it is
over the open country, and much greater over pine
forests than it is over deciduous ones; 3. Deciduous trees intercept only one-third of the rain-water,
while pine trees intercept one-half, which is returned
to the atmosphere by evaporation. 4. This evaporation is nearly four times less from the forest

than from the open, and is greater from a pine forest than from a deciduous one in full leaf. 5. Forests have a more equal temperature than the open, higher in winter and lower in summer. Other and earlier observers, in this direction, have arrived at like conclusions, supported by incontestable facts.

In illustration of these general principles of Forestry, I cite, first of all, the remarks of that accomplished botanist and brilliant writer, Dr. Hugh Macmillan, as to the influences and functions of a pine forest like that of the Adirondacks. He says : " Standing on the mountain tops, the fringed forests of pine catch and condense the passing clouds, which distil from their branches into the shaded soil, and, percolating through moss and grass into the heart of the rocks, flow down by an appointed channel—a rejoicing stream--into the valleys. The pine is, therefore, the earth's divining-rod that discovers water in the thirsty desert, the rod of Moses, that smites the barren rock, and causes the living fountain to gush forth. When the pine forests on the mountain heights are cut down, the springs and rivulets of the low grounds are exhausted, and the climate is rendered drier and hotter. The destruction of the grand pine-woods that once clothed the Appenines, has rendered Italy (the Papal States) a region of poverty, disease, and wretchedness. In Greece the traveler

5

looks in vain for the old legendary fountains, rivers,
and lakes, with which the classic poets had made
him familiar; the water-nymphs have vanished
along with their sorrowing sisters the Dryads.
Palestine has become a parched and sterile land,
on account of the disforesting of its mountains and
hills. Not more poetically than truthful, then, did
the old Chinese philosophers say, 'that the mightiest
rivers are cradled in the leaves of the pine.' On the
the mountain heights, too, in the united strength of
of its serried phalanxes, the pine is a natural fascine
or fortification against the ravages of the elements.
The *ban forests* of Switzerland stay the progress of
glaciers, and arrest the headlong fall of the ava-
lanche, protecting the inhabitants of the valleys
from the fearful icebolts of the mountains. On the
Norwegian hills, the pine forests wage successful
warfare with the bitter winds of the Pole; and in
their sheltered rear the fruits of a milder climate
ripen, and the toils of a happier land are carried on.
Against the fierce storms of the Bay of Biscay, the
pines of the Landes offer an effectual barrier; and
the meadows and pastures, forming the support of
an industrious peasantry, now appear where sand-
dunes once filled the air with choking clouds, and
spread desolation over the far horizon. The pine
is, therefore, necessary to the equilibrium of nature.
If ignorantly and wantonly removed from the situa-
tions where God has so wisely and graciously placed

it, His beneficent arrangements for the good of man
would be completely frustrated. We see the presence and hear the voice of the Lord God amongst
the pine trees, as amongst the trees of the garden
of Eden. Each tree is aflame with Him as truly
as was the Burning Bush " (*Bible Teachings in
Nature*, IV.).

This writer also points out the important fact
that the *coniferæ*, or trees of the pine family, are
not only the most useful in the economy of nature
for the regulation of the earth's temperature, the
character of its seasons, the distribution of the
rain-fall, and the general happiness of mankind,
but also that they are the most widely diffused of
any other kind. Some species may be found from
the snows of Lapland to the hottest regions of the
Indian Archipelago, and from the level of the sea
to the highest limit of trees on the great mountain
ranges, giving not only beauty, but fertility to the
earth. He dwells with special emphasis on the
cedars of Lebanon, the cedars of the Himalayas,
and the cedars of the American Sierra Nevada ;
and his conclusion is, that if the earth were deprived of its trees and shrubs, it would be reduced
to a dreary, inhospitable desert.

Nor is he alone in this fearful estimate of the
disastrous consequences of forest destruction. An
able writer in the *North American Review*, of January, 1879, says : " The physical laws of God can

not be outraged with impunity, and it is time to re-
cognize the fact that there are some sins against
which not one of the Scriptural codes of the East
contains a word of warning. The destruction of
the forests is such a sin, and its significance is
preached by every desolate country on the surface
of this planet. Three millions of square miles of
the best lands which ever united the conditions of
human happiness have perished in the sand drifts
of artificial deserts and are now more irretrievably
lost to mankind than the island ingulfed by the
waves of the Zuyder Zee." We shall see presently
where all these desert lands and irretrievable losses
are.

Meanwhile, let us consider for a moment how it
is that forests maintain the healthy equilibrium of
the atmosphere. Every school-boy and school-girl,
who has paid the least attention to Chemistry, knows
how the air is composed of three main elements,
viz., oxygen, carbon, and hydrogen. The oxygen
of the air sustains all animal and human life, while
the carbon is a deadly poison, in a concentrated
state, to all air-breathing animals, so that an atmosphere containing even so small a proportion of carbon as ten per cent. would be fatal in ordinary respiration. But this carbon is the life of all plants
and vegetation. The air is continually flooded
with it, from human and animal lungs ; from the
combustion of fuel and light ; from cracks in the

earth in volcanic countries; and from some kinds
of mineral springs. Were no provision made to
counteract the deadly influence of this poison and
preserve the equilibrium of the atmosphere, human
and animal life on this planet would be plainly impossible. But such provision is found in all the
forests of our world. What we give out as poison,
the trees and plants absorb as their very life. And
by this act of absorption on the part of trees and
plants, the oxygen is set free and the air is purified
for the sustenance of our own life. All town-air,
therefore, must be more or less unhealthy, not
only because of the presence of a large population
and numerous manufactories and gas lights and
foul streets and open sewers, but also from the
absence of trees enough to preserve the healthy
equilibrium of the atmosphere.

Cholera and the mysterious plague are the products of a dense oriental population that has destroyed its forests. Malarial poisons are the
results of foul decay in districts laid bare to the
burning rays of the sun. The Roman Campagna
is a conspicuous example, which for centuries has
been a sickly uninhabited waste, notwithstanding
the richness of its soil, and the former glory of its
Etruscan occupation and civilization. Roman con-
quests, rapacity and cupidity destroyed the neighboring forests, and turned the fertile and beautiful
plains into a pestilential morass, where now only a

5*

few shepherds and swineherds drag out a miserable
and precarious existence. The planting of the
Eucalyptus in the neighborhood of the Basilica of
St. Paul, and the use of dynamite to break up some
portions of the hard volcanic hard-pan of the soil,
have had some effect in mitigating the deadly influence of the poisoned air. But the Roman Campagna is irretrievably lost to civilization with the
loss of its great Etruscan population. Man has
made it a howling desert beyond the possibility of
recovery in its whole extent. Who will replant the
forests on the desolate mountain heights? Or what
population will permit their growth? The pressing
needs of civilization have cut them down; the
pressing needs of civilization would cut them down
again, even though they might be replanted and
grown. In accounting for the decay and desolation
of ancient Veii, the capital of Etruria, Mr. Dennis
mentions *malaria* as the most probable cause,
owing to proscription, neglect and want of cultivation on the part of its jealous Roman conquerors;
and he expressly says that the unhealthy state of
the neighborhood of the old Etruscan capital spread
to the whole Campagna, " which in very early times
was studded with towns, but under the Roman
domination became, what it has ever since remained — a desert, whose wide surface is rarely
relieved by habitation." (*The Cities and Ceme-
teries of Etruria*, second ed., I, p. 16.) If, for two

thousand years and more, the Roman Campagna has been a desert beyond the possibility of recovery, the natural inference is that it will so remain for all time to come. Once a garden of fertility and salubrity, sustaining a numerous civilized population, the destruction of the neighboring forests has turned it into a sickly, death-breeding fen, dangerous even to the passing traveler.

It is just the same with that wide, beautiful plain, on which the ruined temples of Pæstum stand, the only remaining monuments of a once flourishing ancient civilization. Its only inhabitants now are wild buffalos and a few prowling bandits lying in wait to capture some wealthy tourist for a ransom. It, too, is a desert of malaria and death, only to be visited in the winter. The hills behind this plain have long been denuded of their forests, and the gleaming waters of the emerald sea in front, ripple along silent and deserted shores, once trod by thousands and thousands of busy, happy feet. A desert for long centuries past, a desert it will remain for the centuries to come. Its soil is fertile, but its air is poison. The fertile plains of Lombardy and other parts of Italy are fast relapsing into the same dreadful state. The destruction of the forests on the Alps and Appenines have destroyed both the equilibrium of the air as to its vital elements and as to its humidity and climate, so that malarial fevers abound ;

droughts and floods are common; the *mistral* or cold northwest wind, blowing over the denuded slopes, kills early vegetables and fruits; and the general effect, as already intimated, is poverty, disease and wretchedness. What is thus true of the Roman **Campagna,** Magna Grecia and Lombardy, will inevitably be true of all those fertile portions of our own country in proximity to mountains denuded of their forests. In this view of the case **as to forests** being necessary to preserve the healthy equilibrium of the atmosphere, **it is** not a **matter of** wonder that our own vast fertile prairies of the **West** are **so** unhealthy and full of malaria, **and** that **govermental** encouragement is given to their planting **by the remission** of taxes, **as in some of the States and Territories.**

The next principle **in** the science **of** Forestry claiming our notice is, the equilibrium of atmospheric moisture and the regulation of the rain-fall. This principle is local in its operation. The air over a forest being cooler than that over the open, necessarily condenses more atmospheric moisture and causes much more rain-fall or precipitation, as already stated by the French observer, M. Fautrat. The **forest, too,** as a living organism, restores much dew and many light showers to the air, which do **not** reach the ground; and **it** also screens the ground **itself** from the scorching rays of the sun and retains the moisture in **it.** Trees act as media

tors between earth and air; they are conductors of
moisture from the earth to the air, and from the
air to the earth, just as they are of heat: they absorb from the air and through their roots draw
from the ground the moisture necessary to preserve
a proper equilibrium; so that over a vast forest
the temperature of the air is lowered by the latter
operation, when moisture is poured into it: and it
is this process which condenses the vapor into
water, and precipitates the rain-fall. It is just
here that a perplexing question has arisen among
scientific observers of forestry, as to whether the
forest absorbs more moisture from the air for its
own growth than it returns to it, or does it absorb
from the soil itself more moisture than it shades
and protects for springs and rivers. The general
answer to these questions is, as Mr. Marsh gives it,
that the majority of foresters and physicists maintain that in many, if not in all cases, the destruction of the woods is followed by a diminution of
the annual quantity of rain and dew. This is con-
firmed by recent observations in France, as above
given. A German poet, cited by Mr. Marsh, thus
expresses the principle as to the desert of Sahara:

"Afric's barren sand
Where nought can grow because it raineth not,
And where no rain can fall to bless the land,
Because nought grows there."

Dr. Brown, a more recent authority than Mr. Marsh, admits that the facts are sometimes conflicting, and fairly states both sides of the perplexing question. But his own conclusion is thus strongly put: While moisture is necessary to make and keep the forest, yet the forest in turn conserves and reproduces moisture. These necessary and reciprocal functions should not be arrayed against each other, any more than the centrifugal and centripetal forces of nature, so as to invalidate the fact that forests do retard the rain-fall after precipitation, and have a general effect on the humidity of the atmosphere and the soil (*Forests and Moisture, or Effects of Forests on Climate*, Edinburgh).

Mr. Marsh himself had before arrived at the same general conclusion as to the main effect of forests in mitigating the extremes of moisture and drought, heat and cold. He says: " Trees serve as equalizers of temperature and moisture; and it is highly probable that, in analogy with most of the other works and workings of nature, they restore the equilibrium, at certain or uncertain periods, even though as lifeless masses or living organisms they may have temporarily disturbed that equilibrium. When man destroys these natural harmonizers of climatic discords, he sacrifices one of the most important conservative powers of nature, and does himself great injustice and harm. He must not charge upon the benevolent and wise Author

of nature any suffering that may follow his own
wrong-doing." It would seem as though the primal
sin of mankind in Eden had something to do with
this disturbance of the equilibrium of nature, from
the fact that the ground was cursed with barrenness, so that greater toil became necessary to make
it productive. This curse of barrenness and of
greater toil for bread has ever since followed the
human race in its dispersion over the earth, wherever the forests have been destroyed in whole or
greater part, so as to make humidity and the rain-
fall less regular and certain. Long droughts make
famines.

It is not any part of the claim of the science of
Forestry that the entire annual rain-fall of the
whole globe is much affected by the remaining
forests, seeing that only about one-quarter of its
surface is land and the rest water; and because
these forests, mostly in the cold and temperate
zones, have never, generally covered more than one-
tenth of the earth. But so far as human habitation
of the earth is concerned, the disturbance has been
everywhere a local one and universally prevalent,
producing the same sad and disastrous consequences.

The island of Maita is a barren, treeless rock in
the Mediterranean sea, save where soil has been
brought to it from Sicily; and Malta has been
known to have no rain for three consecutive years.

The rainless territory of Peru and North Africa
establishes the same conclusion that the rain-fall
ceases in woodless regions of the earth.   Palestine
and Egypt, once the granaries of the Roman world,
are now desolate and barren, from the sole cause of
the destruction of their forests.   In fact, nearly all
the deserts of the world are found " on the side
turned towards Asia," the cradle and home of the
human race, as if these deserts were the direct effects
of human agency.   The deserts of Thibet and Mongolia must be considered as exceptions because the
great range of the Himalayas intercept the moisture.
For the same reason Patagonia is a barren waste,
the Andes intercepting and condensing the moisture
arising from the Pacific ocean.   The plains of India
are more or less fertile, because the southwestern
monsoon strikes the Himalayan range and its great
moisture is condensed and precipitated on the side
towards India.   But even so, the destruction of the
forests in India has made a great difference in the
regularity and distribution of the rain-fall, so that
famines are frequent and the loss of life by starvation frightful.

As an illustration of this difference, I cite the
following passages from Dr. E. D. G. Prime's narrative of a journey " Around the World:" " A
striking peculiarity of the great plain of India, and
indeed of the whole of Asia, from east to west, so
far as I have seen it, is the destitution of forests.

With all the beauty of verdure and foliage that
marks Japan, I did not see within the thousand
miles of the empire that I traversed, a single forest
of any extent. The whole coast of China, along
which I sailed more than a thousand miles, and the
interior as far as I penetrated it, had only sparsely
scattered trees. There is not the sign of a forest
from Calcutta to the mountains, although a large
part of the country is jungle. Even the Himalaya
Mountains that I subsequently crossed, and the
second range that I ascended, were only sprinkled
with trees, in comparison with the grand old dense
forests of magnificent growth which form one of
the sublime features of American scenery. The
plain of India has scattered groves of palm, acacia,
guava, mango, and many other oriental trees; but
they are all planted for shade or fruit. Centuries
ago the forests were cut down to supply the necessities of an immense population, but the soil does
not appear to have the reproductive power that is
a marked feature of our own soil. . . . The quantity
of water that falls in the rainy season varies greatly
in different localities, according to the distance
from the coast and the mountains, the sea and the
low marshy lands supplying the moisture which the
mountains condense. Sometimes a short distance
makes a vast difference in the rain-fall. At Bombay
the average yearly fall is 75 inches; on the Ghauts,
south of Bombay, it is 254 inches; while a little

6

further inland, at Poonah, over the mountains, it is
only 23 inches. The rain-fall on the Khasia hills is
600 inches, or 50 feet. This immense fall of water
is attributed to the passing of the air from the sea
over two hundred miles of swampy country, by
which it becomes overcharged with moisture, that
precipitates itself when it strikes the mountains,
and falls in torrents as long as the monsoon pre-
vails in that direction. Only twenty miles farther
inland the amount is 200 inches. I met in India a
veteran army officer who had spent twenty years at
Assam, in the western part of that country, and he
gave me an extract from the meteorological record
that he had kept for many years, which contained
some remarkable statements. In one year, 1862,
there fell at Chorrapoongee, 725 inches of rain, a
little more than 60 feet, probably the heaviest rain-
fall ever noted at any place on the earth. The
rainy season in India is short, beginning in June,
when the heat is greatest, varying from 110° to
130° in the shade for weeks at a time. From
March to June hot scorching winds prevail, that
parch the earth and wither all vegetation."

All this vast difference of rain-fall, from 23 inches
to 725, this tremendous heat and scorching winds
that meet little or no resistance, must be traced, in
chief measure, to the disappearance of the forests
on plain and mountain. It is estimated that from
20 to 24 inches of annual rain-fall, equally and

regularly distributed, are necessary at the lowest
calculation for purposes of agriculture and forest-
growth. But if this lowest possible amount is
precipitated in drenching floods, after drought and
dry wind, crops are uncertain, if not impossible,
except by costly irrigation. But when the water-
supply of the mountains is fitful or insufficient or
fails altogether, because bare of forests, then what
becomes of irrigation? It fails when most needed.
The fields are parched; vegetation dies; famine
begins its dreadful ravages, as in India, China,
Persia, Ireland, and even in the Empire of Brazil.

Another important consideration is climatology,
or the effect of forests upon temperature. Having
spent both winter and summer in the Adirondack
forest, it is simply a matter of daily experience to
affirm that the winter is milder and the summer
cooler than in the open of the same latitude or its
equivalent. The winters of Minnesota are far more
severe and the summers much hotter than in the
Adirondacks, judging from the records of the
thermometer; and it must be borne in mind that
the altitude of the Adirondack region gives it a
higher latitude than that of Minnesota. If the
Adirondack forest were all destroyed the climate
would be changed to that of Labrador or the barren
region just south of it, as Mr. Colvin asserts,
although in his estimate, the effect of the forest
was not calculated. Humboldt claims that a forest

in full leaf receives and emits more heat in proportion to its surface than so much bare ground.
Trees are conductors of heat, and convey the
warmth of the atmosphere to the earth when the
earth is colder than the air and most needs the
heat. On the other hand, trees transmit the heat
of the earth to the atmosphere when the earth's
temperature is higher than that of the air and the
air most needs it. The forest is thus an equalizer
of temperature for the whole region round about,
in summer and winter. Minnesota has no mountain-
range to screen its fertile plains from the piercing
blasts of the Icy Pole, nor any extensive Pine
forest to equalize its temperature by moderating
the chilliness of its winter winds or the ardor of
its summer heats. For all central New York the
Adirondacks serve as such a screen, and their
magnificent forest as a moderator of climate. But
careful preservation of this forest is necessary to
save central New York from some of the direful
consequences that have ensued in Italy and France
from denuding the Alps and Appennines of their
forests. Avalanches and land-slides, burying whole
villages and destroying thousands of people, may
not be among these calamities here; but a radical
change from a healthy to a sickly atmosphere may
be, as well as great changes in climate and humidity
and regular distribution of the rain-fall; here as in
Italy and France, tempests and hail-storms may

become more frequent and destructive, desolating
the fertile lowlands; violent floods here as there
may destroy great manufactories and submerge
whole towns and villages; deluges of rain, as in
denuded India, may cover the soil, or as in Italy,
may sweep away the mountain deposits and choke
up our rivers and harbors with the *debris:* the
mistral or cold north-wind may make even later
springs and nip early vegetation; and all this, in
time, will as surely beget disease, poverty, and
wretchedness in all central New York as in Italy.
This *mistral* or cold north-wind, making our own
late springs, is, as Dussard says, the child of man,—
the result of his forest devastations, destroying the
equilibrium of temperature.

In winter, when there is less absorption and
radiation of heat by deciduous forest trees than in
summer, the dead leaves serve as a protection to
the ground from any deep freezing. In an evergreen forest, especially in the swamps and low
marshy places, the ground scarcely freezes at all.
Here the snow lies undisturbed and undrifted to
the depth of from four to six feet all over the
Adirondack plateau. Protected thus by leaves
and snow, the soft soil retains the moisture received
from the clouds; the snow melts gradually in the
spring, and instead of devastating floods, the water
is slowly and steadily and gently sent forth into
the springs, rills and rivers to fertilize and rejoice

6*

the plains and valleys below. A bare, hard, frozen
soil could not receive or retain the rain-fall, which,
with the melting snows, would rush down in torrents
of muddy water to desolate the lowlands and choke
up the rivers with sand and gravel.

Intimately connected with this part of the subject
is the drying up of springs and water-sources by
the destruction of the forest. The soil of a forest
being always in its normal moist condition, save
perhaps in long continued heat and drought, as is
sometimes the case even in the Adirondacks, when
the soil becomes dry as punk and forest-fires are
frequent, retains its full supply of water for the
distant lowlands. This constant moisture of forest-
soil insures both the permanence of springs and
their regularity, not merely within the forest limits,
but far beyond. When the mountain forests are
destroyed, the springs flowing from them are
diminished both in number and volume; and, as a
consequence, the greater water-courses fed by them,
are also diminished in volume. The Hudson River
is thus diminished already; and the long, dry summer of 1879 so dried up and diminished the sources
of supply to the great canals of New York, as to
confuse and interrupt much of her grand commerce.
If, as the *North American Review* says, " we have
been wasting the moisture-supply of the American
soil at the average ratio of seven per cent. for each
quarter of a century during the last one hundred

and twenty-five years, and we are now fast
approaching the limit beyond which any further
decrease will affect the climatic phenomena of the
entire continent," then it behooves a patriotic and
intelligent people, who love their country and would
secure its present and future welfare, to give more
heed to this subject of Forestry, and save the land
from becoming ultimately a hot and barren desert
like so many countries of the East.

The traveler in Assyria and the central provinces
of Asia Minor tells us of the scarcity of water, the
extreme aridity of the soil, the meagre crops and
the sparse population living in poverty and
wretchedness; and he also tells us that the forests
are gone. Assyria was once the seat of splendid
empire and a numerous population; it is now a
desert and the home of the wandering Bedouin.
Asia Minor and Palestine were once the very garden
spots of the earth, producing large grain crops,
flowers and fruits, having one of the most congenial
and delightful of all climates, luring the Irsaelite
from fertile Egypt and the Roman magnate from
his luxurious villa; Asia Minor and Palestine are
now comparatively deserted; only meagerly tilled;
dry, hot, sickly and barren. All day long, even so
early as April, have I gone from one mean little
hamlet or town to another, broiling and sweltering
under a scorching sun, without meeting half a
dozen persons on the way; no shade anywhere

under which to rest for the mid-day luncheon; no
water to drink away from the Jordan or the Barada;
and great seams and cracks gaping open in the
parched soil like famished mouths for a single
cooling and refreshing drop of water. The brook
Kidron, which in David's time ran full and sparkling along the eastern wall of Jerusalem, is now a
dry and empty channel, serving the sole purpose
of conveying the winter rains which sweep the
barren hills around in muddy turbulence to the
Dead Sea. Arabia, Persia, Greece, Media, Bactria,
Cyprus, Carthage, Tyre, and all the rest of worn-
out and desolated countries and islands of the sea,
whose prosperity and greatness have long since
perished with their forests, seem to have left no
impressive and restraining warning to the succeeding generations of men, who, heedless of consequences and reckless in the pursuit of wealth and
material greatness, have been doing their utmost
for the last two thousand years to make the
countries of Europe and America as waste and
desolate as these Oriental human deserts.

Spain is a conspicuous example of a European
country without forest laws and forest protection.
During the reign of the Moorish Hassan, from 1466
to 1484, the forests of the Sierra Nevada were
protected by a rigid legislation; and in every
district where the original woods had disappeared
the proportion of orchards and grain fields was

not a matter of choice, but regulated by a code of
" field laws." After the conquest of Granada these
laws were abrogated, and the Moorish orchards
and chestnut groves disappeared to make room for
vineyards. The Moslem inhabitants of Andalusia
had created a paradise in southern Spain; but their
Christian conquerors could not prevent that country
from becoming a desert. The children of the poor
Spanish peasant have now to starve because their
forefathers devastated the Sierras, and " preferred
the cultus of the Virgin to the culture of fruit-
trees," and the preservation of the mountain forest.
It is a well-known fact, that in the arid parts of
Spain, wine is so much more abundant and cheaper
than water that builders mix their mortar with it.
Sir John Herschel attributes the extreme aridity
of Spain to the absence of trees, and the proverbial
hatred of a Spaniard for trees, according to the old
adage, " trees breed birds, and birds eat up the
grain." Therefore destroy the trees, and make the
land dry and barren. The Spanish writer, Antonio
Ponz, evidently had a different idea of the utility
of trees from that of his countrymen, when he said:
" Some are declaiming against trees, thereby proclaiming themselves, in some sort, enemies of the
works of God, who gave us the leafy abode of
Paradise to dwell in, where we should be even now
sojourning, but for the first sin which expelled us
from it." Obviously, here is a hint that original

sin or depravity is that spirit of lawlessness and destruction, which, first and all the time, attacks the forest and desolates God's garden.

If, according to recent French observations, a cleared country exposed to greater action of wind and sun, evaporates four times more moisture from its soil than a forest does, then it is easy to see why the soil of the open becomes barren from the failure of springs and water-sources. The plain of Jericho was a pleasure garden in the time of the Roman domination because the fresh water of the Western hills was brought to it by a stone aqueduct now in ruins; but in the time of the prophet Elisha, long before, the principle of irrigation was recognized by the men of the city, who came to the prophet and said : Behold, I pray thee, the situation of this city is pleasant, as my lord seeth ; but the water is nought, and the ground barren. And he said, Bring me a new cruse, and put salt therein. And they brought it to him. And he went forth unto the spring of the waters, and cast the salt in there, and said, Thus saith the Lord, I have healed these waters; there shall not be from thence any more dearth or barren land. (2 Kings, II. 19–22.)

Having visited the site of ancient Jericho in the spring of 1860, I certify my readers that the spring of Elisha is still flowing; and that, although the the water is slightly brackish, it is fresh and copious enough to quicken the soil around, to which

every precious drop is brought by irrigation; and
that, the only fine field of wheat I saw in all Palestine was here. The rest of the plain of Jericho is
barren, yielding only thorn-bushes and the apples
of Sodom. It is therefore a Divine law and a Bible
principle that fresh water and fertility of soil go
together, a law and a principle now at last recognized by the Science of Forestry.

But springs of water fail and lakes diminish
when the surrounding or neighboring forests are
destroyed. Thus, a fine spring in the island of
Ascension, at the base of a wooded mountain,
dried up when the mountain was cleared, but reap-
peared when it was replanted. The streams used
to drive the workshops of Marmato, in France,
were diminished in volume within two years after
clearing the heights from which they drew their supplies; and these works, together with other great
manufactories throughout France were obliged to
stop, thus causing much distress, for a like reason.
In the year 1800, when Humboldt was in South
America, the waters of lake Tacarigua, in the valley
of Aragua, were observed to be receding, which this
great naturalist attributed to the numerous clear-
ings around it. Twenty years later, after political
revolutions had desolated the country and made it
possible for the forest to grow up again, the waters
of this lake were sensibly rising. Another lake in
this same valley had been greatly reduced in size

by the removal of the mountain forest to obtain
fuel for the saltworks in the neighborhood—a reduc-
tion, be it noted, from ten leagues long to one and
a half, and from three leagues wide to one. Other
lakes there remained in undiminished volume and
size, where the forests were undisturbed or where
the valleys had always been bare of trees. The
lakes of Switzerland have sunk to a lower level
since the prevalent destruction of the Alpine forests,
and it will be the same with the Adirondack lakes
as the forest disappears.

Dr. Piper, in his "Trees of America," mentions
the case of a mill-pond near his house, having mills
around it of long date and constant operation,
until twenty years from the time of writing, when
the water began to fail. The pond was supplied
by a stream having its source in hills once densely
wooded. When these hills were laid bare the
stream ceased entirely, except in the spring
freshets, after which it went dry—a thing never
known before. But within the last ten years, he
says, a new growth of wood has sprung up on most
of the land occupied by the primeval forest; and
now the water runs throughout the year, notwithstanding the droughts of many seasons. In a
letter addressed to Dr. Piper, by Mr. Bryant, of
New York, the distinguished poet and journalist,
occurs this remarkable statement: " Fifty years
ago large barges loaded with goods went up and

down that river—the Cuyahoga—and one of the vessels engaged in the battle of Lake Erie, in which the gallant Perry was victorious, was built at Old Portage, six miles north of Albion, and floated down to the lake. Now, in an ordinary state of the water, a canoe or skiff can hardly pass down the stream. Many a boat of fifty tons burden has been built and loaded in the Tuscarawas, at New Portage, and sailed to New Orleans without breaking bulk. Now, the river hardly affords a supply of water for the canal. The same may be said of other streams—they are drying up. And from the same cause—the destruction of our forests; our summers are growing drier, and our winters colder."

More than a hundred years ago, that acute observer and delightful writer, Gilbert White, of Selborne, made this record: "Trees perspire profusely, condense largely, and check evaporation so much, that woods are always moist; no wonder, therefore, that they contribute so much to pools and streams. That trees are great promoters of lakes and rivers appears from a well-known fact in North America; for, since the woods and forests have been cleared and grubbed, all bodies of water are much diminished; so that some streams that were very considerable a century ago will not now drive a common mill."—*Letter XXIX, to the Hon. D. Barrington, Selborne, Feb. 7th, 1776.*

7

In our own time, and right here at home, many a warning voice is raised to the same effect. Ex-Governor Hartranft, of Pennsylvania, in more than one message to the Legislature of that great Commonwealth, earnestly called attention to the rapid disappearance of its forests, especially the pine forests. He says: " Lumbermen of experience declare that in thirty years, with the present alarming destruction of trees, Pennsylvania will not have any saleable timber within her borders. The regions where this timber is found are the natural reservoirs from which our rivers and streams are fed, and observation shows that the rain-fall and the supply of water therein have been materially diminished since they were stripped of their forests. It is alleged, likewise, that decided atmospheric changes are perceptible, and that the winters have grown more rigorous and the heat of summers more intense in these same regions ; and that the dwarfed fruits and stunted crops are plainly traceable to the absence of the usual moisture occasioned by denuding them of their trees. Water-power has decreased in consequence, as well as fertilizers of the soil ; devastating floods and droughts have rendered the rafting season uncertain and the lumber supply precarious ; so that the investment of nearly $28,000.000 in timber lands, and the marketable product of $35.200,000, and the employment of 20,000 men at more than $6,000,000 wages, are all threatened with extinction at no very distant day."

From these principles of Forestry and the facts that establish their certainty, I now turn to consider the dreadful subject of forest destruction and its consequences to mankind. Man is both its agent and its victim. It is estimated that between the years 1750 and 1835 the total aggregate of forests felled in South and Central America, and in the Eastern, Southeastern and Southwestern States of our Republic, has been the enormous one of 45,000,000 to 50,000,000 of acres. Since then, the destruction of the forests in the distant territories of the Far West has been going on steadily and remorselessly, at the same tremendous rate. Fire, more than the axe, is the chief cause. It is alleged that the recent outbreak of the Ute Indians was owing to the attempted arrest of some of their number for setting fire to the woods and the settlements in their reservation; and that these Utes had destroyed in a single year five hundred miles of forest. In Major Powell's report to Congress in 1878, we learn some important facts as to this forest burning and the savage reasons for it. This officer claims that some parts of the great arid Plains of the Far West may be brought under cultivation by irrigation, covering, as they do, four-tenths or nearly half of our whole vast territory, exclusive of Alaska, and destined in time to a necessary occupation by an increasing population. The preserva-

tion of the rain or snow-fall and its regular
distribution over these arid plains by irrigation,
depends upon the protection of the mountain
forests, and is reduced to this one single problem:
Can these forests be saved from fire? A single
winter has witnessed two fires in Colorado, each of
which destroyed more timber than all that has been
used by the citizens of that State from its first settlement to the present day; and at least three fires
in Utah, each of which has destroyed more timber
than that taken by the people of the territory since
its Mormon occupation. Similar great forest fires
are constantly witnessed all over this vast region.

The Report charges these fires in the main to the
Indians for the purpose of driving game. Driven
as they are from the lowlands by advancing civilization, they resort to the higher regions until
forced back by the deep snows of winter. Want,
the desire for luxuries, ornaments, and better implements for the chase, and for trapping, have of late
years greatly stimulated the pursuit of animals for
their furs, which constitute the wealth and currency
of the savages. On their hunting excursions they
systematically set fire to the forests for the purpose
of driving the game. This is a fact well-known to
the mountaineers. The removal of the Indians is
recommended as a possible great curtailment of
these forest fires.

But, cheek-by-jowl with this Report to the government of the United States, recommending the removal of the Indians to prevent forest fires, comes Mr. R. W. Raymond's Report on Mines and Mining Interests of the Pacific States in 1870, which most emphatically declares that one of the worst abuses attendant upon the settlement of the mining regions and other portions of the West is the wanton destruction of timber. This reckless and disastrous practice prevailed in the heavy fir and cedar forests of Oregon Territory, more than twenty years ago. Hundreds of square miles were burned over in a single season, and vast quantities of the finest timber in the world, easily accessible to commerce, were either totally consumed or rendered utterly valueless. The timber was so abundant that to many it seemed inexhaustible, and they took especial delight in its destruction. The same waste of the forest is yearly going on in all the Western States and territories, and particularly in the mining regions of the Rocky Mountains.

It seems from this, that the savage Utes are outdone in forest destruction by civilized miners and settlers; but no recommendation is made for the removal of the latter. For, Westward the course of Empire takes its way, to make its deserts meet those of the east, and thus girdle the earth with a broad belt of desolation and death, ornamented with the grinning skulls and cross-bones of the last races of a famished humanity. After the desola-

7*

tion of America is completed, what hope and place
are left for human kind? With the sure and steady
march of Fate and the inevitably wrathful advance
of an avenging Nemesis, comes the penalty of
violating the laws and destroying the equilibrium
of nature by this wicked and wanton burning of
the forests all over our broad land. This alarming
cry of fire! fire! fire! not only resounds among the
mountains of the Far West, but it is also heard
from Maine to Florida, and from the Atlantic sea-
board to the Mississippi River. And scheming
politicians, mis-called statesmen, in or out of the
halls of legislation, give little or no heed to the
appalling cry, but rather plot and conspire for place
and power and the rich spoils of office; while the
people, either too ignorant or too indifferent about
the consequences, stand idly by enjoying the spectacle of their home and country wrapped in devouring flames. No, no; the charge is neither
false, nor is the statement too strongly put. For,
what legislation has ever yet seriously and vigorously attempted to arrest this forest arson as it
punishes the arson of barns and cow-sheds? And
what great proportion of our people has ever yet
strongly protested against it and demanded a remedy? This is not a question involving the existence of any political party, but the existence of
the nation itself; and before any effectual remedy
can be provided the people must be informed of

the great evil and danger of this thing, and a public sentiment be created against it, demanding severe punishment of all criminals, North, South, East and West, applying the torch to the forest.

In addition to the forest fires already mentioned, comes this long painful catalogue of others. In the years 1860 and 1862, fires of unusual extent and severity overran portions of what is now called Wyoming Territory, and spread so rapidly that neither man nor beast could escape. Valuable timber was not only burned, but also the turf or vegetable matter of the soil, preventing any future growth. The dry, long summer of 1871 will be remembered as one of the most disastrous on record in fires, not only in the Rocky Mountain region and throughout the Northwest, but elsewhere. Chicago was then burned; and the forest fires of Wisconsin, Michigan and New York were of vast extent. In Wisconsin and Michigan, especially, these fires were unprecedented, and swept not only through forests, but even through cultivated fields, and destroyed towns and villages. The area swept by that one year's fires was thousands of square miles, and the pecuniary loss is estimated to have been not less than $215,000,000.

Then, again, in the autumn of 1876, after a very dry, hot summer, the forests of Northwestern Pennsylvania were ravaged by fire, and many destructive fires broke out in the Adirondacks. In the following May, 1877, a most disastrous fire started at Clinton Mills, Clinton County, New York, in the Adirondack region, and besides consuming several lumbering villages and establishments, burned over a vast area, and destroyed timber to an incalculable amount. During the same year these fires raged in the woods of Vermont, New Hampshire, Massachusetts, Wisconsin, the Upper Peninsula and Canada. New Jersey and Florida have suffered in the same way. A conductor of the Camden & Atlantic Railroad counted no less than fifteen forest fires in a single trip from Camden to the sea, in the summer of 1878. In 1866, a fire swept over 10,000 acres, or seven miles, which is now the burnt district from Tuckerton to West Creek; in 1870–71, nearly the whole of the wooded portion of Bass Township, Burlington county, was burnt over. In 1871, two fires in Ocean County burned over 30,000 acres. In 1872, one fire in August burned in Southern New Jersey from fifteen to twenty square miles of timber worth from ten to thirty dollars per acre. These fires not only cause a scarcity of large timber so that importation is necessary, but also burn out the vegetable mould of the soil, so that the possibility of reproduction is reduced to the narrowest limits, or altogether prevented, as Dr. Hough's report of forestry assures us. Some of these New Jersey forest fires are caused by malicious mischief; others spread

from the burning sedge and brush-heaps of the farmers; but it is affirmed that the larger proportion
of them are kindled by sparks from passing railroad engines, falling into the underbrush rendered
inflammable in a region pervaded by little or no
moisture.

So, too, the Florida crackers and cow-boys fire
the pine woods every year, wantonly wasting much
valuable timber. These miscreants burn the fields
to obtain fresh grass for their cattle, and the fires
spread far and wide to the forests, destroying not
only millions of valuable trees, but also the planta-
tions and improvements of enterprising emigrants.
And besides all this immense destruction of our
forests by fire, the vast and rapidly increasing disappearance of them by the axe must be taken into
account, on arable land for farms; for building and
commercial purposes; for railroad ties and telegraph poles; for smelting purposes and brick making; for packing boxes, wagons and farming
implements; for fences, fuel, matches, shoe-pegs,
tools, etc., for spars and ships and boats of every
kind; for casks and barrels, not only at home but
abroad; our staves going by the million to France;
our oak, walnut and pine to England; our spars
and dock-timber to distant Japan, and our shoe-pegs
to Germany. And to supply all these demands, at
least 250,000 acres of forest lands must be cut over

every year, to say nothing of the greater amount
cleared for farms.

The Adirondack forest, which more especially
concerns us, has greatly suffered from both these
destructive agencies. As to the depredations of
the axe for fuel and lumber, and the settlements of
squatters, chiefly from Vermont and Canada, during
the last twenty years only, I cite the testimony of
that careful observer and veteran angler, Mr. Dawson, who has already appeared in these pages to
good advantage, as a plain, blunt man, speaking the
truth from his heart; and he says this: " Many
years ago, when I first came to Corey's, the carry
was covered with a dense growth of beautiful pines.
But the demand for lumber was too pressing to be
resisted, and this delightful spot is denuded of its
most attractive feature. The work of lumbering is
being pushed vigorously within practical distances
of all the water-courses of sufficient volume to
float the logs to manufacturing points, of which
Plattsburg, Potsdam and Glenn's Falls are the
principal. During the winter, the logs are cut and
placed upon the ice, ready for the spring freshets,
and from the time of breaking up until well on in
May, there is scarcely an available stream which is
not filled with these moving masses. And yet the
Rev. Mr. Murray, in his famous book, contrasting
the Adirondacks with the forests of Maine, says of
the former that they retain their primitive beauty

because ' the sound of the woodman's axe has never been heard among them.' If the reverend gentleman's theology is as loose as his facts, it must be a poor commodity."—(*Pleasures of Angling*, c. XXIX.). This poor, clerical horse-jockey and back-board wagoner having now proved to be " loose " in more ways than this, to the great detriment of morals and religion, and having gone to California on business, no contradiction of Mr. Dawson's statement is to be feared or expected. I may, therefore, safely venture to add my dozen years of experience and observation in the Adirondacks to his more weighty testimony.

In or near all the settlements of the Adirondack region, on streams of sufficient water-power, there are numerous saw-mills busy in supplying the demands of the neighborhoods for building materials. Occasional steam-mills are to be found, also. From all such neighborhoods, the majestic pine groves have long since disappeared ; spruce is well nigh gone or rapidly disappearing, both under the axe and by decay, and the remaining hemlock is now vigorously attacked. So close do these desperate lumbermen now cut, that I have seen in the milldam at Saranac Lake, many a little hemlock stick not more than five or six inches in diameter, in violation of the rule that requires all logs for sawing to be at least nine inches. These Adirondack

saw-mills, therefore, are rapidly consuming all the
neighboring forest.

Then, too, every family resident here requires at
least fifty cords of wood for its annual consump-
tion, which for fuel alone, is fast laying bare the
harder wood of the deciduous portion of the forest.
But even this is nothing in comparison with the
stupendous destruction going on continually to
obtain charcoal for the manufacture of iron. This
is most conspicuous at Chazy and Chateaugay
Lakes, and along the road from Ausable to St.
Regis, where miles and miles of forest are completely destroyed, not a single stick left standing,
and the whole ground left as bare as a field of stub-
ble after harvest. Many a tourist or invalid, on
his first visit to the woods, sarcastically remarks
on this grim desolation, and keeps asking his more
experienced friend, 'How soon shall we reach the
majestic primeval forest, so much talked about in
the books?' Not a glimpse of any primeval forest
will he obtain, the whole distance of forty miles
from Plattsburg to the St. Regis Lakes or the
Saranacs; and the little pine grove left around the
enterprising Paul Smith's hostelry is all that will
give him the least idea of what this forest once
was. There are, indeed, remote and almost inac-
cessible parts of this wilderness where the forest is
yet entire in its beauty and majesty, where no axe
or fire has yet made hideous desolation, and where

good pine timber is yet to be had; but if the
nefarious Adirondack Railroad Company ever suc-
ceeds in its monstrous project of crossing the wilderness to Ogdensburg, you may soon thereafter
write *Ichabod* on every barren mountain side
throughout the entire region. The State Railroad,
from Plattsburg to Clinton Prison, is bad enough—
a stupendous job in the interest of the Chateaugay
Iron Company, to which it is rented for ninety-nine
years, at the liberal rate of a dollar a year, which
Iron Company will extend the road to its rich ore
beds, and then lay waste a vast portion of the
forest for charcoal, to make iron; but even this is
not half so monstrous as the other project of cutting the wilderness in twain and destroying it far
and wide on either side, not only by cutting, but by
setting it on fire, as with the pine woods of New
Jersey.

Nearly every spring, before the leaves appear,
and during every long, dry, hot summer, forest fires
here are more or less frequent. They are easily
kindled. A lighted match or cigar-stump, or the
cinders of an emptied pipe, dropped upon the dry
inflammable turf or 'duff' as it is here called, will
start a conflagration in the forest. Much more will
a smudge or an unextinguished camp-fire or sparks
from a locomotive do it. This 'duff' is simply the
decayed mould of leaves and fallen trees. It is
sometimes a foot deep. In this the forest roots

8

itself and grows. Below is sand or rock, no clay.
When dry, this mould is as inflammable as tinder,
and smoulders in the same intense way. When
ignited, the fire burrows rapidly in every direction
under the trees, making a dense smoke, but no
flame. When the mould is consumed, great masses
of trees crash down with a terrific noise and catch
on fire. This communicates with the more distant
parts of the neighboring forest yet standing, and a
vast roaring conflagration is the result, until a long,
heavy rain-storm comes to extinguish it, wholly or
in part. Sometimes these fires smoulder in the
" duff " until the snows of winter come, which alone
effectually extinguish them; but usually the fire
ceases only when there is nothing more to feed it.
In that case, the mould or " duff " is completely
burned up. The naked sand and rock appear, upon
which nothing can grow again, any more than upon
the barren sands of Sahara, or the seashore.
Immense tracts of such barrenness and desolation
exist in the inevitable " fire-slashes " around or near
all the settlements—have so existed for half a century or more, and will so exist to the end of time.
They have been caused mainly by the deliberate
firing of the forest as the most expeditious way of
clearing the land; and every year more " fire-
slashes " are made as the meager soil wears out
upon the poor farms nourished by no fertilizers.
Not only squatters, but owners of land are respon-

sible for all this mischief. A careless or drunken
camp-crew is the occasional cause. Malicious mischief, or spite and revenge sometimes wickedly fire
choice portions of timber lands, and add their
share of desolation to all the rest. These vast
open expanses of barrenness are breeders of fierce
heats in summer, as well as of destructive cyclones
and terrific hail-storms now so common in the
Adirondack region, some of which have laid the
best parts of the forest low for miles in extent;
notably the "windfall," fifty miles long by half a
mile wide, over which a fierce tornado swept some
years ago and cut down every tree and bush like a
mower's scythe. But worst of all these destructive
agencies, are the great hordes of wild and savage
huckleberry-pickers, who sweep down upon the
open places of the wilderness every summer like
swarms of devouring locusts, to make the desolation as complete and perfect as possible. They
come chiefly from the lowlands bordering on the
St. Lawrence River, and are the terror of all the
mountaineers, the intolerable nuisance and standing
menace of every sportsman. They are marauders,
pure and simple ; insolent, thievish, turbulent and
brutal. They are worse than tramps, because they
are armed to the teeth, and it is dangerous to be
near them. Their encampments are usually scenes
of drunken debauchery. Their girls will stone
you, and their men will secretly fire upon you while

quietly fishing, or watching for deer. Their shouting and drumming on tin-pans purposely spoil your hunt, when the dogs are driving your game straight to your watch-ground. If, unsuspecting or inexperienced, you pitch a camp near them, it may be set on fire. And to make wider and fresher picking-grounds for future expeditions after berries, they deliberately set fire to the wooded hills and valleys on their departure for home. This is their chief mischief, and of every year's wicked perpetration. Savage Utes can be no worse in burning the forest to drive game. And this in the great Empire State of New York, with no adequate forest legislation or police force to interpose! In this disgraceful matter, I simply record my own experience and that of some of my friends, hoping that something may be done to make the northern portion of the Adirondack wilderness a safe summer resort, and to preserve it as a sanitarium for the worn-out invalid and for the general welfare in its equalizing effects upon the atmosphere, climate, humidity and regular distribution of the rain-fall.

As a corollary to this forest investigation, I simply cite recent famines in India, China and Brazil, consequent upon the absence of extensive woods. Long droughts in these countries have caused an utter failure of crops, whereby millions of men, women, children and cattle have perished of famine, accompanied by small-pox and the

plague, as in Brazil especially. In the northern
provinces of China the famine of 1878 was only a
little greater in horrible destruction of life than
that of 1832. The whole landscape of Mongolia
in the 17th century, according to M. Huc, was one of
rude grandeur; the mountains were covered with
fine forests, and the Mongol tents whitened the
valleys, amid rich pasturages. For a very moderate
sum the Chinese obtained permission to cultivate
the desert, and as cultivation advanced, the Mongols
were obliged to retreat. From that time forth the
aspect of the country became entirely changed.
All the trees were destroyed, the forests disappeared
from the hills, the prairies were cleared by means
of fire, and the new cultivators set busily to work
in exhausting the richness of the soil. Almost the
entire region is now in the hands of the Chinese,
and it is probably to their system of devastation
that we must attribute the extreme irregularity of
the seasons which now desolate this unhappy land.
Droughts are of almost annual occurrence; the
spring winds setting in, dry up the soil; the heavens
assume a sinister aspect, and the unfortunate
population await, in utter terror, the manifestation
of some terrible calamity; the winds, by degrees,
redouble their violence, and sometimes continue to
blow far into the summer months. Then the dust
rises in clouds, the atmosphere becomes thick and
dark; and often, at mid-day, you are environed

8*

with the terrors of night, or a blackness a thousand
times more fearful. Next after these hurricanes
comes the rain; but so comes, that instead of being
an object of desire, it is an object of dread, for it
pours down in furious raging torrents. Sometimes
the heavens, suddenly opening, pour forth an
immense cascade of water in certain quarters, and
immediately the fields and their crops disappear
under a sea of mud, whose enormous waves follow
the course of the valleys, and carry everything
before them. The torrent rushes on, and in a few
hours the earth reappears; but the crops are gone,
and worse even than that, the arable soil also has
gone with them. Nothing remains but a ramifica-
tion of deep ruts, filled with gravel, and thenceforth
incapable of tillage.

The droughts and inundations together sometimes
occasion famines, continues M. Huc, which well
nigh exterminate the inhabitants. That of 1832 is
the most terrible on record. Spring and summer
passed away without rain, and the frosts of autumn
set in while the crops were yet green; these crops
of course perished, and there was absolutely no
harvest. The population was soon reduced to the
most entire destitution. Houses, fields, cattle,
everything was exchanged for grain, now worth its
weight in gold. When the grass on the mountain
sides was devoured by the starving creatures, they
dug into the earth for roots. Thousands died upon

the hills, whither they had crawled in search of
grass; dead bodies filled the roads and houses;
whole villages were depopulated to the last man.
Neither rich nor poor were left; pitiless famine had
levelled all alike. (*Travels in Tartary, Thibet, and
China*, I, pp. 11–13.)

The famine of the year 1878, in three of the
northern provinces of China, carried off over
7,000,000 of human beings. There had been no
rain in all the land, for three years, of sufficient
amount to produce crops. The little that did fall,
in occasional light showers, was at once evaporated
by the hot sun from a dry soil on which there were
no trees to shelter it and retain the moisture. In
all this stricken region of famine there is said to
be hardly a tree left, and it has become a desert
from the same cause of that devastating policy
mentioned above. Pitiful and heart-rending are
the accounts given of this dreadful famine. For
all these years of drought, men, women and children
desperately toiled to fight off starvation by tilling
a parched soil that could not yield them sustenance;
then, as heretofore, they went to eating grass; when
the grass failed, they dug roots; ate insects, vermin,
and their own dead; mothers, driven mad by the
cries of their starving children, buried them alive
to end their sufferings, or else killed them for food;
and at last, with black and bloated faces, they fell
dead by thousands and millions, at home, on the

hills and fields, and along the road sides, victims of their own blind folly and sin or that of their fathers, in violating the laws of nature and destroying her beneficent equilibrium of climate and moisture in summer and winter, seed-time and harvest, as maintained by the forest.

But the heartless, brutal and cruel policy of two great Christian nations towards these despairing and starving Chinese is far more a matter of tearful and indignant wonder than famine itself and its destruction of millions. When the poor Chinese were crying for bread, some time after the dreadful famine of 1832, the British Government made war upon them and crammed opium down their throats, as if to stifle that cry of famished agony, and forever stupify and silence its troublesome importunity. That most iniquitous Opium War has fastened upon China a heavy carcass of disease and death compared with which even famine and pestilence are but slight evils. These Pagan children asked for bread, and the good Christian Fathers of England gave them poison, bullets, fire and slaughter. The Chinese Government was helpless then; it is just as helpless now; and the opium trade of Christian England still goes on, bearing misery and death throughout the dense population of that vast empire, without a protest from the Church Prelates and Peers of the Realm. A Chinese anti-opium society has been formed to do

what it can in mitigation of the evil which is fast
bringing their country to ruin; and this is the
despairing cry which it utters: "If this evil is
allowed to go on, there will remain no remedy, no
salvation for our country. We ask, in the name of
Heaven, what unheard-of crime we have committed,
that we should be thus punished? *Since the creation
down to our days no plague has so ravaged our
country.*" And what is the natural consequence?
Wolfe, the great English Missionary, thus expresses
it: "There is one thing which the Chinese people
dislike, and which has tended more than anything
else to produce hatred of foreigners, and cause
misery and ruin to multitudes of the Chinese
people themselves; and that one thing is the act of
the British Government in compelling the Chinese
people to buy opium, at the point of the bayonet,
when they virtuously and patriotically protested
against it. I have invariably found in my journeys
through the country that this act of the British
Government is remembered with deep and lasting
hatred by all classes of the people, and is handed
down from father to son as one cause why the
English should be held in everlasting hatred and
contempt."

But Christian England is not alone in meriting
the everlasting hatred and contempt of the Pagan
Chinese people in rejecting the civilization and religion which it thus offers by her charitable opium

trade and naval armaments ; the present Government of the United States is attempting a like
experiment, at the instigation of the Irishman. Denis
Kearney, backed by a mob of hungry Californian
politicians, and even by petitions signed by clergy-
men and a Protestant Bishop, to drive the starving
Chinese emigrants from our shores.   And this, too,
right in the pale face of the dreadful famine of
1878.   Where shall these famished creatures go for
a little bread to keep them alive ?   Thousands and
thousands of starving Papists from Ireland, and
thousands more of blaspheming Jews from all
Europe, and hordes of atheistical Communists and
beer drinkers from Germany, have swarmed like
locusts to our shores, and have found welcome to
the ballot-box stufling of all our large towns and
cities ; but because the poor Chinese prefer hard
work at moderate wages and take no interest in
party politics, they must go — go back to starvation
and death.   Restrictive emigration laws, reported
in Congress, are for them alone.   Pass them ; make
them operative, and henceforth Americans in China
will share with Englishmen the everlasting hatred
and contempt of the Chinese Government and people.   Shall our trade and commerce with China, our
civilization and our Christian schools and enterprises there, be all endangered by the shillalah
tongue of the blatant Irish demagogue, Kearney,
and by the restrictive policy, which it so wickedly

advocates and demands? If sauce for the goose is
equally good sauce for the gander, then, in the name
of justice and fair-play, let these restrictive emigration laws of our present Democratic Congress,
include Denis Kearney and all his Irish race.

The present Tory government of Great Britain
is seeking a "scientific frontier" of its Eastern empire. Had it studied the science of Forestry a
little better, it never would have added sickly worn-
out Cyprus to its domain, nor would it have sent
an army to the present doubtful conquest of Afghanistan. India has ceased to be profitable to the
British exchequer, and is a standing menace to the
British usurpation of her territory. Because the
Hindoo worships any superior power and patiently
submits to it as long as possible; when some other
and greater power appears for his deliverance,
whether native or foreign, then he will rise against
his present oppressors, as in the dreadful days of
mutiny at Cawnpore. Lucknow and Delhi, and
massacre them to the last man. The native Hindoos have no love for Englishmen in India, nor for
any of their ways and doings; they endure and
submit in silent hatred, waiting for a leader. It is
the London *Spectator* which says : " Hindoos feel
oppression like other men. They are as angry when
they are uncomfortable as other men. They are as
ready to fight for their rights, and especially their
right to live out of their labor as any other men.

But none of them will do any unusual act alone.
They cannot act, except together, in an association
which gives them the feeling of being protected
both against force and against opinion. There
must be a band; a band implies a leader, and till a
leader appears, they will bear anything rather than
move. The leader found, the band made, the spell
of their peculiar fear is broken: they are all ready
at once to proceed against the oppressive regime in
a fit of angry desperation, deluging the land in
blood and fire, so that the existing government has
to struggle sword in hand for its very life. It makes
no difference who the leader is, whether a prince or
cowherd, so long as he is competent by mental
power, skill and courage. 'The gods have chosen
him who wins,' say the priests, and the pedigree of
his leader matters no more to the mind of the Hindoo insurgent than to a Roman Conclave in their
choice of a Pope. This profound belief that power
is in itself sacred, and that success proves the ap-
probation of the gods, while it makes insurrection
rare in India, yet makes it at any time probable,
sudden and dangerous."

Add to this the testimony of the late Ex-Secretary
Seward and the present Afghanistan complications,
and famished, oppressed India may be nearer the
time of her deliverance than we suppose. When
Mr. Seward was in that unhappy country, some few
years ago, a wealthy *baboo*, or merchant, confiden-

tially assured him that, "a general discontent with
with the British authority was felt by his countrymen, but without any present idea of an uprising
or resistance—hoping that, amid the chances of war
India will receive a new conqueror, either the
United States or Russia." (*Travels*, p. 357.)

Naturally it must be Russia as nearest the scene
of action; and Afghanistan may be the proximate
or remote occasion. When that clash of arms
resounds along the heights of the Hindoo Koosh,
between England and Russia, the hour will have come
for Indian mutiny and a general uprising; the art
of modern warfare which England has been teaching patient Sepoys, these many years, will be turned
against her to avenge the wrongs and robberies
and oppressions endured from the days of Hastings
to the present time; and advancing Russia, Asiatic
in all her sympathies and modes of government,
will restore the ancient patriarchal regime over the
" palmy plain " of India.

The profound discontent and silent dislike lurk-
ing under the patient and even smiling acquiescence
and submission of the Hindoo, in his subjection to
the power and authority of England, find ample
illustration in an interesting occurrence which I
witnessed on board the Peninsular and Oriental
Company's steamer " Ceylon," in March, 1860.
Being one of a party of sixteen Americans on our
way to Egypt, Palestine, and Syria, to learn some-

9

thing of the present and past condition of those old countries from personal observation, I naturally kept my eyes open to every little passing incident or strange occurrence. The majority of the passengers were English officials and travelers on their way to India and China. Among the rest was Lady Trevelyan, Lord Macaulay's sister, wife of the Governor General of Madras, going to join her husband. One of the ship's company was a native of India, a rich, accomplished and very intelligent Mohammedan Prince, an author of repute in his own country, on his return home after a protracted sojourn in England, where he had gone to study its society, laws and civilization on the spot. This Prince had received distinguished attentions in England, and was one of the lions of London society for a season or two. He was a gentleman in the best sense of that much abused word, and spoke English correctly and fluently, with but slight accent. Our American party was most rigidly ignored the whole distance to Alexandria from Malta, where we took passage on the "Ceylon." It was then the fashion; since, much out of date. The only notice we attracted from our stiff English cousins was as to the extreme singularity of Americans on an actual visit to Egypt and the Holy Land, then not so common as now. The weather was mild and warm; the sea smooth and beautiful under the light of a full moon. There was dancing on board till a late hour in the night, on which we Americans were permitted to gaze in silent wonder. No hint or intimation was given us to join the festive exercises and good fellowship.

It so happened that, at dinner on the last day of the voyage, a certain bluff Major of her Majesty's service in India, whose name I have forgotten, sat at table between the Mohammedan Prince and my wife, while I sat next beyond her. The Major, supposing my wife to be an Englishwoman, after some conversation ventured a final remark upon the American party on board, to this effect: " Really, Madam, it's a most extraordinary thing, that there are sixteen Americans on this ship, who are going to Palestine and Jerusalem. What they mean to do there, except spend their money ostentatiously and get into a row with the natives, I don't know. What a shabby looking set they are, anyway, not fit for genteel society." Some American blood crimsoned my wife's cheeks, and some American pride of spirit sparkled in her eyes, as, with quiet accents in her trembling voice, she replied : " Sir, I am one of that party." Astonishment and confusion disconcerted the Major's complacency, as if some sudden night-attack had been made upon his sleeping bivouac in the field of battle. Without apology, and in gruff, hesitating tones, his only remark was : " La, Madam, I thought I was talking, this while, to an Englishwoman."

And then he turned away to engage the Prince in
a discussion upon religion. The dinner was drawing to an end amid much noise, drinking, profanity,
and rough play among the younger men of the
company, when I heard the gentle ripple of a laugh
from the Prince, followed by a loud smack in his
face from the Major. Pale with anger, the Prince
arose and went out on deck, pacing back and forth
like an enraged tiger. The Major finished his dinner in silent satisfaction, not joining in the revel
going on around him.

When I went on deck to find the Prince, and
express my indignation and sympathy, he said this:
" Sir, I have been grossly insulted in the presence
of this distinguished company,—slapped in the face
by that rude English officer because I defended my
religion better than he did his own, if he had any;
—what am I to do?" My reply was: " Report
his outrageous misconduct at head-quarters, when
you reach home. Of course, you stand no chance
in a duel with an experienced soldier, and assassination is out of the question with so good a man
as yourself." The Prince interposed: " But they
slap us in the face at home; degrade, abuse and
oppress us; call us all niggers, and treat us as
menials; ostracise us socially; give us the lowest
places in any service of the state; load us down
with heavy burdens of taxation; get out of us all
they can, with nothing to compensate; and we are

only biding our time for retaliation and release from the hateful power. Helpless now we are, but not forever." I parted with the Prince at Alexandria, and saw him no more. Some few years afterwards, I learned from a young Anglo-Indian, to whom I gave the above account of slapping the Prince in the face, that a certain Major in India had been dismissed the service for such or other like ungentlemanly conduct. If Lord Lytton were Viceroy of India at that time, a like incident under his administration would have been as severely condemned.

An English resident in Bombay slapped his native groom in the face, felling him to the ground, and he afterwards died. An examination showed that rupture of the spleen had caused his death, and that the blow had indirectly led to the result. The Englishman was fined a trifling sum and dismissed. The Viceroy, Lord Lytton, or Owen Meredith, author of *Lucille*, demanded and investigation by the high court. The court reported that they did not find the sentence open to objection. Lord Lytton disagreed with them, and issued a most scathing review of the whole affair, expressing his abhorrence of the brutal manner in which English masters treated their servants. Naturally, the Englishmen would not listen to such ideas, and the whole community arose in arms. An Englishman had no right to beat a Hindoo? Absurd! From

9*

this moment every official and even every private
act of the Viceroy was held up to scorn. Who was
this Lord Lytton? His father had written novels
and plays; his mother was an Irish girl, who had
composed dry and crabbed essays; and he had
himself dabbled in verse, and in some vague way
had borne a part in diplomatic circles. Prejudiced
against him thus from the start, and considering
him an intruder upon the sacred soil of Indian
politics, their opportunity for his recall came with
this just rebuke of their brutal treatment of the
the native Hindoos. For transatlantic advices intimate that Lord Lytton, after a three years' successful and honorable tenure of office, is about to
resign his position as Viceroy of India, because his
administration of the office was execrable in the
estimation of resident Englishmen.

Now, when all this insult and degradation and
wrong are added to the horrors of famine in India
and China by brutal Englishmen, whose mission on
earth seems to be to go about slapping all weak
and defenceless peoples and nations in the face as
their menials and slaves, the wonder is how long it
is to last. When England once attempts the experiment on Russia, the Bear will undoubtedly
strike back with his ugly and vigorous paw, and
there will be the tight hug of a terrible death.
grapple. For India, any change but anarchy and
perdition would be a relief; and, therefore, in that

coming contest, it would be in strict accordance
with the eternal fitness of things that Russia should
win, and establish her better and more congenial
rule, protectorate or alliance, as the case may be,
over this oppressed and plundered portion of the
Orient.

During our exile at Saranac Lake the Russo-
Turkish War was in progress. After the long siege
and fall of Plevna, the triumphant passage of the
Balkans, and the jubilant march of the Russian
army on Constantinople, there was something so
comical and clownish in the fume and bluster of the
Tory Government of England and the eccentricities
of her Mediterranean Fleet as to give us poor lonely
Exiles about the only bit of real fun we could extract from our New York papers. We understood
it as a game of pure bluff; and when the Sepoys of
India appeared upon the scene, and the solemn
farce at Berlin was enacted by some of the interested Powers of Europe, we laughed all the more ;
and thought of the days of King George III. and
his hireling Hessians, and the issues of his war upon
his own American Colonies. But when we thought
of England even thus doing her utmost to preserve
the Turkish Power in Europe in its most atrocious
misrule, oppression and massacre of her Christian
subjects,—an England most degenerate grown since
the heroic days of the Crusades and her lion-hearted
Richard, then the laughter turned into tearful in-

dignation, and our sympathetic rhymester was impelled to give it vent. His effusion is more
energetic than elegant; but it proved to be satisfactory to the majority of our little company
assembled one stormy Sunday evening for reading
and conversation. It is herewith given as part of
the records and doings of our colony of exiles and
invalids.

TORY BEAR-BAITING--PAST AND PRESENT.

Like pot-house Kearney searching far and near,
For pure potheen his Irish heart to cheer,
Draining the jug with shout and tipsy song,
For will to do, but not endure, the wrong,--
Ben Jingo Dizzy must have had a bee
Under his bonnet, at the Berlin Spree ;
The wine went round ; the feast was rich and gay ;
A roasted Turkey on the table lay,
All smoking hot, well-done, but rather lean ;
Bulgarian doves choice courses serv'd between,
Which Ben disdaining, call'd in hungry tone.
For second joints, Pope's nose, and sweet side-bone :
The Sultan cooked the doves ; the Czar the fowl
Of jealous Europe in perpetual scowl ;
And Bruin meant to have the greater share,
Whatever Jingo Dizzy might forswear.

An Empire lost beyond th' Atlantic Main,
Cyprus is hired, the Queen of Love's domain ;
Zulu and Afghan feel the oppressor's hand,
And every helpless, hapless Pagan land,

Yielding supplies to sate the British greed,
Though millions starve and hungry nations bleed.
The bull-dog Briton flies at every race
Defenceless, timid, snapping heels and face,
And dragging down to tear them in the dust,
In savage pleasure and unbounded lust.
Must not Lord Bishops and Lord Barons dine?
Quaffing great goblets of life's ruddy wine?
Must not the world pay tribute to the Jew?
Making Messiah's Kingdom English, too?
New course of Empire must be now begun,
Marching no more from East to Western sun;
The stars must all their lawful courses change,
To fight for England and her world-wide grange.

When loyal Colonist in Western wild,
Bewailed injustice, pleading like a child.
Thy brows were knit in blackest hues of night,
Swearing and blustering thou wert in the right;
In angry violence crack'd loud the lash,
Into submission this bad boy to thrash;
Chas'd him from home, thy folly to deplore,
Envied his greatness, hated him the more.
And yet sometimes the old man wipes his eye,
Asking himself in vain the reason why,—
"No matter; let it pass,—I'm sick at heart,
Because this lad and I must live apart."

Yet search his ships, impress his tars as slaves,
Does not Brittania rule the ocean waves?
And when he gains the freedom of the seas,
Like Boston harbor, full of floating teas;
When Yankees make the highways of the main,
Safe from thy bandit arrogance and reign;

When flags of nations flutter in the breeze,
O'er every sea, despite thy loud decrees —
Assume a virtue if thou hast it not,
For nigger slaves and their unhappy lot,
Banish the trade from all thy vast domain,
When it has wrought thee more of loss than gain.
Make all trade free to swell thy single purse,
And damn the Yankees with thy harmless curse.

Berate their land in agony of strife,
For Union fighting as its breath of life,
Its slaves to free, thy legacy of ill,
And make for all one law of peace, good-will,
One brotherhood of men, by birth proclaimed
One blood and kinship, as of God ordained.
Aid treason and its rebel Southern brood ;
Buy up its bonds to glut thy envious mood ;
Give aid and comfort to these lords of lust,
To rend the Union and destroy its trust ;
Take bloody traitors to thy fond embrace,
Slidells and Masons, meanest of their race ;
Protect them, pet them,—shot thy heavy guns,
And dare the Yankees take these Absoloms :
Take them they did, but yielded up again,
Not to thy threats, but freedom of the main :
And when the Union waves its victor flag,
Blaspheme and scoff the vulgar Yankee brag.

No more chivalric, and no longer just,
As when the Lion Richard held thy trust,
Fighting the Paynim on the Sacred Sod,
Once trod in mercy by the Son of God ;
Truth fallen that the Turk may riot there,
Cursing the agony of Christian pray'r.

When Peter draws the sword to smite him down,
And guard the Sacred Head from thorny crown,—
When mighty Muscovy, like wrathful Bear,
Advances grimly from his snowy lair,
Avenging Christian wrongs and mournful plaints,
So long gone up from dead and living saints,—
Then whistle forth the slot-hounds to pursue,
Old Kaiser, Frenchman Turk, Italian, too ;
Bait him and tear him in Crimean ring,
And as he growls and bleeds, exult and sing ;
He's down, not vanquish'd ; crippled for a day,
And will again confront thee in the way
Of other pastime to thy hoary locks,
Then baiting bears and running hounds and fox.

For now, again, when all the northern pines
Sing joy and peace with merry Christmas chimes ;
When Moslem wrong lies helpless and undone,
A rotting carcass under Orient sun,
And soaring eagles come from far and near,
To cleanse the land and fill it with good cheer ;
When Plevna falls, and Balkans' iron gate
Is pass'd, and Turkey finds her Kismet,—Fate ;
Then puff and bluster ; split with fear and rage ;
Roar like a lion in his iron cage ;
Go mad with envy ; rack thy scheming brain.
To balk old Bruin in the Porte's domain.
Fling treaties to the winds ; break faith with all ;
Add treachery to insult, spleen to gall ;
Hunt for allies, and hunt them up in vain ;
Send forth thy navy—send it back again ;
Then try again,—then prudently hold fire ;
Vote thy munitions in hot haste and ire ;—

The game is bluff, old Falstaff, to the strong,
To win more sack for brawling tavern song.
Alone and single, thou didst have a care,
To go and meet the rampant Russian Bear ;
Erect he stood, mouth open for the fight,
Filling thy soul with horror and affright.
Some pretext must be sought to save thy name,
And vaunted prowess from contempt and shame ;
Mob Gladstone, drunk with sophistry of words,
Denouncing cruel Turks and bloody Kurds ;
Send to the Berlin Spree some Tory sons,
With secret treaties backed by Sepoy guns,—
Ben and his Sal to make a grand display
Of brag and bullion, pomp and pother gay ;
Call Wolseley or Sir Ham Pennywon,
To lead thy niggers to the baiting fun ;
Bruin is waiting in his snowy lair,
Sucking his paws to sharpen and prepare.

Poor starving India writhes in sleepless pain,
Under the wrongs of thy detested reign ;
Hastings there are who yet oppress and kill,
If plundered Rajahs dare resist thy will.
When mutiny breaks forth among her sons,
Blow them to atoms with thy scrapnel guns ;
When Princes claim the prestige of their race,
Trample them down and cover with disgrace,—
Niggers they are to serve the British crown,
And add new lustre to its old renown.
When China, for her people sore afraid,
Protests against thy poisonous opium-trade,
Then show her all the might of Christian power,
In sack and slaughter, burning town and tower ;

Must not fat Bishops and lean Barons dine?
Quaffing great goblets of life's ruddy wine?
Nemesis frowns and shakes her golden rod,
Calling the vengeful Furies all abroad.

What if the Bear o'er India's palmy plain,
And China's deserts, spread his vast domain?
The Hindoo Koosh may be the rocky lair,
His giant thews to shelter and prepare ;
And issuing thence in sure and solemn might,
To smite the wrong and give the Orient right ;—
What millions then shall hail his glad advance,
Where Double-Eagles in the sunbeams dance ;
Old England's royal banner must go down,
From every ravaged plain and plundered town ;
And over all, by conqu'ring Czar unfurled,
The flag of Peace shall shield the Orient world.

III

ENVIRONMENT.

Environment, or our external surroundings and condition, is of two kinds, viz.: nature, as wild or as cultivated; and man, as savage or as civilized. It would puzzle a Philadelphia lawyer to disentangle from the jumble of contradictions in our environment at Saranac Lake any consistent definition or description, inasmuch as nature had been suppressed; and a real man was hard to find. Nature had been cropped like a convict,—lopped off like the legs and arms of a Union soldier, and reduced to a mere stump, without a single artificial contrivance to improve her appearance or aid her movements. She only hobbled and squatted by turns, and was altogether unlovely. Man was reduced to the hardest of all struggles for existence, and stood moping on one leg like a crane in a bog watching for hours together for a fine fat frog. This was his sole occupation all the fair summer long; and during the long dreary winter he turned into a sleeping bear and hibernated on the fat of his paws. He could not migrate to better regions because of excessive poverty of purse and poverty of spirit. Shorn of all manly pluck

and ambition, he was content to be a mere dawdler.
Too dull, slow and stupid to learn anything for his
improvement, he was also too obstinate to have any
greatness thrust upon him. Shy and suspicious, he
rejected all new ideas and suggestions for his benefit, and looked upon all physical and mental
superiority with aversion or disdain. All science
to him was mere humbug; art, a pretense and a de-
lusion; religion, a sham and a cheat. He had cunning and courage enough to club deer to death in the
water or slaughter them in their yards when the deep
crusted snow prevented their escape. He trapped
a little, and too often sold the pelts for whisky and
tobacco instead of procuring food for his hungry
wife and children. The law of purity and marriage
was unknown to him, and he scrictly followed the
rule of Henry VIII and his Paget Nobility, or
the better practice of the Mormon bishops. His
ideal man was the fire-eating juggler and commun-
ist, Denis Kearney, and not his own former neighbor, the heroic John Brown, about the only real
specimen of manhood ever produced in the Adirondack wilderness, and seldom produced anywhere
else. Brag, bluster, drunken brawl and bloody
fight, licentious revel and dance, rape, incest and
bastardy, were about the only pastimes and enjoyments of which he was capable. All his loud talk
was obscene and profane. When he could read at
all, his choice books were coarse vulgar dime novels.

Shakespeare was incomprehensible, and Dickens was too refined, too dull and uninteresting. Churches there were none until a very recent period, and even Bibles were exceedingly rare. School houses have been recently built here and there by means of the taxation of non-resident owners of land, and they are kept open a few months in the winter for the instruction of children too small for cutting or burning down the forest for new land to grow potatoes and oats. This was the state of things at Saranac Lake and elsewhere up to a recent time ; and although Sunday shooting-matches and street fights have ceased, there still remains a vast amount of rudeness, vulgarity, ignorance and vice to make the environment anything but attractive and improving. And some of us have survived an eight months' endurance of it to tell the winter tale of our dismal exile.

A short time since, I met young Borlase at one of the pleasant weekly gatherings of scholars, poets, jurists, diplomatists, statesmen and other notables, that informally met to discuss various topics of interest, at the hospitable mansion of a friend on, the Fifth Avenue, New York ; and this archæological enthusiast, inheriting the disposition and energy of his great-grandfather of precious memory, had crossed the Atlantic to explore some of the ancient remains of our American prehistoric civilization. He brought me the drawing of an Asiatic *swastica*,

which he had that day made in one of our museums
of native antiquities, and asked me to tell him what
it was. I informed him that it was the oldest form
of the cross known, and that it first appeared in
ancient India, and was found at Troy, Herculaneum,
and in the Christian Catacombs at Rome. How it
ever came to North America was to me a mystery,
unless it was a universal symbol among all nations
and peoples, ancient and modern, of life and its
eternal perpetuity. He told me that he was going
to the Far West to examine the mounds and rock-
buildings of prehistoric times, and possibly to Central America. When he reached San Francisco,
Borlase inquired of one of its busy and sprightly
citizens whether there were any antiquities in the
neighborhood, such as temples or tombs or ruins of
any kind. He was confidently answered in the affirmative, and then directed to an old dilapidated
shanty having the extreme antiquity of forty years.
Borlase told this in one of his London lectures as a
good joke, illustrating the average American ap-
preciation of its own antiquities.

If young Borlase had gone with me to Corey's farm
at the foot of the Upper Saranac, he might have found
stone implements and fragments of ancient pot-
tery ornamented with zig-zag lines and *swasticas*, to
his heart's content ; but which there attract no attention whatever, except from some collector. They
are ploughed up every year and cast aside as

10*

worthless.   A bottle of whisky is of far more account.   There is a log hut not far away fifty years
old, which is of greater interest and pointed out
with more pride and enthusiasm than this old Indian encampment and graveyard.   And this half
century of intrusion and settlement in this part of
the wilderness has produced sad havoc and destruction of the forest, and wrought as frightful a desolation almost as that of Sahara itself. The miserable
hamlet of Saranac Lake,—its present name twice
changed from that of Baker's and Harrietstown, as
if the people were ashamed of having it long known
under one appellation,—consists of about fifty or
sixty log and frame houses, and has a population of
three or four hundred souls.   It is in a little deep
basin of hills on every side of it, on the main branch
of the Saranac river, a few miles from its leaving
the lower lake of that name, and one mile below
Martin's.   It is nearly forty miles distant from the
terminus of the branch railroad from Plattsburg to
Ausable, and is reached by daily stage.   The Mon-
treal Telegraph Company has a station here from
which despatches can be sent anywhere.   It is this
sheltered position of the place in winter, this daily
stage and the telegraph that have given Saranac
Lake its main attraction to invalids, aside from the
pure invigorating mountain air.   It has two country
stores of the usual heterogeneous assortment of
coarse dry goods, boots and shoes, groceries, hard-

ware and quack medicines, but no books or maga-
zines. An old rickety saw-mill supplies the place
and neighborhood with building materials; and a
steam-mill occasionally makes shingles and clap-
boards. There is also a small grist-mill; one shoe-
maker, but no tailor. The barber of the place is a
peripatetic on crutches, going from house to house
or from room to room, on call, to discharge his ton-
sorial duties and do the main head-work of the
community, at the rate of twenty-five cents for each
clipping and manipulation, which must be considered as a fair price, and the usual average of all
other head-work, except that of legislation and railroad management and stock gambling. But when
the Saturday stress of business came round and
the calls were too numerous to be answered by the
slow process of stumping over the village buried in
snow, an appointment was made and an assembly
called at the popular store, which was central and
convenient, and at the same time, the post office,
telegraph station and general lounging place. The
head-work here done was marvelous, and there were
many admiring spectators. With one leg, one wife,
ten children and twenty-five cents a clipping, our
peripatetic managed to get his whisky and tobacco,
and trusted to good luck for the rest of his and his
family's support. It must, however, be set down
to his credit that he subscribed two dollars for the
erection of the new village church, which he agreed

to pay in the best possible head-work of which he was capable.

To the everlasting honor of Saranac Lake, it must be said, that it has no lawyers or newspaper editors to do the mischievous and harassing head-work of keeping the community in an uproar of needless excitement and agitation. No newsboys din your ears to deafness or startle your nervous sensibilities by their loud, shrill cries and startling announcements; no lawyers plot for fat fees or manufacture bogus cases; all is peace and quietness. Far distant Malone, the county-town of Franklin and the residence of lawyer, Vice-President Wheeler, is rather the place of these tumultuous cries and harassing trials. One good doctor of medicine, Saranac Lake, perforce has, during the winter, the intrepid and heroic invalid, Trudeau, who for some years has here sought to regain his shattered health, and not sought in vain, despite the wretched lonely environment. Ready and willing to give his best advice to his needy sick friends, and to the very poor who cannot afford to send for some distant physician, without money and without price, it was also by his good management and great energy that the enterprise of our little colony of exiles and invalids in church building was carried out to a successful issue on the 10th of July, 1879, when the Bishop of Albany, the first who had ever visited this region in an official capacity, consecrated the

beautiful and commodious Church of St. Luke the
Beloved Physician, to the worship and service of
Almighty God, as he had already, a year and a-half
before, consecrated the Church of St. John in the
Wilderness, at St. Regis Lake. Both these churches
owe their existence to the earnest suggestions and
faithful oversight of the Rev. Dr. Lundy and Dr.
E. L. Trudeau, aided by the generous gifts of Christian visitors and sojourners of various names; and
nowhere in the world are churches more needed.

Saranac Lake has one flourishing tavern, whose
landlord, it is needless to say, is the richest man in
the place; and who, publican and sinner as he is,
gave us the choice of a half-acre lot on which to
erect our church. A traditional blacksmith shop
and two large boarding houses, of which "The
Berkeley," our home, was one, completes the list of
attractions in our immediate environment. But,
when a solitary rare day of bright sunshine comes
to melt the thick fantastic frost-work from our
small window-panes, let us look out upon the scene
beyond. It is white and dazzling in its thick
mantle of snow to such a remarkable extent and
degree of brilliant purity and lovliness, as to make
one envy the descriptive power of that fine French
writer. GAUTIER, recently dead, in his fascinating
account of a *Winter in Russia*. But instead of the
splendid churches and palaces of St. Petersburg
and Moscow, we here behold nothing but low cabins

and dilapidated stables or tumble-down fences, that
have never seen a drop of paint, or here and there
a better human habitation, harmonizing in whiteness with the surrounding scene. The fields, far
and near, are full of charred and blackened stumps,
intermingled with great boulders rolled down from
distant Labrador in the ice-floes of remote ages.
The steep, conical hills around, are stripped of their
evergreens, and stand bare and trembling in the
keen winter blasts. The distant mountain ridges
are seamed and scarred, where great gashes and
blisters have been made by the axe and by the
demon, fire. It is all a vast and silent amphitheatre
of desolation and death. It chills you to the bone.
It sends a convulsive shudder to the very tips of
your toes and fingers. It is enough to make better
saints than we pretend to be, swear in righteous indignation.

There is, however, one object in the desolate
scene commanding especial attention; it is a noble
mountain with two rounded peaks, so arranged as
to bear a striking resemblance to the female bosom,
and hence this mountain is called, in the vernacular
of the woods, "Nipple-Top." Mr. Colvin's mod-
esty would change the name, but to no purpose.
Nipple-Top it is, and Nipple-Top it will remain so
long as it stands in its pleasing suggestiveness.
This is more especially the case when the mountain
is covered with snow and the peaks are still more

rounded and softened, and adorned with a purple
and crimson glow every clear morning and evening,
when, if ever, the very royalty of womanhood is
suggested, either as the bride decked for the marriage altar and adorned for her husband, or as the
more queenly mother nourishing her tender and
helpless offspring in the natural queenly fashion,
and not with that modern contrivance necessitated
by female degeneracy and physical delicacy and
weakness, the bottle, with its simulated gutta-
percha nipple. Think of Virgin Mary so nourishing her Divine Child!

This mountain, thus made and adorned, recalls
Erasmus Darwin's mechanical theory of Aesthetics,
—that same Erasmus Darwin, whose works contain
the seeds of his Grandson's, Charles Darwin's more
elaborate and now generally accepted theories of
Evolution, Origin of Species, Natural Descent, and
Natural Selection. In the first part of that remarkable book, Zoönomia, now almost forgotten, Erasmus Darwin thus states his doctrine: "When any
object of vision is presented to us, by its waving
or spiral lines bearing any resemblance to the form
of the female bosom—whether it be found in a
landscape with soft gradations of rising or descend-
ing surface, or in the form of some antique vases,
or in the forms of the pencil or chisel,—we feel a
general glow of delight which seems to influence
our whole senses; and if the object be not too

large, we experience an attraction to embrace it
with our arms and salute it with our lips, as we
did in our infancy the bosom of our mother."
Whereupon, the keen wit of that day sought to
turn this fiddle-faddle into ridicule, as in our own
time it has ridiculed Charles Darwin's more sensible
and considerate theories; for Sheridan replied in one
telling brief retort and soul of wit : "I suppose that
the child brought up by hand, would feel all these
emotions at the sight of a wooden spoon." Had
Sheridan now lived, he would probably have said,
gutta-percha and the bottle : unless, indeed, as in
the case of such mothers as object to bringing up
their children on the bottle, for the reason, as one
of them recently gave when urged to do so with
her first-born, "I shall do no such thing; look at
Grandpa's nose."

Sir Humphrey Davy was perhaps nearer the
mark, when he said of Darwin's theory : "I will
not allow my views as to the varieties of trout and
dogs being produced by differences of food and
habits, in a long course of ages, and transmitted to
their offspring from one primitive type, to be
assimilated with the somewhat unsound views of
Darwin, who, however ingenious, is far too speculative; whose poetry has always appeared to me
weak philosophy, and his philosophy indifferent
poetry ; and to whom I have been often accustomed
to apply Blumenbach's saying, that there were

many things new and many things true in his doctrine; but that what was new was not true, and
what was true was not new." (*Salmonia*, 2d ed..
London, pp. 72–74.)

That ardent child of Nature, Mr. John Burroughs,
came to the Adirondacks on a summer visit to his
old mother, to inquire after her health; but he did
no more than feel her pulse and recline in peace
and quietness at her feet, along the shady banks of
her clear trout-streams and beautiful lakes. It is
doubtful whether even his boyish enthusiasm and
infantile reminiscence of maternal delights would
have been equal to the task of embracing with his
arms and saluting with his lips the bosom of that
mother, even when covered with snowy and crimson
splendor on the bleak heights of old " Nipple-Top,"
with the thermometer 30 or 40 below zero. The
scientific Colvin never did anything more than
plant a signal station there, and strive to change
the dear maternal name; and not a single resident
Saranacker, far and near, was ever heard to express
the slightest pleasure in view of the maternal
bosom. To his untutored mind and obdurate heart
this motherly mountain was nothing more than a
choice spot for rousing and stalking deer, or for
seeking fire-wood and lumber. And, therefore.
Darwin's theory of æsthetics fails in its maternal
application here, although in certain other respects
appertaining to the seventh commandment of the

11

Decalogue, it may hold good.   On all this delicate
subject the talk of these mountaineers is very
coarse and ribald, and their conduct is like that of
the mere animal.   As with the men, so with the
women.

   Doubtless, environment has much to do with
that physical health and prosperity which give the
opportunity of mental and moral culture; but it
has yet to be proved that it uniformly excites and
stimulates such culture. Buckle, Spencer, and Hux-
ley to the contrary, notwithstanding.   The potency
of matter is doubtless very great; but that it is of
itself capable of originating and developing all
mental and moral activities, is thus far an unsolved
problem.   Matter and mind may be modifications
of one and the same Force, but we must still wait
for the proof of it, or some reasonable probability.
Speculation is not science.   Dogmatism is not
truth.   One fact is worth a dozen arguments.   If
a race of dogs or monkeys can be found with
germinal poetry, philosophy, and morality existing
among them, even to the faintest trace of an Iliad
or a Hamlet or a Plato's Republic or a Decalogue.
it would be something to the purpose.   Or if canine
instinct can, in the remotest sense or degree, be
assimilated with man's achievements in music and
the fine arts, or even with his cultivation of the
soil and his manufactures, his trade, commerce,
and legislation, then mere environment might be

claimed as the inciting stimulus. But dogs have
been dogs, and men have been men, with precisely
the same environment for ages upon ages, not only
showing no disposition to change places, but without ability to do so. The environment of the
Negro races in Africa and elsewhere has for thousands of years been the same magnificent scenery,
richness of soil, delightful climate, forests, game,
lakes, rivers, proximity to the abodes of civilization
in Asia and Europe, and ancient Egypt at their
very doors; and yet these black savages have never
yet even tamed an elephant to do their bidding, or
invented a Winchester rifle to bring down game or
defend themselves from lions and gorillas. No
literature, no science, no progress, have these
Negroes ever yet developed; no nationality, no
agriculture, trade and commerce, as other races of
men have. As they appear on the oldest Egyptian
monuments, thick-lipped, woolly-headed, black
slaves and captives, so they have been ever since
and are now. Prehistoric races they may be, but
no environment has ever improved them or changed
them. All their modern betterment in the abodes
of civilization is nothing to the purpose, for as
soon as the Negro is left to himself or returns to
his native wilds, he becomes a savage again. And
yet the Negro is a man, of the lowest type, indeed;
but still a man.

This matter of environment is not lugged into

our winter's tale by the ears to display itself; it
was the subject of much long and animated discussion among the members of our little colony, one
of whom was a very intelligent Darwinian and a
graduate of Yale; and therefore it forms a legitimate part of our story. Hence, this chapter is devoted to its consideration.

A new, commodious, frame house was built for
the accommodation of this invalid Darwinian and
his little family, into which three other families
were invited and one young bachelor, a law student,
in impaired health. They were all intelligent, cultivated and agreeable persons sent into exile for
purposes of health. One of these families occupied
a high position, and was well-known in the best
society of New York, the widow of a distinguished
jurist, sister of an Ex-Governor of New Jersey, U.
S. Senator, etc., with her two accomplished daughters. It was by one of these that our new house
was named "The Berkeley," still retained, after the
good bishop and philosopher who came to America
to further the progress of westward empire, and do
what he could to make this Republic time's last, best
legacy to the human race. To make "The Berkeley" worthy of its name, literature and philosophical discussion were quite in order during "the
long, long winter nights." Our rooms were made
cheerful and comfortable by blazing old-fashioned,
open fire-places, adorned with the quondam brass

andirons of our grandmothers, and the old-time
spinning wheel in the corner out of respect to their
memory. Guns, fly-rods, bird and beast pelts
mounted, hung over the walls and lay upon the
floors for ornament. Geranium plants in vases of
our own adorning stood in the deep recesses of
some of our windows. Most conspicuous and better than all, each sitting-room had its bookcase well
filled with attractive volumes in the best domain of
literature, art and philosophy. Let *The Atlantic
Monthly* take notice that some of us were proud of
our Plato, Epictetus, Marcus Aurelius, Descartes,
Leibnitz, Spinoza, Berkeley and Henry More ; that
others of us delighted in the company of Shakespeare, Dickens, Thackary, Bulwer Lytton and his
son ; that some others rejoiced in the possession of
White's *Selborne*, Walton's *Angler*, Davy's *Salmonia*, and Jesse's *British Dog;* and that Lord
Lindsay's *Christian Art*, Lübke, Mrs. Jameson's
Works, Schleiman's *Troy*, Di Cessnola's *Cyprus*,
as well as Irving, Hawthorne, Prescott and Motley
were there or easily accessible. The stage drivers
swore at our trunks and boxes, and wondered if we
had lead or iron in them, when we entered upon our
exile. No matter ; these books were the chief elements of our civilization and delight, whatever they
might be to the uncultured Saranacker who had
never heard of them. They were far more to us
than any Adirondack environment that had thus far

11*

failed to dispel any native ignorance and stupidity.
Without them our exile would have been intolerable.

Once settled in "The Berkeley," we were, of
course, the observed of all observers, of which the
entire population of the miserable hamlet constituted itself a committee of the whole. We were
the first city-folk to spend a winter there. The
maid-servants and guides were the chief spies. All
our movements and conversations were closely
watched and carefully noted as matters of future
comment and gossip; but chiefly to be reported to
the high and mighty Pontiff of the place, a ranting
and irascible Methodist parson, called the Reverend
Jehu Wagtongue Coonscratcher. This illustrious
personage took great umbrage at our invasion of
his special and exclusive field, inasmuch as we were
a proud pretentious set of "'Piscopals" without
vital piety, who had come to Saranac Lake to corrupt its innocence and pervert its serene simplicity
by a mere formal book worship, and not one of the
heart. Not deeming it necessary to ask this Pope's
permission to say our prayers in our own way, in
our own house, and not dreaming that we could
give offence to any one by so doing, we nevertheless incurred the displeasure of the jealous parson
and his meddlesome busybody of a wife, together
with their zealous adherents in Saranac Lake.
They all pounced upon us as hawks do upon smaller
birds, even flying into our windows and doors,

when open, to seize their prey. No seclusion or
privacy could keep them out. With a ferocity
and a rapacity peculiar to all zealots and fanatics,
they impaled us on their sharp tongues as the Emperor Nero did flies, and picked us to pieces with
childish delight. If any of our poor, emaciated
invalids drank a little Sauterne or claret at dinner, or took a milk-punch to aid their infirmities,
they were publicly stigmatized and denounced as
rum guzzlers and drunkards. If, as it sometimes
happened, Sunday was the one and only bright,
sunny day of the week, and any of our number
went out to get some fresh air and exercise by
a short walk or drive, the wrath of Parson Jehu
Wagtongue Coonscratcher would flame forth on the
next Sunday at their vile and wicked Sabbath
breaking. If we gave a supper to the young people of the starveling hamlet, and enlivened the after
part of the evening with an innocent dance, then
how the eyes of the parson and his pure wife rolled
in chaste horror and indignation; and what a rich
subject it was for the next Sunday's pious and
charitable denunciation of these city lepers and
lechers—an Adirondack dance being always the
synonym of a licentious revel. If that devoted and
saintly churchwoman, Miss Virginia H., pitying
the forlorn destitution of the poor children of the
place, visited them in their bare homes and gave
them toys, candies, picture cards and little bright

books, with a kind word or two of wholesome instruction; or if she went about by the solicitation
and appointment of our chaplain to prepare their
mothers and aunts for the sacrament of baptism,
and in both these respects acted like an angel of
mercy, ever busy and willing to serve these hapless
ones notwithstanding her weak and invalid condition, it is scarcely credible, yet perfectly true,
that even she was publicly denounced by name in
the school-house, before the crowded assembage of
a Sunday night seance or experience-meeting, by
our heroic Jehu, as a painted Jezebel, who must be
thrown down and trodden under foot. She was too
successful in enticing the true Israelites to her vile
idolatry and soul-killing formalism. " Throw her
down," shrieked this modern Jehu, like his name-
sake of old; and just then Fitz Halleck picked up
a billet of wood to fling at his head, as the valiant
hero of slander on gentle womanhood sank into his
chair exhausted by rage and fury.

This outrage found its parallel, not long since,
in the case of the Rev. J. R. Henderson, pastor of
the Methodist Episcopal Church at Van Wert, Ohio,
who censured the organist of his Church, Miss
Norma Comer, before the whole congregation, for
attending several innocent and respectable dances;
and for which public censure the indignant organist
played the horsewhip on his back and shoulders
publicly and vigorously, to the tune of the " Rogue's

March." Or, it is still better illustrated in the case
of that gay, young Methodist Lothario, or Don
Juan, the Rev. Mr. Trumbower, of West Hoboken,
N. J., who carries a revolver for protection in his
various amours; and who declared from his pulpit,
a short time ago, that a certain young lady of his
congregation had "set her cap" for him; which
young lady was the means of his exposure in an
intrigue of elopement with the wife of one of his
flock, when the enraged and jealous husband burst
in upon them in his own house, and drove the loving pastor through the streets of the town to punish
him, and was only stopped by the aforesaid revolver
pointed at his head, with the pastor's mandate,
"Stop, man; or I'll shoot;" and who, after a brief
incarceration, was released and the affair settled for
decency's sake, and the pastor permitted to reassert
and vindicate himself in two or three eloquent sermons, before going to seek other fields and pastures
new of fresh amours and pistol practice.

Our Jehu was not certainly known to have carried
a pistol since leaving the army, having been chaplain
of one of its regiments; nor was he guilty, perhaps,
of any worse things than the issuing of forged
passes and permits to some of the men for a consideration,—a small matter in which he nevertheless
took some pride, by his own admission long after the
Rebellious war was over; but his persistent, violent,
public assaults upon the character and private

doings of some of our people, stigmatizing them
by name as drunkards and worse, at last roused
the slumbering fear and suspicion of the more
thoughtful ones of his own clan, that Methodism
would soon become a stench in the nostrils of the
little community of Saranac Lake, and beget a
strong sympathy in favor of our colony of Church-
men and Churchwomen. He must therefore go;
and go he did in high dudgeon and chagrin, leaving
us to our work of gathering together the largest
congregations ever assembled in the place, and of
building the only church there, after two other
village failures in the attempt. It would be a
strange thing, indeed, if this slanderer of his
Christian brethren should long go unwhipped of
justice, and have meted out to him the same
measure of severity which he had dealt to us. It
came at last, after a year's delay, and still hangs
over his head like the sword of Damocles, in the
form of a criminal libel suit. The further development of this winter tale, in the next chapter, will
disclose the whole nefarious business and all the
persons implicated.

Meanwhile, there is to be noticed other things in
our environment besides these howling storms of
slanderous Methodism, not yet quite lulled. The
great Presiding Elder of the district comes to
collect the church taxes of the poor, half-starving
community, lest some of its means and help might

go into the church 'Piscopal. He warns them that
the clergy of that church are miserable "Gospel-
tramps," let loose upon the flock like lean and
hungry wolves to tear and devour them. Whereas,
the simple truth is that these clergy made their
services gratuitous, so that it became a matter of
inquiry among some Methodist adherents themselves as to whether they never asked for money
like their own ministers were constantly doing.
The missionary clergyman settled at Saranac Lake
is sustained by the voluntary gifts and offerings of
summer visiters, a Diocesan fund, and what the
poor resident population choose to give him. The
two churches in the neighborhood are free to all
comers, without pew rents or subscription lists.
Therefore, the shoe fits on the other foot, and our
Presiding Elder may put it on and be the Gospel-
tramp himself, or be the beggar on horseback.

But what a strange spectacle it was to see the
estimate placed upon the pecuniary ability of the
chaplain and members of our colony. We were all
as rich as Crœsus, and must divide with all sharpers
and applicants. Sheep-shearing and goose-plucking
time had not yet come, but the gentle sheep and
silly geese of our colony must be shorn and plucked
as much as possible. The meat-shop at which some
of us procured extra-thick steaks of tough, stringy,
tasteless beef, raised its price from ten cents per
pound to twenty. Partridges advanced in the same

ratio. Venison was scarce and dear. The telegraph wires were tapped to ascertain what messages
we were sending to our distant friends or receiving
from them, touching any possible increase or decrease of our number, and any consequent gain or
loss to the business of Saranac Lake. Letters
containing bank bills were sometimes opened, rifled
of their contents, sealed up again, and sent to their
destination. Bank books, with adjusted balances
coming from New York, were brought from the
Post-Office with their sealed envelopes torn open
by the fingers of some curious and unknown bung-
lers at crime. No investigation could discover the
culprit. The rough apologies for roads endangered
life and limb, and caused heavy bills of expense for
broken vehicles and sprained shoulders and arms.
Gloomy skies and furious winds were as nothing in
comparison with the dark scowling faces and blustering solicitations of a desperate poverty that en-
compassed us on all sides. Rough, grisly men, in
party-colored rags, boldly accosted you with more
of demand than of entreaty in their looks and
tones for large sums of money to purchase teams
of oxen or new fishing boats, or to cancel heavy
mortgages. Great, strong farmers, whose cabins or
stables had been burned, came with childish impor-
tunities for loans or gifts of cash to build them up
again. Lean, hungry beggars walked miles to
" The Berkeley," to solicit a little alms to keep

them from starvation. Wrinkled and decrepid
crones invaded your privacy with their tedious
chatter and unclean gossip, smoking strong clay
pipes, and inquiring for some trifle of good tea,
better tobacco than their own, or, if you pleased,
a spare bit of money. Or, instead of this, they
would make their appearance about meal time, just
for sociability, and drive a shrewd bargain for an
old spinning wheel or pair of brass andirons long
since discarded and stored in the loft. A Christmas tree for the sad-faced village children and
their disconsolate parents, with the usual present
for each person, was somewhat costly. Your
oysters and fruit sent for and expected from home,
froze by the way. The sameness and monotony of
plain fare and plainer cooking could be had at the
rate of $50 or $60 per month, including room and
fire-wood. A necessary guide or man-servant's
wages during the winter months were $20 or $30
dollars more. The requisite horse and sleigh or
buggy would be cheap at $30 per month, and a
double team at $50. A hunting dog could be hired
at 50 cents per day; his master at $2.50. With
the usual extras and tips for washing, boot-blacking
and eye services, what an environment of pecuniary
perplexity is all this, when your best investments
in Railroad stocks yield you no dividends for
two or three years together, including your prolonged invalid sojourn in this barren wilderness.

12

The poor dumb beasts, too, needed some sympathetic Bergh to protect them from neglect and cruelty. There is no quality of mercy here to be strained ; it is altogether unknown. An old Jewish proverb, not Shylock's, founded upon a Divine injunction, is this : " A righteous man regardeth the life of his beast : but the tender mercies of the wicked are cruel." It is a text quite beneath the notice of a Coonscratcher, but inspired by the same good sense and wisdom that gave this wholesome advice : " Give strong drink unto him that is ready to perish, and wine unto those that be of heavy hearts. Let him drink and forget his poverty, and remember his misery no more." Or, as an illustration of its meaning and effect, read this : " Wine maketh glad the heart of man ; " therefore, " Drink no longer water, but use a little wine for thy stomach's sake and thine often infirmities." We poor exiled invalids at Saranac Lake did this at our peril, as has just been seen ; milk would have been a good substitute but for its poor quality in the skimmed state of its being set before us, and the miserable sickly condition of the poor cows that gave it. These cows were but vagrant masses of skin and bone, so weak and lifeless as to be hardly able to walk to some distant swamp for a little possible wild grass or twigs, covered as they were with huge bunches of hardened excrement requiring an axe to chop them off; wandering over

the place and along the road, all winter long,
lowing piteously and examining carefully every bit
of soiled paper, old boots and shoes, rags, chips
and discarded hats and caps for something to eat.
A little bucket of dish-water constituted their
morning and evening meal; a little dry wild hay,
without much nutriment, their nightly cud of contentment and bliss. During the summer they fared
better, and give us richer milk. Meal and vegetables were far too costly to be given them in the
winter. Corn fodder there was none, and good English hay or timothy was for the horses. And yet even
many of the horses had so little good hay and oats,
and were so neglected by their owners as to be
poor and emaciated; and they sometimes lost their
hair through disease and vermin. In fact, food of
any kind was so scarce and dear that a long severe
winter produced starvation and death of both cows
and horses. Think what the native beef of such a
barren region as this must be, and eat it if you can,
especially on the next day after the slaughter, as
the custom here is with all fresh meat.

The dogs, too, man's most affectionate and stead-
fast friends, are objects of the deepest commisera-
tion. After hunting for their masters from August
until November, or the close of the season by ice,
they become a heavy burden of care and cost; and
if kept chained up at home, they are fed on a little
corn meal scalded with hot water and the scraps

that fall from their masters' scanty table. If let
loose to forage for themselves, these dogs become
nuisances around every household, or they kill
sheep, or hunt deer and hare; and thus many of
them are shot or poisoned, or they become lean
and sick and mangy, and then die. Many a fine
hunting dog comes to such an end every season;
and what is far worse, the jealousy and spite of
the guides among themselves often cause the
wicked destruction of dogs that have been too
successful in the chase. Beaten, kicked, and
almost starved as they are; run every day in the
burning heats of August and September until their
eyes are blinded or ooze out, and their feet become
too sore even to stand upon or to touch; and shot
remorselessly as they are by still-hunters in the
western part of the wilderness, or lost in the woods
during a long chase from camp, to be devoured by
wolves or bears, surely the Adirondack hunting
dog has a dog's life of it, and is to be pitied and
protected.

The Saranac guide is the wonder of humanity.
He has the doubtful reputation of being the best
guide in the woods, saving a few exceptional cases.
He sits and watches every coach load of tourists
and sportsmen like a hawk, and selects his victim
with unerring precision. He is all smiles and
promises before going to camp; all glumness and
apology in camp; all sourness and disappointment

after camp. His chief expectation is the largest
of gold watches, Winchester rifles, suits of clothing, abundance of whisky and tobacco, fine camp
stores, and bank bills enough to buy a house and a
small farm, in addition to the much smaller consideration of his paltry wages at $3.00 per day and
found. He knows all the best fishing and hunting
grounds in the wilderness, but seldom finds them.
He boasts of his great hunting prowess and success, but the camp is often without venison. He
is always a dead shot at deer, on the jump; but
prefers a club in the boat because it makes no
noise. He goes to bed early, so as to be up at
four o'clock in the morning for a timely hunt, but
sleeps until seven or eight, unless sooner called,
and the hunt comes to grief. He is strong as
Samson, but his light boat must be drawn over
every little "carry" where there is a horse and
sledge or wagon. He disdains gentility and
despises effeminacy, but wears gloves to keep his
fine hands from tan and blisters. He is no vain
coxcomb, but mounts a cherry-colored cravat and
spends an hour in dressing his hair. He has no
useless book-learning or very little, but he will
argue every possible question and discuss every
conceivable subject louder and longer than a
senator like Webster or a philosopher like Franklin. He severely condemns city immoralities, and
lives in all available concubinage. If his wife

12*

remonstrates, he turns her out of doors to follow his example. He believes like a devil in God and true religion; but he is profane and never goes to Church, because he has no fine coat. He has no obtrusive or violent obstinacy, but he is never convinced. He is meek as Moses and patient as Job; but fights like Hector and storms like Achilles. Faithful and true, he is all your own to do and dare; but he is full of ingenious tricks, practical jokes, and long-winded stories. He takes you fishing, and dumps you in the mud. He takes you partridge shooting, and tears you and your clothes to pieces in dense thickets of briers and young evergreens. He sends you after a bear, and has made impressions in the soft sand with a claw which he carries for the purpose. He is playful and sportive as a kitten, but prowls around camp at midnight with the growl of a wolf whose flaming eyes glare through two holes made in his hat, by the aid of your candles. He is tender and respectful to youthful inexperience, and frightens green city boys into fits with his horrible 'swamp-saugus', or the panther's piercing cry of some neighboring screech-owl. He is a quick and trusty messenger with your mail-matter and additional camp-stores, and stays at the house to enjoy himself on a sly spree for two or three days. He inspires the hope of a fine saddle of venison, and brings you an old horse saddle neatly done up in a

bag. He is very industrious and enterprising, and
there is never enough wood for a big camp-fire at
night. He is incapable of fatigue, and lounges around
camp for hours together. He anticipates all your
wants and wishes, and must be specially told what
to do and when to do it. He is the very soul of
honor, and can not be trusted out of your sight.
He knows all the paths and trails of the wilderness,
and gets lost with a compass in his pocket, all
wrong of course, and to be broken to pieces on the
spot. He will drive you a fine, fat buck, and
expect a ten dollar Greenback. He is grave and
truthful as a judge, and lies like Ananias and
Sapphira. He is uncommonly poor and hard beset
with difficulties to make a living, and has money
loaned out at usurious interest. He has an old
leaky boat which you wish him to substitute with
a new one and give him $50; and he takes the gift
for a fresh investment and loses a good friend
worth to him ten times the amount. He is saving
and frugal with his hard-earned wages, and gambles
them away at cards. He is honest and careful of
your property; but guns, pistols, camp-stores,
watches, pocket knives, pelts, and other possessions
disappear, and are only found when the law and its
penalty are invoked. Finally, he knows you better
than you know yourself, what you wish to do, and
where you ought to go; and acts accordingly.

The portrait is an aggregate and may be some-

what highly colored, but it is no caricature. It is
the likeness of other guides at St. Regis and elsewhere, as well as of some of those at Saranac Lake,
making them the wonder and glory or shame of the
wilderness. Not all, indeed,—far from it; but of
so large a proportion that great care and long experience are necessary to the choice of a good one.
Good guides there are, whom to know and accompany
on your fishing and hunting expeditions, is a real
pleasure and satisfaction. Year after year they
serve you faithfully and well, and you never tire of
them or wish to change them. But like angelic
visitants, they are few and far between.

The guide's little sweetheart or sister is a shy,
demure creature, who, when a good chance offers,
marries at twelve or fourteen, the longer period of
sweet sixteen being too distant to wait. The
gawky, blushing lad of eighteen or twenty is her
choice. Children as they are, they either grow
tired of each other, disagree, and separate after a
while; or they live amicably together in the faithful execution of the Divine commandment to
increase and multiply, until a dozen and more of
yearly, flaxen-headed and blue-eyed gradations of
young humanity sprout up like plants in the narrow
household, from a foot high to six feet-three. Care,
anxiety, and hard work make the mother thin and
pale. She has insufficient clothing and food. Her
cabin is bare and open. She and her shivering

brood keep close to a hot stove for warmth. Lonely
days and nights pass, with little in the house to
quiet the clamors of hunger, while the bread-winner
is on some distant trapping expedition or lumbering job. She does not complain; she only weeps
and moans. It is one of the sorriest sights in the
world to see these poor women so sad and woe-
begone, with all these children clinging to their
thin skirts and looking up with tearful eyes and
wan faces for a morsel of bread. Or, when the
guide loses his life in the hard struggle, is shot, or
drowned, or deserts his post, it is only a little
worse; the outside help that comes is only a little
more uncertain. Widows and orphans everywhere
else have some provision made for them; but here
the universal poverty, and utter want of regular
employment of any kind for such as these, make
their lot one of complete destitution and woe. The
little, meagre town, or county alms is but a drop in
the dry and empty bucket. In such a case as this,
is it any wonder that young women, widows or
orphans, are here most easily tempted into evil
courses of life, and think it no great wrong?

Here, then, is the perplexing problem of environment,—a native population almost lawless and
savage, well-nigh bestial and depraved, in the midst
of pure air and magnificent scenery and forest
growth; and cultivated men and women coming
here from distant towns and cities to find benefit

and enjoyment of life. The best and greatest of
the land,—statesmen; college presidents and professors; artists; Bishops and clergy; lawyers;
physicians; bankers and brokers; students; scientific scholars; ladies of culture and refinement and
high position in society, all come here for rest and
health and the innocent sports of the wilderness,
and alike find profit. What mere external environment of nature made them to differ? Why had
Coonscratcher no library like our own? and why
did he disdain to consult it? Why were Adirondack ideas so meagre? its intelligence so narrow?
its manners so rude? its morals so bad? Even
Charles Darwin admits, that it is just as hopeless
a task to discover in what manner the mental and
moral powers of man were first developed from the
lowest organisms, as to discover the first beginning
of life itself; and that we have no reason to suppose that the lower animals have any moral capacity
at all, while their mental powers are immensely
lower in degree. And as to civilization, Mr. Darwin asserts that it is very difficult to form any
judgment, or give any true account as to the reason
why one particular tribe of men and not another
has been successful and risen in the scale of civilization; and more especially, that the problem of
the first advance of savages towards civilization is
at present too difficult to be solved. When science
thus acknowledges itself baffled in the solution of

the origin of man's complex being in mind, soul
and body, or rather of mind and soul in body, as
well as his civilization; and when Mr. Darwin
admits in his last edition of the *Descent of Man*,
that many of his own views as to Evolution,
Natural Descent and Natural Selection are highly
speculative, and that some of them will doubtless
prove to be erroneous; then, what are we to do but
wait for more light as the future researches of
science and the generalizations of philosophy may
give it to us? It is just as likely as not, that this
whole origin of things rests entirely with the
Originator to disclose, whose ways have hitherto
been past finding out.

Is this fondness for fishing and hunting or camping in the woods, on the part of men and women of
the highest culture and refinement, an inherited
taste and propensity derived through a long line of
ancient kings, princes and nobles so fond of the
chase, from our unknown prehistoric ancestors?
Is this duality of savagery and civilization, co-
existing and co-extensive in all ages and continents,
necessary to the equilibrium and stability of human
society, as the centripetal and centrifugal forces of
nature are necessary to the equilibrium and stability of the material universe? Were the first
men barbarians and citizens at one and the same
time? So long as the aspiring soul of man is attached to a grovelling body, savagery and civiliza-

tion must needs coexist and be coextensive.
Civilization, overdone by the refinements of mere
intelligence and the excessive accumulation of mere
material wealth, begets a luxurious case and corruption of which the body politic and social, at last
dies, or else barbarism comes to make an end of it,
and to organize a new state of things.   Human
nature weakened and depraved by the excessive in-
dulgences of civilized life needs the new blood and
stronger muscle which barbarism gives.   Or rather,
the nervous and worn-out denizens of our cities
and large towns must return to the simplicity and
invigorating influences of nature to recuperate their
wasted energies and restore the equilibrium of
mind and body.   They must go to the woods, the
first " native life-element of the human race ; and
our homesickness, an instinctive yearning after the
garden home of our forefathers, haunts the nomad
of the desert as well as the inhabitants of luxurious cities."   Abel, unambitious tiller of the soil
and simple herdsman, is superceded by the jealous
and barbarous Cain, who nevertheless becomes the
builder of cities and the progenitor of all such as
handle the harp and the organ, as well as of all ar-
tificers in brass and iron.   And these two brothers
are but types of all that savagery and civilization
that have ever coexisted in the very same environment.   Moses and Darwin are agreed on the point
that man was not first placed in a desert, or a cul-

tivated field or a city, but in the forest, in a garden
or park; and if this park be utterly destroyed,
then we should lose all health-giving influences and
means of subsistence, the sweet music of song-birds
the purest enjoyments of our early years in fishing
and hunting, and " nature's remedies for the mental discords of manhood." We should starve and
die.

In this view of the matter, it is not surprising
that the Adirondack Wilderness produced, at least,
one great prophet, hero and martyr of human liberty, John Brown. His simple gravestone in his
old favorite resort* behind a great boulder in his
beloved North Elba, where he came to read his
Bible, pray and meditate, is the noblest monument
here standing to perpetuate the name and the memory of human greatness. As a prophet, he foresaw
and foretold the great war of the Rebellion made
by the South in the interest of slavery and for the
destruction of the American Union. As a hero,
he did what he could, almost single handed, both
in Kansas and Virginia, to rouse the nation, or at
least the servile portion of it, to make this Republic in reality what it was only in name—a land of
freemen. He would be another Spartacus and lead
his slaves to the liberation of a second Italy. His
confidence in the negro character being misplaced
and mistaken, there was no uprising; and John
Brown became a martyr, being executed on the

13

gallows at Harper's Ferry, December 2d, 1859. It was unquestionably one of the most memorable executions that have ever occurred in history, according to the estimate of the New York *Times*. It produced a profound impression throughout this country and Europe, and did much to make John Brown one of the foremost figures of the Western World. He was one of the bravest and best of men. His tragic end did as much as anything else to precipitate the long and fruitless war of Slavery against Freedom. His name alone well-nigh redeems the Adirondacks from all their gigantic iniquities. Let us sit down by his grave in North Elba, and read his last touching letter written to the Rev. L. Humphrey, twelve days before his execution, dwelling more especially on these passages: "So far as my knowledge goes as to our mutual kindred, I suppose I am the first since the landing of Peter Brown, from the Mayflower, that has been either sentenced to imprisonment or the gallows. But, my dear old friend, let not that fact alone grieve you. You cannot have forgotten how and where our grandfather, Capt. John Brown fell, in 1776; and he too might have perished on the scaffold, had circumstances been but very little different. The fact that a man dies under the hand of an executioner or otherwise, has but little to do with his true character, as I suppose. * * * Whether I have any reason to be of 'good cheer,' or not, in

view of my end, I can assure you that I feel so; I
neither feel mortified, degraded, nor in the least
ashamed of my imprisonment, my chain, or my
near prospect of death by hanging * * * When
I think how easily I might be left to spoil all I have
done or suffered in the cause of freedom, I hardly
dare risk another voyage, even if I had the opportunity. It is a long time since we met; but we
shall now soon come together in our Father's house,
I trust. Thanks be ever unto God who giveth us
the victory through Jesus Christ our Lord." And
now, indeed, his " soul goes marching on " with all
that great company of heroes, martyrs, and saints
that have fought a good fight here against sin and
iniquity, and have gone hence rejoicing in view of
the incorruptible crown of righteousness that fadeth
not away. Under the shadow of old White-face,
" John Brown's body lies a-mouldering in the
grave," as the most precious treasure held in the
trust and keeping of these everlasting hills, until
the time of the restitution of all things, when he
shall again walk over the new earth and under the
new heavens to enjoy the fruit of his toil and self-
denial and heroic endeavor, in the better environment of everlasting peace and righteousness. The
name of William Tell is forever associated with
the Alps and Swiss freedom; the name of John
Brown, shall, for all the ages to come, connect the
Adirondacks and human liberty together—old

Whiteface and the cleaner, whiter face of our land purified from the foul blot and deep stain of slavery. And this is all; but it is enough.

A desolated and ruined paradise as our winter environment, occupied in the main by a poor half-starved population, whose men are drunken and depraved in morals; whose women, young and old, are pale, wan and half-clad, the very ghosts and spectres of real womanhood; a population without books, lectures, museums, libraries and theatres, but with vile taverns in abundance, gave us all the heart-ache and the home sickness which scattered our colony in the spring to more welcome and congenial surroundings. Three of our number died. Others who received no benefit left before the winter was over. The nervous, dyspeptic and rheumatic ones complained loudly of the continuous damp and stormy weather, only occasionally relieved by a snapping cold day of sunshine. But truth compels the statement that, despite our surroundings and discomforts, the most of us gained so much health and strength of body, as well as cheerfulness of spirit as to be able to enjoy life again and its various pursuits. All's well that ends well.

It was during the early part of our sojourn at Saranac, that a continuous heavy down-pour of rain, sleet and snow of two weeks' duration, only once broken by a brief gleam of sunshine revealing

a blue spot overhead, caused our sober Darwinian
to make a waggish remark about it, one day at
dinner, and our wise and witty dame, Mrs. O. H——
to observe that the sky had a new color which was
blue; and this grim playfulness of spirit called
forth the following downright doggerel, as best
suited to give expression to the general disgust:

OUR SARANAC PARADISE.

"It seems to be raining," observed Mr. T.,
With a mischievous face and mock gravity—
For, pouring it was, like a great spout at sea, —
As we sat one day imbibing our tea,
And he, devising some plausible plea
For this vagabond spouter, come on a spree,
In this home of the brave and land of the free :
An accomplished imp, with a promising way,
But not safe to be trusted, a single day.
Bright in the morning, and scowling ere night ;
Coming over the hills with smiles of delight
To roll in the mud, a contemptible sight ;
Blustering and roaring and spoiling for fight,
And the Berkeley colony all in a fright.
Mixed up very much, it is needless to say,
Like the snow and the sand, November and May ;
Not blithesome at all, not youthful and gay,
But wrinkled and old, cross, gloomy and grey,
Groaning all night long, and swearing all day
At every poor creature that came in his way,
Like any old soaker squared off for the fray,
That nobody ventures to drive away :

13*

Red eyes in the morning, dull, heavy and wet,
From the night's debauch with an earthquake set.
Eyes darting at noon tide an impudent stare,
And lit up at night with a frenzied glare ;
Always capricious   a fine confidence man,
With new tricks in his head, or some artful plan
To cheat and to dupe all the strangers he can,
The doctors themselves. and their invalid clan
Who are made to believe there is health to gain,
By the process of drowning in mud and in rain, —
A remedy sure for rheumatic pain,
The limping and lounging that go in its train,
A quick cure for phthisis - for being too stout,
Bronchitis, dyspepsia, soft-corns, and the gout.

"It seems to be raining" again, Mr. T. ;
But look through the window, and changefully see,
Before he's done speaking, some snow and some sleet,
Assisting stray sunshine to fall in the street,
With venturesome ladies who can't keep their feet,
Going out like the Parsees, the bright sun to greet,
On snow shoes to roam this Paradise sweet,
And go down in the mill-dam, rushing and fleet.
Blest Eden of Saranac, how shall I sing
The joys or the sorrows thy winter may bring?
Or skies so resplendent — at least, once a week,
Not so often, indeed, the Muse bids me speak,
And record what was said by a witty dame,
Bearing well all her ills and an honor'd name,
As one day she espied a change in the view
Of the low black sky with a rift broken through, —
" It has a new color, the color is blue."

When, when shall thy frost-king resume his bright reign,
O'er the lakes and the streams of his forest domain?
Where the partridge yet drums in the hunter's ear,
Believing that spring-time still lingers here ;
Where the hare turns white, though of nimble feet,
In the doubtful struggle for something to eat ;
Where old legends tell of the home of the deer,
And trout in cool waters crystally clear,
In the far distant past of ages gone by,
When for all there was found exhaustless supply,
Only now to be sought in the red man's sky.
The tables are groaning with little good cheer,
As the hungry sit down with a sob and a tear,
To feast on potatoes all through the year,
And wonder why " cakes and ale " are so dear.
The manners are simple, though not much refin'd,
Good morals, like game, are not easy to find ;
Yet some few keep sober whenever they must,
And swear they will pay when they drink upon trust ;
What care they for Coonscratcher's fiery tongue ?
The dance they will have, and their song shall be sung.

Sweet Eden of Saranac, when did the sin,
And the tempter thy borders come crawling in?
Poor Adam goes forth with a tear in his eye,
And Eve trudges after just ready to die.
A Beverland tells us the first sin was lust,—
Explaining THE SCRIPTURES more worthy of trust ;
The pure love of mortals grew strange and debased,
Transgression the sweetness of virtue effaced ;
The good *tree of life* was sapped to the core,
The man was a lecher, the woman —— was more :
However this be, there can be no mistake,
It is true in the Eden of Saranac Lake.

For often and often these facts have been told
Of original sin here open and bold.
A lumberman drove his poor wife out of doors,
And looked for another to do his odd chores :
A neighbor there was, who had a fair spouse,
Too poor to indulge in a tipsy carouse ;
For a pair of old breeches, a ten dollar bill,
And a gallon of whisky his guzzle to fill,
The lumberman hired his wife for awhile.
And then o'er his cups indulged a long " smile ; "
But when all was spent, and a famine began,
He went for his spouse and that lumberman,
To find the fond woman content with her place,
And himself booted out with contempt and disgrace.
A land owner, grasping and rich and severe.
Had two houses and harems established here ;
Nobody complained,—he brought grist to the mill,
The poor man to hire and the hungry to fill.
Not many miles hence, in poor rocky Duane,
Where live many sons of the vagabond Cain,
Two monsters abide, whose daughters have been
Like Lot's in the crime of incestuous sin ;
And others there were who drove a brisk trade,
As in cattle and horses for wife or housemaid,
Exchanging the woman, not asking her will.
For an old bed-quilt and a two dollar bill :
All a primitive way of barter and trade,
By the Lords of the South more extensively made,
In the good old times of Calhoun and of Clay,
By the soul of John Brown done forever away ;
Yet dancing in rage round his lonely grave,
Contemning the Power, Almighty to save
From wrath and from ruin, and passion so fell
Going down to the darkness and blackness of hell.

"It seems to be raining," groaned out Mr. T. ;
And raining it is, as we all must agree,
Raining and pouring all manner of ills
Over these valleys and over the hills,
Brutal manners and customs, and Herrick's pills.

Lot journeyed to Sodom his Eden to find,
And ran for his life, leaving Lottie behind ;
He should have come here to Saranac Lake,
His Eden to seek and his sheep-farm to make,
His wife would have run at the very first halt,
And not stopped to become a pillar of salt.
If she wept over Sodom its burning to see,
Was it not that she lived there happy and free ?
She had plenty to eat and plenty to drink,
And not very much about which to think,
Save parties and bonnets, and what gossips said
About her flirtations and tossing her head, —
For she liked to be noticed as one of the *ton*,
Because of her dinners and what she had on.
Her father was rich, but not very genteel,
Being only a dealer in mutton and veal ;
From a good ancient stock her husband had come,
Though too fond of drinking old brandy and rum ;
Her daughters were stylish. quite haughty and proud,
And as it turned out, rather fast and loud.
She loved this dear Sodom because it was gay,
She could go every night to a dance or a play ;
The shops were attractive along its Broadway,
Just as brilliant at night as during the day.
To Stewart and Arnold she had bills to pay,
And Tiffany shared even more than they ;
But her purse was full as the blossoms in May.
And she sailed like a ship in gallant array,

Till the tempest burst, on that fatal day,
Which wrecked all her fortune and swept her away ;
But a place there is at the turn of Broadway,
For the statue of folly, cold, naked and grey.

Now, Saranac Lake is the most hum drum place,
Without these attractions, with never a trace
Of fashion, or pleasure, or blue-blooded race ;
Its Lots are all stumpy—its wives without grace,
Its annals obscure, and repulsive its face ;
Its matrons and maidens, pale, shrivelled and sad,
Have no other Broadway along which to gad,
Than a three plank walk to a school-house grey,
Which they crowd once a week to chatter and pray, ·
And slander their neighbors as much as they may,
Or the Berkeley colonists drunken and gay.
Dame Lot among these would never abide,
Her spirit was lofty, and great was her pride ;
She would take a nice boat and a first-class guide,
And, like Mistress Merry, would pleasantly glide,
Wherever she liked and as long as she pleased,
Even though the mosquitos tormented and teased, —
Some fine Antinous very handsome and strong,
Attractive and blooming, and merry with song,
With a form like Apollo, and muscular arms
Like a Hercules showing his manly charms.
She would visit St. Rex, o'er the Saranac Lakes,
And feast on the dainties of syrup and cakes,
Nice breakfasts out-vying Delmonico's trash,
Grand dinners of veal, pork and beans, succotash,
And suppers of slapjacks with plenty of hash.
She would don her fine laces—her velvet train,
Her jewels and gimcracks – be at home again ;

Only nod to great people of kindred tastes,
And see what ladies had delicate waists,
Little feet, white hands, real jewels or pastes ;
Hunt up the rich bachelors having no home,
And pity their blessedness, single and lone.
She would shine in mild splendor and do nothing rash,
And yet on the sly she would cut a great dash ;
She would set up a camp and give dinners to all,
Have tableaux and picnics—a full dress ball ;
Would lead all the fashion and be of the first,
One season at least though worse came to worst ;
For, so it might happen, nobody could tell,
Her daughters might marry ambitiously well.
Meanwhile, her liege lord was sporting away,
At fond Saratoga. Newport or Cape May,
He missed all the sweet curtain lectures at night,
That gave him and dear Caudle their choicest delight.
So she hastened away with vexation of heart,
To comfort her lord, and narrate all the part
She had acted in vain for the peace of her soul ;
And for comfort then turned to the flowing bowl.
Her Sodom was reached not long after that day,
And a statue there is, cold, naked, and grey,
To be seen at the turn of the city's Broadway.

" It seems to be raining," concludes Mr. T.;
Let it rain evermore on the land and the sea,
On city and country, on mountain and lea.
Rain fire, rain brimstone, if so it must be,
The land from such pride and pollution to free.

IV

DEVELOPMENT.

DEVELOPMENT or evolution is both downward and upward, backward and forward. Society, like the athlete, must sometimes run far back in order to make the better leap forward. The great hulks of animals and reptiles that revelled in the jungles of remote Geological ages and continents, have left a very degenerate posterity, if we may take the small alligators and snakes of the present era as specimens; and this is evolution downward. If we could be sure that the intelligence of the present races of animals is an improvement and an advance over the intelligence of their remote ancestors, we might call it development upward. Between the spermatic stuff of a bog, a sponge, a mollusk, a rhizopod, a frog and a human being there is a vast difference and distance, in which evolution upward has made most gigantic strides. But after all, is it anything more than mere physical and organic development? The stuff or matter of which the world is made seems to have in it the seeds of all life, vegetable and animal; and it also seems as if one and the same plastic Force or Life-Power developed these seeds into various growths accord-

ing to circumstances and the necessities of an
advancing order or law of progress. Admit these
seeds or germs of life, and admit this Plastic
Power, and the doctrine of evolution is as old as
the time of Moses and the book of Genesis. What
we want to know beyond this, is, just how the
development is made, which our modern science is
laboring hard to find out. The origin of these
germs and of this Life-Power is beyond investigation, but not the mode of their combined development. It is a hidden duality of course, producing
visible results according to an invisible law or
order of evolution; and these results are certainly
proper objects of scientific investigation for the
purpose of ascertaining the law or mode of their
appearing, in a regular rising gradation of animal
life from its lowest forms to the highest.

Evolution, as applied to civilization and human
society, finds a hard nut to crack in the native
population of these remote parts of the Adirondack
wilderness. All the little wit and wisdom of our
Berkeley colony were fully and constantly occupied
in devising ways and means of improving the condition of our poor neighbors and of developing
whatever germs of goodness yet remained within
them. If any germs of a higher and better life
were there, as we thought there might be, then
something could be done for their development into
a nobler manhood and finer womanhood. The

14

undertaking was difficult, but not utterly hopeless. We would do what we could and strip ourselves as close as we dare in the service and endeavor of providing for their mental and moral wants, somewhat as poor Bridget did when ordered to serve the tomatoes undressed, and she presented herself to the astonished family group, whose most amazed and confused member was the mistress presiding at table, in no other garment than the close-fitting and unmentionable one, exclaiming: "Indade, Ma'am, I'll not take off another stitch if I lose me place." Occupation for the welfare of this wretchedly ignorant people would of course re-act beneficially upon ourselves and be its own reward. We would, in some measure, forget or brood less upon our discomforts and surroundings. We would be more disposed to forgive our cruel autocratic doctors for sending us here to improve our health and spirits amid such depressing influences and repulsive surroundings. We would give them credit for good intentions at least, and a somewhat sharp Yankee practice. It was an experiment, and we were the victims. It was a hobby, and we were tied to its tail. Said a dear old lady of our acquaintance, when summoned from her luxurious city home in mid-winter, by the death of a member of her family amongst us: "All doctors rides their hobbies, and them as rides this'n is the worst of all,"—meaning by this tart and homely observation,

not strictly grammatical, that Saranac Lake was
not the best place in the world for restless and dis-
satisfied consumptives to get well.

The fact is, that some of these doctors living at
a distance had ridden their hobbies here to some
purpose. Our Chaplain's good wife had been
thrown out a sleigh and sprained her arm and
shoulder. A surgeon of fair repute was summoned
from Plattsburg by telegraph to consult with our
own excellent Dr. Trudeau about the injury which
was serious enough; and for this one visit a bill of
$50 was sent to the clergyman, who was himself an
invalid in receipt of no salary. Receiving no
benefit, this lady was obliged to shorten her
sojourn and go to New York to consult one of its
leading surgeons. Thence she returned to her
own Philadelphia home, as soon as able, where
some relief was obtained under the careful treatment of her own family physician, Dr. L. and two
eminent surgeons of his selection. Another case
is that of a gentleman from Portland, Me., who
had long lived in the woods for the benefit of his
rapidly declining health as a consumptive, and
who had grown stout and well in consequence,
only to be attacked with Bright's disease and die
among us; whose poor distressed wife, in his
declining days, as a last desperate struggle to save
his life if possible, telegraphed to New York for
one of its physicians who had been recommended

to her as competent to treat the case; and who
came and went at the rate of $10 an hour from the
time he left his office until his return to it, *i. e.*,
just forty-eight hours at the least and lowest possible calculation of making the one visit.   Still
another case there was of a summer visitor at St.
Regis, an aged maiden lady from Stamford, Conn.,
who had exposed herself to an attack of pneu-
monia, most severe and dangerous, for whose
treatment a young sickly doctor of New Haven,
spending the summer at St. Regis, was secured by
the officious interposition of his friend, Mr. H.;
and as the lady was beyond all medical aid and
rapidly declined, there were only a few visits made
by this young doctor, and one consultation by
another of more skill and experience just before
her death; for which the one sent a bill of $200,
and the other $50, to her executors.

Now, when invalids are thus cut off from all
certain medical aid and from all medicines, as they
necessarily are in this remote part of the wilderness, and when they are subjected to such charges
as these for the services of physicians summoned
from a distance or sojourning here, together with
·the long delays and nervous anxieties incident
thereupon, is it any wonder that a suspicion sometimes arises whether a winter sojourn at Saranac
Lake is not after all, a mere doctor's hobby?   One
thing is certain, that a more ample fortune than the

most of us possessed, and more reliable dividends than some of us received from our best railroad investments, were necessary to such a costly experiment. The air is a tonic, indeed; but, like pure Champagne wine, it is only for the very rich.

Surrounded as we were by a hard and grinding poverty, which had something to do with the manners and morals of the people; and contemplating with most scrutinizing eyes as we must do, the possibility of doing even a little for the relief and improvement of our more needy neighbors, we were compelled to develop our little wit and wisdom in the solution of the present grave problem of the Gradgrind philosophy respecting the relative position of rich and poor. For Gradgrind was here in the wilderness with his furnaces and mills and wood-chopping and charcoal burning and railroads and high-priced country stores and steamboats and exactions and oppressions. Here, as elsewhere in all ages and countries, was presented to our pitying gaze what Mr. Froude styles, "The endurance of the inequalities of life by the poor as the marvel of human society. When the people complain, said Mirabeau, the people are always right. The popular cause has been the cause of the laborer struggling for a right to live and breathe and think as a man. Aristocracies fight for wealth and power; wealth which they waste upon luxury, and power which they abuse for their own interests" (*Cæsar*,

14*

p. 85). Democracies are liable to the same charge, when by fraud or force opposing parties attempt to annul the expressed will of the people through the ballot-box. Poverty is a hard and solemn fact all over the world, under every form of government and in every condition of advancing civilization. If we can never get rid of it, we can at least strive to mitigate its hard lot and alleviate its pain and suffering. If Charles Dickens was an ingrained English snob, he had some sense, nevertheless, and a strong sympathy for the poor. Whatever may be said and done to get rid of poverty, he maintained, in his *Hard Times*, that it could not be effected "by utilitarian economists, skeletons of schoolmasters, Commissioners of Fact, genteel and used-up infidels, gabblers of many little dog's-eared creeds; the poor you will always have with you. Cultivate in them, while there is yet time, the utmost graces of the fancies and affections, to adorn their lives so much in need of ornament; or, in the day of your triumph, when romance is utterly driven out of their souls, and they and a bare existence stand face to face, reality will take a wolfish turn, and make an end of you."

What possible graces of the fancies and affections could there be here in a people whose hard struggle for a bare existence pressed upon them continually? Gradgrind owned his thousands of acres of timber and woodland, which he would not

sell at all or sell at higher prices than it was worth,
far beyond the means of squatters or native buy-
ers : he owned rich iron mines, furnaces and forges,
saw-mills and planing-mills, for which immense
tracts of forest-growth must be devastated ; lakes
and rivers dammed so as to overflow and ruin other
and greater tracts; and hundreds of poor men
must slave and toil night and day at low wages, to
make him rich and prosperous, and then send him
to the State Legislature or the National Congress,
to do what he could there for the protection of his
great industries and interests. Did all this give
employment to these needy men ? Yes; it kept
soul and body together ; but there was no fair and
fit proportion of gains out of which to cultivate
the graces of the fancies and affections. In all
this, Gradgrind is only thinking of himself and
his greatness, like the rich fool in the Gospel parable, who tore down his barns to build greater ; and,
in the terse and graphic words of the *Theologia
Germanica*, Gradgrind says to himself: " Now I
am above all other men ; therefore it is just and
reasonable that I should be the lord and commander
of all other creatures, and that all creatures, especially men, should serve me and be subject unto me.
He seeketh and desireth fame, and taketh it gladly
from all ; thinketh himself worthy of it, and that it
is his due, and looketh on men as if they were
beasts of the field, to minister to his life in profit

or joy or pleasure, or even passion and amusement ;
and he seeketh and taketh it wherever he findeth
opportunity." The passage is especially commended to the consideration of our Gradgrind city
politicians of the Boss Tweed ring persuasion, as
well as to the Weeds and Pilsburys of Chateaugay
Iron Company distinction.

It is now nearly a half century ago that an
earnest and sagacious Spanish philosophical writer,
Balmes, forecast, in his admirable history of *Modern
Civilization in Europe*, the present depressed and
troubled times in which we live, in such startling
language as this : " Society is on the point of
attaining the wishes of that materialistic school in
whose eyes men are only machines, and which has
not imagined that society can undertake any grander
or more useful object than the immense development of material interests. Misery has increased
in proportion to the increase of production ; to the
eyes of all provident men it is as clear as the light
of day that things are pursuing a wrong course,
and that if a remedy cannot be applied in time,
the *dénouement* will be fatal ; the vessel, which we
see advancing so rapidly, with all sails set and a
favorable wind, is about to strike upon a rock.
The accumulation of riches, brought about by the
rapidity of the industrial and commercial movement, tends towards the establishment of a system
which would devote the sweat and lives of all to

the profit of the few; but this tendency finds its
counterpoise in the levelling ideas which agitate
very many heads, and which moulded into different
theories, more or less openly attack property, the
organization of labor, and the distribution of pro-
ductions. Immense multitudes, overwhelmed with
misery and in want of moral instruction and education, are disposed to promote the realization of
projects not less criminal and foolish, whenever an
unhappy concurrence of circumstances shall render
the attempt possible. * * * While the poor
should respect the property of the rich, the rich
should in turn respect the condition of the poor.
Such is the will of God."

It is from the dangerous lack of this mutual respect on the part of rich and poor, and from the
more fatal prevalence of a Gradgrind materialistic
science and philosophy, obscuring faith in God and
well-nigh obliterating all hope and charity for men,
that society in Europe and America is hastening to
a serious crisis of some sort, as in the days when
the materialistic teaching of Lucretius and Epi-
curus, and the vast accumulation of wealth in the
hands of the few, together with the unbounded
luxury and corruption which it brought, as well as
universal distress and want, sent the old Roman
society of a tottering empire to swift destruction;
and the very same agencies in the France of Louis
XIV. brought on the horrors and disruption of the

revolution. The cause of American Independence
was imperilled and well nigh lost by the abundance
of a cheap and almost worthless Continental Currency and the abounding luxury and corruption
of the times ; and the few honest and good men
who raised their warning voices against these
things were published as enemies of their country. Among these was Pelatiah Webster, who laid
down this sound maxim : " That the riches of
a nation do not consist in the abundance of money,
but in the number of its people, in supplies and
resources,   *   *   *   in good laws, good public
officers, in virtuous citizens, in strength and con-
cord, in wise councils, and in manly force." Plenty
of money there was in the dark and doubtful days
of our Revolutionary struggle and some time after,
when the Secretary of War, Timothy Pickering,
could not live on a salary of $14,000 a year, and
paid $4,000 rent for a very indifferent house ; when
flour was a dollar a pound, a pair of shoes fifty dollars,
a pair of leather breeches three hundred, a hat four
hundred and a whole suit of clothes sixteen hundred :
above all and worst of all, when fish hooks were half
a dollar a piece, and few could go trout fishing.
Plenty of money there was for the War of the Rebellion, and for gigantic speculations then and
afterwards ; but what of prices for all the necessa-
ries of life, and the amazing luxury that has come to
taunt and madden the struggles of the poor for

bare subsistence? What of governmental high
tariffs to enrich a few manufacturers at the expense
of toiling farmers and artisans? The Greenback
craze is not yet ended in Maine and elsewhere; and
if it shall only end in the warm spring flood of
equal justice and right that is surely coming to
break up the heavy ice over all our streams of high
social and business life, it will be well, and as it
should be. But if it come, which God avert, in
bloody and burning riots all over the land, like
those at Pittsburg, in 1877, what disaster and ruin
will sweep us down the turbulent stream!

The Emperor William, of Germany, still smart-
ing under the vivid horror and hurt of his own
attempted assassination, is said to have remarked,
on receiving the news of the attempt on the life of
the Czar of Russia: "If we do not change the
direction of our policy, if we do not think seriously
of giving sound instruction to youth, if we do not
give the first place to religion, if we only pretend
to govern by expedients from day to day, our
thrones will be overturned, and society will become
a prey to the most terrible events. We have no
more time to lose, and it will be a great misfortune
if all governments do not come to an accord in this
salutary work of repression." Repression, indeed,
rather elevation into general content and happiness.
Dickens is justified; and Balmes's prediction is
that of a true prophet, and no idle dreamer. " Cul-

tivate in the poor the utmost graces of the fancies and affections to adorn their lives, so much in need of ornament; " " society is on the point of attaining the wishes of that materialistic school in whose eyes men are only machines."

There is a materialistic religion as well as a materialistic philosophy. There is a Gradgrind narrowness, hardness and severity of religious teaching and requirement, just as there is a Gradgrind oppression of the hireling in his wages and contempt of the wretched condition of the poor laborer in manufacturing and commercial life. Dives may be in the pulpit as well as in the palace at his perpetual feast, utterly regardless of his poor neighbor Lazarus starving at his door. This materialistic religion consists in utter selfishness,—in putting us on the torturing rack of saving ourselves from the eternal pains and punishments of a material hell of fire and brimstone, and of seeking ease and safety in a material heaven of mere happiness. This is what Mallock justly calls " Atheistic Methodism."

This Atheistic Methodism minus Christianity is a striking instance of development downward and backward. It was born of the lively fox-hunting card-table piety of the Church of England under the anxious *accouchement* of the Rev. John Wesley, a priest of that Church; and as long as this devoted nurse ministered to the child's welfare, it

was quiet, docile and obedient. But hardly had
Wesley left the house, which he never did till the
day of his death, when the brat, missing his firm
hand and gentle voice and wise counsel, began to
be peevish, cross and quarrelsome. It put on airs,
and in the old slippers, caps and faded finery of the
mother, strutted about to display itself, or posed
before the glass in childish admiration of its ma-
tronly charms. Its superintendents assumed the
title and played the role of Bishops and successors
of the first Apostles of Christianity. The good
old Book of Common Prayer which Wesley put in
its hands, somewhat mutilated, with strict injunc-
tions to be diligently used on all occasions of public worship, the Litany especially on Wednesdays.
Fridays and Sundays, with the regular weekly celebration of the Eucharist, was soon laid aside or
only retained as the broken toy of its childish
days. The restoration of the devout spirit of
primitive Christianity, which Wesley sought to
bring about within the Church of England, soon
became a noisy and swaggering independency that
must have some outside and separate establishment of its own. Some say that the brat was
driven from home by undue harshness and severity.
But it had become too proud of its superior excellence and sanctity, and was too conceited and arrogant to be long kept in the house on any terms.
That dear old home, so picturesque, ivy-grown,

15

gabled and turreted, and hallowed by more than a
thousand years of precious memories, it would
have torn down and built a plain red brick meeting
house in its place. The grace, gentleness, and
sobriety of worship gave way to shrieks, groans
and wild orgies of camp-meetings and miscalled
revivals. And even worse than this, the sweetness
of the religion of the Sermon on the Mount became a rhapsody of words about free-grace and
unattainable perfection and absolute impeccability,
without an experience of which God's hapless and
helpless children were consigned to everlasting
hell-torments. And just here it is, in this relic of
the old Zend fire-worship, that atheistic Methodism minus Christianity has reached its last and
lowest debasement of evolution. The Church of
England by the deliberate rejection of the 42d
Article of Religion, which affirmed endless punishment, left it an open question; so that men like
Maurice, Kingsley and Farrar could preach " Eternal Hope " to men as much as they pleased and not
be prosecuted for heresy.

Methodism has made more atheists than Thomas
Cooper, whose conversion to Christianity was
mainly due to the fearless and great-souled Charles
Kingsley. This poor man was sceptical about the
Incarnation of the Son of God, and he put himself
in communication with Kingsley, who, among other
things, wrote him; " He is in heaven which is as

near you and me as the air we breathe, and out of
that He must reveal Himself; neither priests nor
books can conjure him up, Cooper. Your Wesleyan teachers taught you, perhaps, to look for Him
in the Book, as Papists would have done to look
for Him in the bread; and when you found He was
not in the Book, you thought Him nowhere; but
He is bringing you out of your first mistake and
idolatry, aye, *through* it, and through all wild wan-
derings since, to know Him Himself, and speak
face to face with Him as a man speaks with his
friend." Cooper was a lecturer on scientific subjects, and when he went over to orthodox Christianity, his atheistic hearers were furious and deserted him in a body. As a man of science,
Cooper knew that the infraction of natural law
always brought with it its own punishment. When
applied to wrong acts and sins, his Methodistic
training had taught him that this punishment was
endless. Kingsley, while believing that punishment of every wrong thing was just and inevitable,
and only inflicted in order to produce reformation,
also communicated to Cooper this conviction: "As
for saying of any human beings whom I ever saw
on earth that there is no hope for them; that even
if, under the bitter smart of just punishment, they
opened their eyes to their folly, and altered their
minds, even then God would not forgive them; as
for saying that, I will not for all the world and the

rulers thereof. I never saw a man in whom there
was not some good, which God Himself put there;
and, therefore, it is reasonable to believe that He
will educate and strengthen that good, and chastise
and scourge the holder of it till he obeys it, and
loves it, and gives himself up to it."

But against hopeless, endless, ineffectual and
useless torment, Charles Kingsley most emphatically protested to Thomas Cooper, on these grounds:
That the doctrine nowhere certainly occurs in the
Old Testament, the usual passage in Isaiah cited
to prove it as to unquenchable fire and the undying
worm, having reference only to the burning of the
offal and dead carcasses thrown out of Jerusalem
into the valley of Hinnom, a constant necessity to
keep the city clean and healthy: That the doctrine
of endless torment was brought to Palestine from
Babylon on the return of the Exiles, it being a
very ancient and primary doctrine of the Magi, an
appendage of their fire-kingdom of Ahriman, and
may be found in the old Zends, long prior to Christianity: That St. Paul never makes the least allu-
sion to the doctrine: That the Apocalypse only
repeats the imagery of Isaiah and of our Lord,
but asserting distinctly the non-endlessness of
torture in the declaration that at the consummation
of all things, not only death, but also Hell shall be
cast into the Lake of Fire: That the Christian
Church has never really held the doctrine exclu-

sively, till now, remaining an open question till the age of Justinian, A. D. 530; and 200 years before that, when endless torment for the heathen was a popular theory, purgatory sprang up along side of it, as a relief for the conscience and reason of the Church: That since the Reformation, it has been an open question in the English Church, and the Christian Platonists of the 16th and 17th centuries always considered it as such; and that finally, the Greek word used for endless applies to an age, epoch or era of time. When our Lord took the popular doctrine as He found it, His object was to correct and purify it, and to put it on a really moral ground, as the Parable of Dives and Lazarus shows us. It was the emancipation of the true doctrine from the pagan Tartarus and the fires of Ahriman. Dives is still Abraham's son, under no despair, not cut off from Abraham's sympathy, and under a direct moral training, of which the fruit is seen. He is gradually weaned from the selfish desire of indulgence for himself, to love and care for his brethren, a divine step forward in his life, which of itself proves him not to be lost. The impossibility of Lazarus getting to him, or *vice versa*, expresses plainly the great truth, that each being where he ought to be at that time, interchange of place, that is, of spiritual state, is impossible. But nothing is said against Dives rising out of torment, when he has learned the

15*

lesson of it, and going where he ought to go. Fire
and worms are only the appointed agencies for
destroying dead and decayed matter, and of setting
free its elements to enter into new organisms,—
beneficent and purifying agents in this lower life
of ours, to evolve the germs of a higher and better
future life. If God is said to be a consuming fire,
it is in the spiritual sense of a Love that enlightens
and purifies and burns until all shams, lies, hypoc-
risies, tyrranies, pedantries, false doctrines, and
every other abomination goes up in smoke like the
blackness of old decayed Empires, Oriental and
Occidental,—Babylonian, Hebrew, Roman, French,
and Puritanic. Methodism is only a question of
time, like the vanished Kingdom of Prester John.
Out of its ambitious rule, the bastard Mormonism
has sprung; and the ex-Methodist Brigham Young
was its foster-father, and the most successful guar-
dian of its interests.

Development downward always comes of lies
and wrongs. When the Christian Church forgets
its doctrine of the Communion of Saints, and
ignores the Intermediate State of the Departed,
the soul of man, yearning after its dear ones gone
from sight across the dark passage called death,
invents Spiritualism to supply the want. When it
becomes idolatrous and corrupt, Mohammedanism
arises to correct the one evil, and bring about
other and greater evils. When it allies itself with

the despotism and corruption of the State, as in
the France of Louis XIV, a tremendous and bloody
Revolution is the consequence. When, as in Russia, it puts the Emperor in the place of God,
atheistic Nihilism comes to tear out of the hearts
of men all belief in God, and to reduce everything
in Church, State and Society to chaos. When the
Church becomes exclusive and chiefly courts the
rich and prosperous, Communism and Socialism
enter into dangerous alliance against her. When
she parades her logomachies in turgid rhetoric or
bitter pamphlets or controversial tones of discord-
ant Theology, then men of sense become disgusted,
and not knowing where to turn for religious truth,
take refuge in scientific atheism or literary indifference. And when she gives her children the stones
of mere pomp, parade, dumb show and overladen
ceremonial, instead of bread, they starve and die.

Having passed through the numerous revivals
and horrors of both Methodism and Calvinism in
my childhood and youth, which never had any
Christmas with merry-making on cakes and ale
and tokens of Christian affection, but were made
as gloomy and silent as the grave; and having
escaped positive atheism through the more gracious,
cheerful, and benign teaching and practice of the
derided Episcopal Church of my native village, I
was fully prepared to encounter " the slings and
arrows of outrageous fortune " in Saranac Lake,

Gradgrind Methodism rose in hideous deformity
before our little colony in the dark and sinister
form of its chief representative and minister, The
Reverend Jehu Wagtongue Coonscratcher, to
whom reference has been made in the preceding
chapter. His special graces and attractions claim
brief mention. Of medium height, with large,
bony frame and stooping shoulders, a downcast
look, shuffling gait, bushy, black whiskers, heavy
eye-brows, coarse, sensuous mouth oozing tobacco-
juice at the corners, snub nose, and dark, dull eyes,
he was certainly no Apollo in manly beauty. Opposite The Berkeley was the School House in which
Coonscratcher declaimed Methodism minus Christianity. His voice was as loud as a bull's, and
could be heard on stormy winter days and nights
above the roar of the wind and through tightly
closed doors and windows, sometimes in shouts as
of defiance or in tones trembling with passion. It
was never my privilege or pleasure to hear him at
any closer quarters than the Berkeley, of which I
was the chief offender and object of public animad-
version. Had I ventured to put in an appearance
at the School House, it would doubtless have acted
as a red flag shaken in the bull's face, and sent the
roof aloft like a balloon. Being an utter stranger
to the place and people, and for a time living
within a few feet of his house, he never once called
to give me welcome or speak a kindly word,

although he was coming and going through my garden every day for spring-water. A young schoolmaster boarded awhile with him, but soon changed his quarters for the more congenial Berkeley, where our Chaplain married him to a devout member of the Methodist flock. Coonscratcher's rage knew no bounds, and this hapless couple were publicly reprimanded. It was from this schoolmaster that I learned of the dreadful lies and slanders which Coonscratcher and his great red-haired Amazon of a wife were in the habit of uttering publicly and privately against the members of our colony. From our own guide, with whom he had quarreled on some trivial point of Sunday School management, I learned the subject-matter of his preaching, which for the most part was the cheerful theme of everlasting hell-fire torments. He was no Greek scholar, no theologian, and therefore, did not know the difference as to Hades being an intermediate state between death and the general Resurrection; and hell to him was the final gloomy Tartarus of the old Pagans, to which sinners went at death, without hope of escape, improvement, or pardon. Coonscratcher compared this dreadful place to red-hot furnaces, to burning forests or prairies, through which ran a river of blazing petroleum; not a drop of water to be had, as in the parable of Dives and Lazarus; not a single drop, from silver cup, china cup, gourd or

calabash, and in vain sought even from the finger-
tips. "You call the floor of this School House
dirty now, when **we** ask you to get down upon **it**,
but in hell you would take a drop of water from
the foot of any saint in glory, if you could get it.
Think of it ; the smallest prayer cannot be answered
there. No conveniences **are** there for guests, no
seats, no cushioned chairs, no carpeted rooms, like
those of The Berkeley, for card-playing **and** guzzling whisky-punch, no revels **or** dancing **parties**;
no windows or doors to the prison-house of **the**
damned ; **only a** fiery lake of blazing waves. In
order to escape it, come here and kneel down **at**
this anxious bench and get religion. Never mind
the dirty **floor; it's** not **as** hot **as hell.** Come
right along, **and in five** minutes **you can make**
your 'title clear **to** mansions in **the skies.'** Now
or never."

The benevolent doctrine of remedial punishment
in Hades, and the final restoration of the whole
human race **to** purity and blessedness, as taught
by Origen, one **of** the ablest **of** the Christian
Fathers, and **held** by many modern theologians,
was beyond the knowledge and comprehension of
such a ranter as this. For saying that this doctrine
was **not** necessarily heretical, **a more** intelligent
and thoughtful Methodist minister, **named** Bullock,
was recently tried **for** heresy **in** northern New
York, and obliged to retract or go elsewhere. **So**

that we must conclude that Methodism is a materialistic religion like Mormonism or Mohammedanism,
minus Christianity.

When Coonscratcher had left Saranac Lake in
disgrace, and I had learned his where-abouts, I
addressed him a short note, asking him whether it
could possibly be true that he had applied the
epithet of rum-guzzler to me or any of my friends.
In reply, is this characteristic and frank admission :

"Sir, in reply to your note I would say that part
of it is a base falsehood. I never applied the
epithet of rum-guzzle to you and your friends at
the Berkley House. Secondly, I did use the term
of whisky guzzler in relation to you, based on a
report to that effect." J. W. C.

Having committed himself in writing to the
slander, I addressed him another note to this
effect : "I am not much surprised at your frank
admission as to the difference 'twixt tweedle dum
and tweedle dee.' Will you please favor me with the
name of the person or persons who told you I was
a whisky guzzler? As I have never in all my life
guzzled whisky, and as this false report is calculated to do me injury, unless it is retracted or cor-
rected, I fear that I shall be under the painful
necessity of bringing a criminal suit for defamation
of character against you and all concerned."

This note seems to have made Coonscratcher scratch his head to some purpose, as the following reply will show :

" Dear Sir, your note of the 2d is received. In reply I would say * * * I feel at liberty to address you more freely in the matter, so far as I am connected to the matter. I am willing to do all that is honorable in the case. As to the idea of resorting to the courts, seems to me would be a surrender of those broad christian principles which should govern all good men. I deplore the thought of courts as I am a poor man, and have no money to lavish on the Lawyers. Now you will allow me to fully explain my meaning in the use of the term guzzler. It was intended to imply and convey that you was an habitual drinker of whiskey or strong drink. Since you called my attention to the matter I finde it was a word implying more than I intended to express, and I must confess, that I was ignorant at the time of its full import, and the implication was based on report to that effect. Now Dear Sir, as a christian I am willing to act the honorable part in the matter by removing the statement out of the way so that you may receive no damage from it. Now, as to the charge of libel their was none intended on my part. As it was based on the report of your drinking you desired me to furnish the names of the persons in the matter, this I am able and willing to do, if it is strictly necessary, deeming it advisable first to adjust the matter. As it would involve several poor men, and to prosecute them would only add to the poverty and suffering of their innocent wifes and children. And for their sakes I defer at present. As I desire if possible to close this matter between ourselves.

"Now my Dear Sir you are aware that this is an age of talk, and the human family are given to it, and that it is well said ' The tongue is an unruly member.' Now Dear Sir I am greatful for the privallege of explaining myself, and will most hartily add that I am sorry that I did allow myself to speak evil instead of *good*.

"Now I submit the statement for your kind consideration and await a reply as to the tearms of your decission.

"I remain yours truly,

"J. W. COONSCRATCHER."

Commending this letter to the special attention of all Grammarians, Orthographers and Phonetic Reformers of the English language as to the exact form in which it lies before me, I have only to say of it, that the part which most appealed to my sensibilities was that about the poverty and suffering already great, to be increased by prosecuting the matter in a court of law. It was easy enough to forgive a poor whining dog like this, and with-

16

hold the hand from merited punishment; but to
have one's good name kicked round the mud of
Saranac Lake like a foot-ball, was out of the question. Neither a proper defensive pride, good sense,
nor charity admitted its possibility for a moment.
Accordingly, another and final letter was addressed
to Coonscratcher to this effect: That so far as he
was personally concerned in the slander, his ex-
planation and apology were sufficient: That he
must use his best influence to arrest the vile talk
about me in Saranac Lake: That he must exact
an apology like his own from his informers, or I
must adhere to my purpose of prosecution: That
the talk of that portion of the human family living
in this miserable hamlet, about its sojourning invalids, had already done them and the place much
injury, so that none of them would ever come there
again: That when these invalids drank a little
wine or whisky-punch for their infirmities, it was
under medical advice and according to the injunc-
tions of Solomon and St. Paul; and that as he had
retracted his own slander, his informers must do
the same. Can it be believed that this was Coonscratcher's reply?

" December 27th, 1878.

" Dear Sir your letter of the 13th inst. came to
hand. I should of answered it at once, but absence
from home and occupation since my return prevented. Now in relation to the reports of Saranac

Lake by that people. I do not consider that I am
responsible as I had no hand in geting up the
reports only made a remark about the reports.
And for said remark I gave you the former explana-
tion and apology, and will write a note to that
effect to Saranac if you desire it. As to the securing an apology from them is out of my power.
Now as to who first made the statement I do not
know, but this I do know that it was quite general
in the community. * * * Now my Dear Sir
if you wish to follow this matter farther I will
refer you to the following named persons of whom
you may make inquiry G. Berkly, Charles Manning,
G. Washer, Theodore Fisk, Will Sheldon, John
Slater, some of them may be able to tell you what
they know of the matter.

"Yours Truly,

"J. W. COONSCRATCHER."

As this letter was beneath contempt, no reply
was possible. The opportunity given to shield his
friends from prosecution and additional poverty
and suffering, was perverted into an unmanly exposure of their names. Not one of these men had
any personal knowledge of the matter in contro-
versy. Not one of them could swear without per-
jury that they had ever seen a single member of our
colony drink a drop of wine or whisky at any time
or in any place. They were all utter strangers to

us with two exceptions. One of them was our own
chore-boy, who served us awhile, struck for higher
wages, and was discharged. The other had been
the guide of my friend and kinsman, Mr. C., on a
fishing expedition which we took together in the
Spring of 1878. But even they never saw any
guzzling of whisky on our part. All the rest knew
nothing of our personal habits whatever. They
were ardent Methodists, and their attainment of
complete perfection and absolute impeccability
must have made them consider that lies and slanders in the interest of Methodism, and to the detriment of the Episcopal colony quartered upon them,
were no sins and crimes.

Development, indeed; to which our medical ad-
visers ought to give heed, when they send invalids
to this part of the Wilderness, to be so annoyed,
slandered and turned away forever in disgust. But
not to blow one's own trumpet too loudly, it can
be modestly whispered that our little colony had
vigorously set about the project of certain improvements in Saranac Lake. A plank walk was laid
through the principal part of the village. A reading room was established, and well supplied with
the best periodical and pictorial literature of the
day, choice works of higher fiction, history and
travel, and the New York daily papers. This reading room was used for awhile by the better class of
guides, but it was too high-toned for the roughs,

some of whom took a mischievous delight in making it untenable and impossible. The enterprise
came to grief after about a three-months' trial. A
weekly musical meeting was held at The Berkeley
which was far more successful. Christmas festiv-
ities were not neglected, and a large Balsam was
adorned and hung with gifts for more than half the
village,—in fact, for all who cared to come. And
Sunday services, with simple expository preaching
and teaching of the Gospel, were surprisingly well
attended, resulting in numerous baptisms, reformed
lives, and the establishment of a beautiful and commodious church.

Inasmuch as a walk on a bright sparkling day
should not be aimless, and inasmuch as society is
for the most part better than solitude, some of
us were accustomed to visit our neighbors in
companies of three, four or a half dozen persons.
One such visit to old grandam Runnie deserves
brief mention. She lives on the outskirts of the
village in a little, low, red-painted frame house, surrounded by stables, pig-sties, and dog-kennels.
She was then a widow of about three score and ten
years, having a numerous progeny of sons and
daughters, and their equally numerous offspring.
She is small of stature, somewhat bent down with
the weight of years, cares and troubles; but her
hair is yet unsilvered, her small black eyes undimmed, and her natural force unabated, more especially

16*

in the muscular pliability of the tongue, sweet
woman's last and best unfailing organ. Our first
acquaintance with that marvelous instrument and
its fortunate owner, began in extensive negotiations
for an old-fashioned spinning-wheel, and in subse-
quent minute instructions as to its use. Her farm
consisted of eighty acres of the best sand, stumps
and boulders in the neighborhood; and its chief
recommendation was that the mill-dam submerged
it every Spring when the lumbermen were driving
logs, and no early crops could be planted. Its
price was $2,000, and a bargain. She managed this
farm herself, with the aid of one of her sons, for
many years; but at last she took compassion on
one of her neighbors, a recent widower of about
her own age, who had been burned out, and secretly
married him. This man's chief attractions were, a
tall, commanding figure of about six feet three; a
most witty tongue; a few more adjoining acres of
sand, stumps and boulders: and a remarkable pony
without hair, which he often rode in triumph
through the village, and was not for sale at any
price. When he and Mrs. Runnie came together
as man and wife—for nobody else knows who per-
formed the marriage ceremony—it was a sight worth
seeing and sketching as they went in mutually restored connubial bliss, on their seven miles' wed-
ding trip to Bloomingdale, in a small buckboard
wagon, drawn by this hairless pony. His name is

Shortcut Tenk or Tank, spelled Tenk, but pronounced Tank, christened Shortcut from the fondness of his ancestors for the tobacco of that name. He is the tall, lank and lean, but witty father of the still taller and wittier and leaner guide at St. Regis Lake, so well known under the familiar designation of Hank Tenk, or Tank, which patronymic most probably had its remote origin in the great capacity of the family for whisky and dirt. This capacity is still a full and complete inheritance by the law of heredity, especially in Hank.

When our little walking party of two ladies and two gentlemen arrived at Mrs. Runnie's cottage, the first obvious thing to do was to knock three times, and answer the summons to enter by pulling the leather latch-string. The low door creaked open, revealing a room of moderate size, with low ceiling, bare floor, except where two or three circular rag mats lay, a table, a few wooden chairs, a large spinning wheel, and an enormous cooking stove, occupying a third of the space. We all bowed profoundly, from the necessity of the case, as if we were entering some grand cathedral. Mrs. Runnie met us with pleasure sparkling in her eyes and mantling her face. Her timid, unmarried daughter and child retired to a place behind the stove, where they sat silent and abashed during the interview. Wiping the dust from four chairs with the check apron which she wore, Mrs. Runnie

asked us to be seated. "Set down, an' stay a bit,"
she said: "I'm right glad to see ye; ye hav'nt
come to make fun of us an' our poor house, have
ye?" Assuring her that we had come for no other
purpose than to make her a friendly visit and to
get better acquainted, she went on to say with surprising volubility and freedom: "Why did'nt ye
come sooner? It's so lonesome-like here, an'
nobody ever comes to see sich an old critter as
me. If you've got eny more of that good tibaccy,
I'll light a pipe, an' set down to talk a bit." This
remark being addressed to myself, as chief spokes-
man, I handed her my tobacco pouch, which she
eagerly seized, and then filling her short clay pipe
and taking a long whiff or two, she said, "That's
good tibaccy; they've none like in the store; what
we git there is very bad an' dear."

Before her last marriage with Shortcut Tenk or
Tank, Mrs. Runnie was anxious to dispose of her
farm. On this occasion she expatiated upon its
excellence and cheapness somewhat after this
fashion: "Ye see, this farm is all me own; it has
eighty acres of as good land as the sun shines on;
I'll sell it for $2000, jest to spite them good-for-
nothin' boys of mine, who are only waitin' till I
die to git hold on't; an' I'll leave all the money to
Sally an' Jim, so I will. That's Sally over there
behind the stove, an' that's Jim a-settin' in her lap,
—he's sich a nice boy, an' fond o' books. He

knows some of his letters a'ready, an' he's only six years old."

There was some family feud between this old woman and her sons, two of whom are well known at Saranac as good men and guides; and as for Sally and Jim, whom most mothers would have turned out of doors in shame and disgrace, she rather took them to her heart with all the more tenderness and consideration as poor unfortunates. Jim was her pet and darling; and she cared not a whit who his father may have been. He was hers by the great law of nature, and she meant to provide for him and his weak-minded mother as well as she could. She recognized no pride of life or of society that would make them outcasts. Her daughter may have sinned like the adulterous woman of the Gospel narrative, but she would throw no stones at her, or drive her away from home to perish. Like all of his kind, Jephthah, or Edmund and Faulconbridge, of Shakespeare's plays, Jim was a boy of high spirit; he had good mettle in him. He had disobeyed orders once; tied the dog loose; taken him in a boat on the deep, full mill-dam of rafting time; had upset, and came near being drowned.

Mrs. Runnie's account of the matter was this: "Last spring Jim had bad spells, an' he was told not to go on the water. But one day he went, an' had a spell, an' fell in, an' was drownded. Poor

boy, he's been ailin' ever sence. I tried to cure
him with spruce-gum, an' balsam tea, an' wild-
cherry, an' birch-bark, an' skunk-cabbage root, an'
wild plants from the woods, an' he only got worse.
The doctors charges so much for killin' folks, that
I hated to send for one. But I had to do it. I
don't like old Bill Martin an' his humpethy pellets
an' powders; an' so I sent to Vermontville for good
old Doctor Quackenbosh to cure Jim's spells. He
come, an' gin him some stuff that done him some
good; but, ye see, when a poor boy is drownded
an' has sich spells, it'll take more money than I've
got to pay for curin' him. Mebbe, he'll outgrow
the spells an' drowndin'. But I gin the doctor a
pair o' chickens an' two dozen eggs for his trouble,
an' he went away smilin'."

No doubt, Mrs. Runnie was frightened into sending for a doctor, by the recent death of one of her
grand-children from diphtheria, a new disease in
this region. The parents, supposing it a case of
croup or ordinary sore throat, sent for no physician.
As the child grew worse, and the parents became
alarmed, they were persuaded to apply the unfailing remedy of a dead cat to the child's throat and
chest. The cat must be a black tom, just killed
and split open, and applied while yet warm. The
cure and charm would be most effectual if all this
were done about midnight. A great crowd, filling
the house to suffocation, assembled to witness the

wonderful performance and to gloat over the suffocating spasms of the dying child. Before morning the poor little creature was at rest.

Mrs. Runnie was there ; and this is what she said about the matter : " When they were all a-cryin' and a-goin' on at sich a rate that, abody could'nt hear her own ears, I jest sot still an' said nothin'; but thinks I to meself, what's the use o' cryin' an' a-sobbin' so for the dear little thing? She'll know nothin' o' this world's troubles, as I've done, an' as poor Sal has done. When I looked at it arterwards a-layin' in its little pine coffin, dressed out so nice an' clean in its white muslin frock, an' its dear little hands folded across its breast, an' its face so sweet an' smilin', jest like the prettiest wax-figger ye ever saw, I could'nt cry a bit,— indeed, I could'nt; for it seemed to me so wicked-like to mourn for an innocent little baby jest gone to Heaven to be a blessed angel."

Surely development of a higher and better character was here than we usually meet with under better circumstances and surroundings of Christian life and society. Heroism, self-command, and a practical belief in immortality, like that of the early Christians singing hymns of victory and rejoicing over their dear departed ones, gone to God forever out of the tyrant's fiery persecution, were all here to justify this poor old grandmother's seeming indifference at the death of the child.

She did not wring her hands, or tear her hair, or weep her eyes out, or rave like a mad woman on the point of suicide, like an infidel or a Pagan, or charge God with an unjust interference with her happiness, like a blasphemer. Nor did she often go to the child's grave, merely to bewail her own loss and renew her fits of weeping and wailing, or exclude herself from the society of her friends, and find her only genial occupation in adorning herself and the water-pitchers and other bed-room vessels with sombre crape, to mourn the loss of those who had used them, like some of the poor distracted and despairing ones I have known. But, rather, she fell back upon the simple faith of her early years, as she had learned it from her New Testament, and as the yearnings and prompt-ings of her own soul called that faith into active exercise on this fitting occasion. Her faith, not her grief, was too deep for tears.

Here was a favorable moment for speaking a word about religion and religious duty, and I thus addressed her: "Mrs. Runnie, not having seen you at any of the services which our clergyman is holding at The Berkeley, I suppose you attend the meetings at the School House." Something like contempt and anger darkened her face, and unmis-takably gave this animated utterance: "I us't to go sometimes, but it does a-body no sort of good. The preacher don't know no more than I do meself;

an' he hollers an' yells so much about hell, an'
drinkin', an' dancin', an' damnation, that he scares
the young gals into 'sterics, an' then they set up a
scream like so meny wild-cats an' painters, an' git
religion. An' there's the preacher's wife, too,
curvetin' round with her talk an' blab, coaxin'
people to come to her experience meetin's jest to
hear her speak, an' be converted. She aint eny
better than the rest of us, an' her hair is red
enough to set the School House a-fire. It's a
queer religion they git there, for it don't last a bit
longer than a snow squall in May or a hurricane of
hail in August. The gals will take the first chance
they can git to play the fool."

We were now getting upon that delicate ground
where this strange compound of a woman was said
to be fond of treading; and, as our ladies showed
signs of uneasiness, we rose to take our leave, with
an invitation to Mrs. Runnie, that we would be
glad to see her at The Berkeley service next Sunday morning. Making an excuse about her poor
clothes and the fine city company, she nevertheless
thought it might be a good thing to try it once, at
least. On our way home we met old Mr. Shortcut
Tenk or Tank, mounted on his bare-back, hairless
pony, his long legs and feet nearly touching the
ground, going towards the widow's cottage on a
courting expedition. Numerous visits of like kind
in and around Saranac Lake revealed much dis-

satisfaction with a Gradgrind Methodism minus
Christianity; and when a subscription list was
opened for the building of our new church, it was
a matter of astonishment to us with what readiness
and alacrity it was soon filled up to the extent of
nearly a yard long. Most of the subscribers gave
services or materials or the use of teams to a given
amount, reaching the handsome sum of about $900,
of which about one-half was realized. Mr. Blood
gave us the choice of a lot. The Bishop of Albany,
in whose Ecclesiastical jurisdiction we were, gave
his sanction and encouragement to the new enterprise. The members of our colony each gave
liberal donations in cash. Our friends at home
rallied to our aid. On the 28th of January, 1878,
a meeting was held in the parlors of our Chaplain,
to organize, appoint a building committee, and
choose a name for our parish Church. At Easter-
time twenty-five persons were baptized, some of
whom were the principal adult members of the
community. Since then nearly a hundred more
have been added to the church by baptism. On
July 10th, 1879, the church was dedicated, when a
large class was presented for confirmation; and
when, strange to say, the local Methodist exhorter
communed, and said it was one of the best meetings he had ever attended. As in the case of
St. John in the wilderness, there was a balance in
bank after the consecration of the Church of St.

Luke, The Beloved Physician, that is, after both churches were completely furnished and paid for. And all this without the existence of any such things as wardens and vestrymen. An experience of more than a quarter of a century had taught our Chaplain that in such enterprises as this, and in fact, in all church management and administration, wardens and vestrymen were generally more of hindrances than of helps. We would have none of them, either at St. John's or St. Luke's; and the results prove the wisdom of our decision and action. The title deeds of our church property in the Adirondack wilderness are held by the Board of Missions of the diocese of Albany, some of whose funds go towards the support of the resident clergyman, who, in turn, is appointed by the Bishop, according to primitive and rightful church usage. And Christ's blessed Gospel will never be preached to the poor of this land, as it was its Divine prerogative and credential to have been so preached in the days of the Son of Man on earth, until the Church is taken out of the control of the few rich men who now manage its affairs for their own selfish and social ends. The sooner, the better, or society will have nothing to give it stability, grace, beauty, coherence, or order. Think of a wealthy and prominent member of church society in New York, declaring, that unless the Ecclesiastical authorities in Council assembled conformed

to the wishes of such of his kind as would have
the Constitution and Liturgy of the Church altered
to suit their notions, the supplies would be cut off;
and you have the whole matter in a nut-shell. And
think, too, of a faithful minister of Christ and His
Church, driven from his work and injured in his
sacred calling, exposed to hardship and suffering
and the humiliations of a grinding poverty, that
tend to destroy all his manhood, because he gently
warns a rich parishioner not to come to the Holy
Communion for causes that would convict him in a
court of justice; but who, persisting to come, is
passed by, and a tumult is raised, and the parish
is injured, and the Bishop is appealed to, and the
rich offender is sustained, and the minister must
resign and go on his weary and hopeless round of
parish hunting. Let the great axe fall on such
iniquity as this, and make a speedy and utter end
of it, or a Gradgrind Churchmanship will ultimately
succeed in grinding the Church to powder, and
blow society itself to atoms.

What our colony could do here in the wilderness
by other methods formed on the primitive model
of a truer and better churchmanship, was done in
order to cultivate to the utmost, in this rude and
ignorant population, the graces of the fancies and
affections, so that its wolfish nature would not turn
upon us and make an end of us, or of our enterprises for its welfare, bodily, social and spiritual.

To stimulate the endeavor somewhat, our verse-maker read, one Sunday evening, to the assembled colony, the following artless effusion :—

SARANAC EREMITES—ST. SIMON, THE PATRON.

St. Simon Stylites stood on his tower,
By day and at night, in sunshine and shower,
Summer and winter, for many a long year,
With nothing but rain-drops his spirit to cheer.
His principal diet was very pure air,
And his sole occupation was silent prayer ;
When tired, he stood on one leg like a goose,
Tucking down his beard in his vestment loose ;
For he stood all the while in this upper air,
With no inch of space for a couch or a chair ;
Besides, if he nodded or ventured to sleep,
He might tumble down to a mangled heap.

All round lay the desert in silence and night,
When a sound struck the ear of the Eremite,
Like the note of the Hermit's soft plaintive cry,
Or the sigh of an infant laid down to die :
And Stylites started like one in a dream,
To look and to listen what the cry might mean ;
And it came like Undine in a ghostly shape,
At the base of the column its station to take.
'Twas a fair young girl, all her golden hair
Tearing, and wringing her hands in despair ;
"St. Simon," she moans, "for the dear love of Him,
Who came to deliver from sorrow and sin,
Come down to our aid ; there's one famished and ill,
A pilgrim, just come from dear Calvary's hill,

17½

He loves me, good Father, with heart and with soul,
Come down to our help ; come, and make him whole."

St. Simon stood up like a man at the call,
And taking his rosary, let it quickly fall :
Then lifting aloft his white bony hands,
And his streaming eyes to the bright starry lands,
He fervently sought all their merciful aid,
The pilgrim to bless, and this sorrowing maid.
" Come, take up my beads," he tenderly said,
" And hang them right over the poor pilgrim's head ;
While I will stay here 'twixt the earth and the sky,
And pray the dear Lord that he may not die."
In a tumult of anguish mingled with hope,
She hastened away through the desert to grope ;
Bewildered and frenzied, — in love's tempest tost,
She fell in the tangle exhausted and lost.
The pilgrim made search. and one fatal day,
He found where her bones in their whiteness lay.

Ye Saranac Eremites, come from afar,
To these lone bleak heights near the Northern Star,
Go down yourselves from your pedestals high,
And guide the poor souls that here wander and die ;
They cry for your aid in the pathway of peace,
From Gradgrinds and sorrows to give them release ;
Something more than a prayer, — a light in the way
Through the night of their weeping to brightness of day.

St. Simon, the Fisherman, stood by his boat,
Quite busy with fish-nets — divested of coat ;
A net had been split by a fine lucky haul,
And his boat had capsized in a sudden squall.

He was swearing a bit—a bad habit he had,
And savagely mauling his hireling lad,
Because he was lazy, and told him a lie,—
When, like one from the skies, there came walking by,
A strange stately man with a heavenly air,
Making Simon afraid that his God was there.
Pale, silent, and trembling all over his frame,
And touched to the quick with anguish and shame,
This stranger, God-Man, spake a word to him then,—
" Follow me, and I'll make thee a fisher of men."
He stopped not to parley, nor question to ask
About loss or gain, or what was the task,
But straight as the arrow flies to the mark,
He left all his catch, his nets and his bark,
And followed this Stranger to learn what he could
About fishing for men and doing them good :
Not yet all converted, impulsive and brave,
A rugged old tar, and nobody's slave ;
Denying his Lord ;—yes, thrice in sore fear,
With great oaths and curses that cost him right dear,—
When the Lord turned on Simon one sorrowful look,
And his heart swelled and burst like Kidron's full brook.
With vision undimmed on the Bethany height,
As at Hermon, he gazed on His splendor and might,
Going up to His throne and Kingdom on high,
To save all the lost that here wander and die.
When the Pentecost glory came down on his head,
As a light in the darkness and life to the dead,
What thousands received it their sad hearts to cheer,
Dispelling all doubt, and the way making clear :
The sick came for healing, the weary for rest ;
None ever departed untaught or unblessed.
No Simon was he on his high lonely tower,
But a man among men with beneficent power ;

He shook all the world like an earthquake throe,
Breaking down its vain idols, dispelling its woe.
The keys of the Kingdom were put in his hand,
Keys of knowledge, the Gospels, to bless every land,
To open the prisons, the captives to free,
Deaf ears to unstop, blind eyes to make see ;
Sad hearts to rejoice, hard toil to relieve,
Give peace to the stricken wherever they grieve ;
Shed light when the darkness comes down on the soul,
And tempests of passion over it roll ;
The erring to guide with all gentle restraint,
And lovingly soothe all despair and complaint.
Still held are these keys,—this their object sublime,
To glorify God, and give peace in our time.
St. Simon the Fisherman Peter became,
Because he was solid, and henceforth the same
Blessed Rock of the Faith, transmitting since then
His knowledge through Bishops and Pastors to men.

Ye Saranac Eremites, hear what I say,
Simon Peter the Fisherman points out the way,
How we must go forward at Saranac Lake,
Not counting the cost our fishes to take,—
With a bait, or a fly, or the great Gospel net
Of the Church's compassion and charity set.
Build a shrine for the Lord ; let it soon arise,
To lighten the darkness, and point to the skies ;
Follow close the God-Man. like Simon of old,
And gather the wanderers into the Fold ;
Be fishers of men ; and the Feast on the Shore
Shall be sweetness and gladness with Christ evermore.

V

PHENOMENA.

IN these days Science has put on her nose binocular and spectroscopic glasses, to examine all the near and remote phenomena of Nature. The dear, old lady,—she was once a young and beautiful Muse—tells us with a quiet chuckle of satisfaction, that so far as she can see into the matter, there appears to be one and the same law of life in all vegetables and animals, and one and the same mysterious Light pervading the entire universe as the seeming cause of this life. With dignity and emphasis she raises her forefinger, and tells us with placid tones of motherly wisdom and admonition that Nature never lies and slanders, and that hre phenomena are bound together by a seven-fold band of truth that cannot be broken. She also assures us that Nature, being fixed and stable, can not deceive or hurt us if we will not violate her order, but obediently follow her guidance; that, being full of life, beauty and harmonious activity. she is a perpetual pleasure; and that through her transparent robes of Rainbow-Light we may behold the stately steppings of her indwelling, all-pervasive, life-giving and life-evolving spiritual Essence or

Force. If we fail to note or heed her rightly.
through incapacity or wilful preconception of what
she ought to be, dear, old Mother Nature quietly
pursues the same undeviating course, however
much we, her children, may pout or suffer. Her
oracular responses are only made to reverent
suppliants endued with superior mental and moral
light.

Therefore it is, that Science bids us now turn
from all the miserable ignorance and superstition,
the hateful ingratitude and treachery, the abomin-
able wrongs, lies and slanders of human kind, to
seek in Nature some peace and solace for the soul.
Her skies may lower for a time and the mountains
may shake, but the glad sunshine comes again and
stays, and all is still and serene. Her old primitive chaos was reduced to order and filled with life
by the Light—the warm, brooding, dove-like Spirit
of Love. All the howling winter of our human
discontent and suffering shall have a merry Christmas and a resplendent Easter. Our life shall not
always be a stumble and a struggle in storm and
darkness, beset with fears, doubts, and anxieties:
a bright day of illumination and of deliverance
must come at last, or wherefore have all men been
made in vain? The storm travels on beyond the
smiling scene of our coming restoration, over
which hangs the bow of peace, and it carries before
it all that mass of dust into which this world's

iniquity has been slowly ground very small by the
neverceasing mills of the gods.   All the Gradgrinds
of society, from first to last, that have been grinding their grists out of a suffering humanity, shall
feel what the grinding process is before the tempest
comes to blow them away.

And now to our winter tale again.   Two months
of incessant storm and darkness at Saranac Lake
begat in some of us the apprehension that we might
possibly share the fate of Dr. Kane and other
Arctic explorers in a visitation of moping melancholy, scurvy, weakness, home-sickness, and distress incident to a long absence of the sun.   If the
very sledge-dogs died in great numbers in this
prolonged darkness of the Arctic regions, might
not the poor Saranac horses die, too, and no means
of escape be left us?   We were not much skilled in
the use of snow-shoes, and if we were taken sick,
how could we get out of this horrible wilderness to
our friends and homes?   Mope we did over our
books, games, and enterprises of reading-room and
church building; but when at last the dark curtain
lifted upon a scene of marvelous light and matchless splendor at the lowest point of our depression,
there was a glad and spontaneous revulsion of
spirit that sent us all forth into the dazzling snow
and sunlight, and crisp sparkling air, on long
merry sleigh rides, walking parties and hunting
excursions.

This snow is everywhere for miles around, pure and undisturbed, as it fell from heaven; on the mountains and their remaining evergreens; on the valleys and their habitations; on the lakes and ponds over which we now glide in sleighs instead of boats. It is all a fairy-land of supreme enchantment. This atmosphere glitters and sparkles with myriads of dancing crystals, finer than the points of cambric needles, and just as sharp, pricking your face into a crimson glow, and yet turning the tips of your ears and nose into dead whiteness. Have a care, and rub them with snow, or you will have no ears and nose worth taking home to enjoy the sweets of civilization. This sun, too, did it ever seem so resplendent before? Did it ever before shed such clear brilliant prismatic light on the earth, or on the diamond-dust of the air, filling both with a vast blaze of commingled radiance of the finest jewels? Rubies, emeralds, topazes, carbuncles, sapphires, amethysts, diamonds, etc., are all here perfectly faultless, adorning the earth like a bride for her heavenly Lord. The sky is a grander dome, more intensely clear and blue than one sees in Italy or Egypt—and that is saying a great deal—but so it seemed to me; the sunlight is even a stronger flood of purity and splendor here than there; the deep rich purple glow on the tops and sides of the mountains, and along the morning and evening sky, is more royal than in the Orient.

or even as one beholds it with fine emotion on an
early morning trip across the Adriatic from Trieste
to Venice, over and among the great Alpine peaks,
where cloud and mountain are almost undistinguish-
able, and the rosy splendor is quite entrancing.
And more than all this, we have here, in this pure
atmosphere and high elevation, a more marked and
clearly defined appearance of the mysterious Zodiacal light during the months of January and
February. It is here a great cone of deep rosy
red rising into the evening sky just at sundown
and sometime after, in the track of the sun and
pointing towards the zenith, as if it were the bright
finger of God Himself tracing the way into infinite
and unexplored space towards the far distant and
as yet hidden source of the one Primal Light. It
is a wonderful phenomenon upon which I have
gazed with ever increasing questioning and delight,
as an evidence that the sun may not be the only
source of light, but that when he has gone down
there still remains something more than his mere
reflection or projection of his luminous atmosphere
to assure us that light is an independent existence.
At any rate, science is not yet certain what this
Zodiacal light is, as we shall see further on.

A bright clear day, with the thermometer nearly
down to zero, may not be the best for hunting;
but nevertheless, let us take a short sleigh ride,
with dogs and guns, to the great swamp which lies

18

beyond Colby Pond. Foxes, hares, skunks, partridges and red squirrels are here in sufficient numbers to warrant the experiment, and recent report
has it that a panther, or wolf, or bear, or something
of the kind has been lately seen or heard there.
The recent snow is full of tracks and paths. The
still air is laden with the strong odor of Reynard,
and the still stronger scent of our dear little meek
friend *Mephitis Chinga*. They are both the most
cunning and adroit of politicians in our woods, but
easily tracked and more easily hunted down by
reason of their ill-savor. The evergreens are laden
with snow, and every branch is gracefully bending
under its light burden of feathery purity and prismatic brightness. If our friend, John Burroughs,
were here, he would surely retract that saying of
his about "the deep wilds of the Adirondacks,
where few birds are seen and fewer heard;" for
birds are here in flocks—snow-birds, chickadees,
pine-finches, blue-jays, partridges, ravens; and a
little later, winter-wrens, thrushes, robins, etc. Red
squirrels and chipmunks run up a tree at your
approach, whisk their tails, and chatter like school
girls at vacation time going home to see their
beaux. As the sun approaches the zenith, there is
a regular fusilade of small arms among the trees,
which snap and crack under the combined action
of frost and heat. Arctic explorers tell us that the

very rocks give out sounds of cannon and thunder
under the same influences intensified.

Brush away two feet of snow from the end of a
fallen log, and sit down awhile to contemplate the
scene until the dog's deep bay is heard in the depths
of the forest on the fresh track of a hare or fox.
It must be the hall of Odin. All the purity, brightness and glory of heaven are here. Snow, hoar
frost, icicles glittering on miles of forest trees far
and near make up such an array and spectacle of
splendor as to dazzle the eyes and bewilder the sensibilities. These white flags of peace are hung out
everywhere. What was it that suggested to the
old Norse imagination the splendid halls of Val-
halla but such a scene as this, so bright, so sheltered
and comparatively warm, so still and peaceful, and
so secluded and safe? Cold piercing winds do not
enter here; bird and beast come here for shelter
and safety and food; and man himself finds it a
bright and cheerful resort, warmer in Winter and
cooler in Summer, than elsewhere. Heaven it is
compared with Saranac Lake; and heaven it must
have suggested to the Norsemen; but a heaven
without skunks and foxes and fiercer beasts that
prey upon the innocent, defenceless and helpless
denizens of the place. A heaven where no poor old
Lear shall ever come to bewail ingratitude; nor
widow and orphan to mourn over the frauds and
losses of bank or railroad funds; nor cunning lob-

byist to charter combinations of capital against the poor and pervert justice; nor Tweed can come even to die.

Bang! bang! goes the double-barrelled shot-gun of our guide. It was a fox, but the shot was too fine to kill. Reynard jumps up two feet into the air as the shot strikes him, and then makes off as swift as an arrow with one of the dogs after him, who does not return for three days, after which he comes in a poor miserable skeleton. One after another slip along, like animated snow-balls, great white hares, which we shoot at on the swift run, and bag only three or four of a morning. Their fur is thick, and they are not easy to kill even when hit; and, perhaps, like wounded deer, they go into the depths of the woods to die. Partridges are always plump and in season for the sick. John Burroughs shall describe one just put up and booming past our quiet watch. "The partridge (*Bonasa umbellus*) is one of our most native and characteristic birds. The woods seem good to be in where I find him. He gives a habitable air to the forest, and one feels as if the rightful occupant was really at home. The woods where I do not find him seem to want something, as if suffering from some neglect of Nature. And then he is such a splendid success, so hardy and vigorous. I think he enjoys the cold and the snow. His wings seem to rustle with more fervency in midwinter. If the snow falls very fast, and promises a heavy storm, he will complacently sit down and allow himself to be snowed under. Approaching him at such times he suddenly bursts out of the snow at your feet, scattering the flakes in all directions, and goes humming away through the woods like a bomb-shell —a picture of native spirit and success."

Our dog, Major, was running a hare, and had put up a partridge out of the newly-fallen snow in this fashion. Marking his swift flight and the place where his booming wings ceased their noise, pursuit was slow and toilsome. The sweat rolled down my face in great drops, although I was clad in my old summer velveteen fishing and hunting clothes; and presently he was seen strutting along most proudly, turning his head and flirting his tail for another flight, when as he rose to take a long and final leave, he was brought down and bagged. Two others treated in the same way, with our two braces of hare, made a prize worth taking to The Berkeley for our invalid lady friends and ourselves. A blue jay is shot and taken home to be mounted on a small board covered with gold paper for dear little May Morris. The pelts of the hares are cured and kept for linings of slippers and protectors of weak lungs from cold. In this way we make occupation and waste nothing.

Somewhat later in the season, say in the latter half of April, when, this year at least (1878), the

18*

southerly breeze began to blow and open the lakes
and ponds, and melt the snow on the sunny sides
of the mountains and hills, and fishing excursions
are in order; there is no more welcome and thrill-
ing sounds in the woods than the drumming of the
partridge and the song of the winter-wren. As the
mode of this drumming is variously described, and
observers are not agreed about it, I must add my
own careful examination of the process, on more
than one occasion, to the unimpeachable testimony
of so careful and accurate an observer as Mr. Burroughs, when he asks and answers the question:
" Who has seen the partridge drum? It is the
next thing to catching a weasel asleep, though by
much caution and tact it may be done. He does
not hug the log, but stands very erect, expands his
ruff, gives two introductory blows, pauses half a
second, and then resumes, striking faster and faster,
till the sound becomes a continuous, unbroken
whir, the whole lasting less than half a minute. The
tips of his wings barely brush the log, so that the sound
is produced rather by the force of the blows upon the
air and upon his own body, as in flying. One log
will be used for many years, though not by the
same drummer. It seems to be a sort of temple
and held in great respect—not a dry and resinous
log, but a decayed and crumbling one, generally
covered with moss. If a log to his taste cannot be

found, he sets up his altar on a rock, which becomes
resonant beneath his fervent blows."

The song of the winter-wren, especially when
first heard, is a marvel of sweetness and melody.
Trolling one day, in latter April, on the Lower
Saranac for salmon-trout, and growing tired of the
poor sport, I landed in one of the wild and retired
jungles to eat luncheon. While thus engaged, all
at once there rose and filled the whole place such
a joyous and fervid and varied bird-song as I had
never before heard. It seemed to be a combination
of flute and piccolo. I looked everywhere, high
and low, far and near, to discover the songster in
vain. Again and again the sweet and well-sustained
melody flooded the still woods; and at last I saw
a diminutive and lively bird hopping about in search
of larvæ, now on this stump and then on the very
log where I sat, seeming to know nothing of fear,
when again it disappeared and the song began anew.
This, then, was my dear little songster, about as
big as the end of my thumb, of a brown color, and
with a pert square tail, erect and pointing towards
its head. He was an utter stranger to me, and I
asked my guide what bird it was. It was that
same pious guide who carried a small copy of the
New Testament in his pocket and watched for deer
with it, who entertained me in the boat with Moody
and Sankey songs, who pronounced Shakespeare
too vulgar or obscene to read, and who, of course,

knew nothing of Ornithology, and not much of
anything else.   Giving the winter-wren three times
three hearty cheers, and swinging my hat lustily
and in such exuberance of hilarity as I had not indulged for years, I went home determined to find
out something about the matter.   Audubon could
inform me, and so could John Burroughs.

Identifying my sweet serenader in Audubon's
plates, I turned to the text and read as follows :
" The song of the winter-wren excels that of any
other bird of its size with which I am acquainted.
It is truly musical, full of cadence, energetic and
melodious; its very continuance is surprising, and
dull indeed must be the ear that thrills not on hear-
ing it.   When emitted, as it often is, from the dark
depths of the unwholesome swamp, it operates so
powerfully on the mind, that it inspires by contrast
a feeling of wonder and delight, and on such occasions has usually impressed me with a sense of the
goodness of the Almighty Creator, who has rendered every spot of earth in some way subservient
to the welfare of his creatures." (II, p. 129).

John Burroughs found our little friend in the
remotest wilds of the Adirondacks, so late as
August, and a few weeks afterwards, on the banks
of the Potomac River; and wonders whether he
travels by easy stages from bush to bush and from
wood to wood, or whether his compact little body
has force and courage enough to brave the night

and the upper air so as to achieve leagues at one
pull. His musical talent is thus described: "The
winter-wren is another marvellous songster, in
speaking of whom it is difficult to avoid superla-
tives. He possesses the fluency and copiousness
for which the wrens are noted, and besides these
qualities, and what is rarely found conjoined with
them, a wild, sweet, rythmical cadence that holds
you entranced. I shall not soon forget that perfect
June day, when, loitering in a low, ancient hemlock
wood, in whose cathedral aisles the coolness and
freshness seem perennial, the silence was suddenly
broken by a strain so rapturous and gushing, and
touched with such a wild sylvan plaintiveness, that
I listened in amazement. And so shy and coy was
the little minstrel, that I came twice to the woods
before I was sure to whom I was listening. * * *
His voice fills these dim aisles, as if aided by some
marvellous sounding-board. Indeed, his song is
very strong for so small a bird, and unites in a
remarkable degree brilliancy and plaintiveness.
I think of a tremulous vibrating tongue of silver.
He has a pert, almost comical look. His tail stands
more than perpendicular, it points straight towards
his head. He is the least ostentatious singer I
know of. He does not strike an attitude, and lift
up his head in preparation, and, as it were, clear
his throat ; but sits there on a log and pours out
his music, looking straight before him, or even

down on the ground. As a songster he has but few
superiors " (*Wake Robin*, pp. 12. 28, 55).

Another sweet songster and a rival of the winter-
wren is the modest and lonely hermit thrush, who
morning and evening, in sunshine and shower, and
all day and night long, seems never to grow weary
of singing his short, tender, plaintive and melodious
song. He is the pet minstrel of the camp, and,
like the tame flocks of cross-bills, does not seem to
fear the presence of man or dog. Such companions
as these in the silent forest are a source of perpetual pleasure. No orchestral or operatic music
can for a moment bear any comparison with that
which pours from the throats of hundreds of such
songsters in the early spring, filling all the woods
with a symphony almost celestial. No pride and
ostentatious rivalry of dress here distract the
attention, and make the music a secondary consideration. No fashionable frivolity and social
gossip and dark-browed envy and malignity are
here to vex and annoy. No religious bigotry or
pharisaical pretension and intolerance, or sectarian
bitterness and calumny disturb the peace or interrupt the enjoyment of the place and time. Is it
any wonder that such solitudes of Nature have
been sought, in all ages and countries, as a refuge
for contemplative minds against man's inhumanity
to man, where the mind may have some peace in
its sole communion with the God of Nature?

We were passing through a trying and stormy scene at Saranac Lake, and it would be a strange thing, indeed, if some rainbows did not come to brighten it and bring relief. One Sunday afternoon in March, a vast snow-cloud came slowly rolling through a gorge of the mountains to the east of Saranac, and spreading along the sides and over the twin summit of old Nipple Top. It was clear in the west, and the sun was shining brightly. The snow cloud must have been heavily charged with moisture, or such a strange and startling phenomenon as that of a snow-bow could not have been produced. All the prismatic colors of the rainbow, from red to violet, were distinctly visible, though not so bright and glowing as in the rainbow, nor in the usual narrow band of seven-fold color ; the whole expanse of the cloud was covered with broader belts or stripes of iris colors and prismatically arranged, presenting an appearance at once novel and transcendently beautiful. The vast cloud was itself a frozen ,and spectral rainbow, moving slowly and majestically along, just like some aurora borealis I have seen in this region. None of our colony had ever before seen anything like it, nor had any of the native Saranackers with whom we conversed about it. It was to us all an entirely new phenomenon of nature. Some of us were well aware of the fact that orthodox science attributes the aurora to electric or magnetic influences, and calls it a magnetic shower or storm according to its greater or less intensity. But notwithstanding this, there was suggested by this spectral phenomenon the possibility that the aurora itself might be a like reflection from some gigantic snow-cloud or mist. whirling about the North Pole. Magnetism is an universal agent or force; why. then, is the greater frequency and brilliancy of the aurora confined to the Polar regions of the earth? Has the frosty atmosphere there anything to do with the question? Arctic explorers are almost ecstatic in their descriptions of the aurora borealis. which, after all that is said about it. amounts to this: that it simply presents the colors of the rainbow. Sometimes there is nothing more than a mere luminous sheet of light widely difused, sometimes long golden draperies float overhead, folding over each other in a thousand ways like waves agitated by the wind; and most often. a luminous arc is spread towards the North, separated from the horizon by a black segment, out of which dart brilliant rays of white or red, which in turn extend. divide. and form themselves into a luminous fan; and then mount to the zenith where they converge and unite to form a corona. darting luminous jets in every direction. Then the sky appears like a vast cupola of fire; blue, green, yellow, red and white join in the palpitating rays of the aurora. But I never remember to have seen more than one

such display in our latitude, and that was in a very
cold midwinter; whereas, in the Arctic regions this
light is the common substitute for the long absent
sun, emanating from his reflected rays upon the
lofty mountains and thick mists composing the atmosphere of the glacial zone. During the absence
of the sun in the midwinter of the Polar regions,
the night there is never so dark as elsewhere, because the moon and stars seem to possess twice as
much light and scintillation, while their rays, reflected by the snow and ice with which the earth is
covered, shed so bright a glow as to enable one to
read without the aid of a candle. The moon, too,
is nearly always bright in these regions; and in addition to this, there is a continuous light in the
North, the varied shades and play of which are
amongst the strangest phenomena of nature; while
the sky is a marvellous spectacle of splendor there,
with its vast sheets of opal, sapphire, emerald and
ruby, under the influence of the sun, which still
seems to shed its brilliant glow long after its disappearance. Such is the account of the aurora
borealis as I gather it from Guillemin's *Forces of
Nature*, and Rambosson's *Popular Astronomy*. I
was not far wrong, then, in my conjecture that the
aurora might possibly be refracted and reflected
sunlight acting on the misty atmosphere of the
Polar regions. ·

But the present magnetic theory of the aurora is

19

not the only one entertained by scientific inves-
tigators. Some trace it to a cosmic gaseous matter
in space, far beyond the limits of our atmosphere,
at least 125 miles distant from the earth's surface.
Others attribute it to unusual perturbations in the
sun itself, or identify it with the Zodiacal light;
while so long ago as 1787, Dr. Elliott maintained
that the sunlight itself was emitted from what he
called a dense and universal aurora borealis.
Another theory, once presented to the French
Academy of Sciences, is that, inasmuch as not only
solid bodies, but also mists of uncondensed matter,
penetrate our atmosohere, both of which contain
magnetic metals, the main cause of the aurora
borealis is the magnetic action of these mists upon
the earth. Inasmuch as hail-stones have been
found which contain iron and nickel, just as aero-
lites do, the inference is that these Polar mists are
magnetic and produce the aurora, seeing that its
most frequent occurrence coincides with the period
of meteoric showers or asteroids.

Is this strange continuous light of the Polar regions, which is neither the direct light of sun,
moon, or stars, a reflection, or an emanation? If the
Polar mists are magnetic, what cause sets them in
motion and into such a brilliant glow, in the absence of the sun? If the aurora is identical with
the Zodiacal light, as spectrum analysis makes it in
both as *giving a brilliant ray of nitrogen;* and the

Zodiacal light is not, according to Laplace, a mere extension of the sun's atmosphere, then, in the name of wonder, who can tell us what the aurora borealis is, or explain its origin?

But I must hasten on with my tale, and now give an account of a complete circular rainbow which I had the joy of seeing in latter April. 1878, on my return from a fishing excursion with a good mess of spotted brook trout, which were as brilliant and beautiful in their way as the rainbow itself. It was a matchless spectacle to behold on so vast a scale as that of Round Lake, between the two Saranacs; and, like the iris snow-cloud it was the first I had ever seen, surpassing in extent and brilliance the contracted circular rainbows of the gorge below the Falls of Niagara, and of the Yosemite valley. What a leap my heart and hands took upward towards the heavenly vision, as Wordsworth's verse escaped from my lips:

> My heart leaps up when I behold
>   A rainbow in the sky;
> So was it when my life began,
> So is it now, I am a man,
> So be it when I shall grow old,
>   Or let me die !
> The child is father of the man ;
> And I would wish my days to be
> Bound each to each by natural piety.

Round Lake is in a wide, deep gorge made by

two ranges of mountains on either side, old Ampersand dominating the range on one side, and I
think, Boot-Bay Mountain on the other. A heavy
thunder storm had just gone along the Ampersand
range, as we entered Round Lake on our way to
Bartlett's. The mass of black clouds was piled on
the Whiteface range to the East, while the sun was
shining low in the West. The lake was now smooth
as glass and a perfect reflector. The rainbow
spanned the entire heavens, forming a complete
circle in the lake. Round and round gleamed the
glorious seven-fold band of prismatic light, as
though it were indeed, what Plato claimed it to be,
the girdle which encircled the entire universe and
held it together; or what Moses said it was, the
sign of peace to the warring elements in earth and
sky, land and water; or as the vision of the Seer
of Patmos makes it, the light and life of all, encircling the throne of God Himself. Here is matter
enough for investigation; and our Chaplain was
called upon to reproduce and repreach his discourse
known as the " Rainbow Sermon." I am permitted
to give it entire, after revision, although, for obvious reasons, it was not all delivered just as here
written. The text was *Revelation* iv, 3, " There
was a rainbow round about or encircling the throne,
in sight like unto an emerald."

Friends and Brethren: Such a complete circular
rainbow as some of us saw, the other day, is one of

the most beautiful objects in nature, and is such as
the prophet and evangelist John mentions in the
text. It is the joint production of clouds and
sunshine, and can only be produced when sun and
cloud are in opposite directions. The rainbow can
only be a complete circle when it is reflected from
below as it is from above, in some deep place or
gorge filled with rain-drops or mist, or reflected
from the smooth surface of river or lake—such a
lake or sea, smooth and clear as glass, like that
which the prophet saw in a vision before the
Heavenly Throne, doubtless a reproduction of his
own sea of Galilee, where he had so often fished,
or of the sparkling waters of the Mediterranean
around the island of Patmos where he was now
banished by order of the Roman Emperor. The
deep gorge in which the sea of Galilee lies would
reflect a circular rainbow, and doubtless the smooth
waters around Patmos did the same. This circular
rainbow St. John transferred to the very seat of
Deity as its chief attraction. I propose to examine
the matter in the light of modern science, philosophy and religion.

Science tells us that sunlight is white; but that
when it passes through transparent glass or water
it is both refracted and reflected, and that then,
this one white light is decomposed or resolved into
seven visible colored rays, which appear in the following invariable order, viz.: red, orange, yellow,

19*

green, blue, indigo or purple, and violet. A clear piece of triangular glass is called a prism, and the sunlight passing through it produces the spectrum or this seven-fold picture. Two refractions and one reflection are necessary to form this colored image or picture of the sunlight, which is called a continuous or complete spectrum—an unbroken spectrum, having all the seven colored rays in regular order. A partial spectrum is that in which only some of the colors appear, with dark spaces between. A refraction is simply the bending of the light when it enters the prism and leaves it. The reflection is from within the prism as from a mirror; and this prism may be a snow-cloud, mist, or rain falling continuously, as well as clear glass.

The throne of God encircled by a rainbow suggests some dark clouds of mystery on which this rainbow must appear above it; and the sea of glass clear as crystal is the reflector of it from below. It is implied, I think, that the light which produces this circular rainbow is an emanation from God himself. Inasmuch as *ex nihilo nihil fit*—nothing comes of nothing: God said, let light be, and light was; His spoken Word or Divine Logos, therefore, and most expressive living symbol of all knowledge, enlightenment and wisdom to mankind, existing and perpetually manifesting itself in and from God as the one only source. The light of the burning bush on Horeb, not consuming; the light of Israel

in the wilderness, guiding and consoling; the light
of the Gentiles in prophetic announcement and
joyous fulfilment; the light of Job on his dunghill
whose way is not known; the light of all men and
their life; the true light that enlightens every man
coming into the world; He who claimed to be the
light of the world, whom to follow is life; God who
is light, and in whom is no darkness; and the light
of the New Jerusalem, of which it is said by the
Apostle John: "The city had no need of the sun,
neither of the moon to shine in it: for the glory of
God did lighten it, and the Lamb is the light
thereof." Or, as the prophet Isaiah had long before
said: "The sun shall be no more thy light by
day; neither for brightness shall the moon give
light unto thee; but the Lord shall be unto thee an
everlasting light, and thy God thy glory."

If these conceptions and expressions have any
definite meaning beyond mere figures of speech,
they surely convey the idea of God as the one only
source of all light, whether material, intellectual,
moral or spiritual, and that His seat or throne is
the centre of all power, all life, order and beauty,
concealed in darkness and mystery, out of which
comes, like the aurora of the Arctic circle, the
rainbow to relieve the gloom and to inspire us with
hope and courage that the storms of our own
troubled life will soon end in a lasting peace. It
is a revelation of God; first, in nature; second, in

ourselves; third and greatest, in the Logos, His
Son.

All science is modest in its definition of light.
Of its true nature and original source it professes
to know little or nothing. Sir Isaac Newton claimed
that it was composed of infinitely small particles or
corpuscles of matter; but the researches of Descartes and Huygens rather prove it to be an undu-
lation or wave-like motion, which is now the accepted theory. Bishop Berkeley, after whom this
house is named, as an ideal philosopher advanced
the doctrine that sound and light are both only vibrations or motions, and that colors are inherent in
light, and are not the sensible qualities of things,
but only more or less rapid vibrations of the different colored rays of light. This anticipation of
Berkeley has lately been verified by natural science,
and we shall soon see what the number of vibrations is in the seven colored rays of light (*Works*,
New Oxford Ed., I, pp. 277-78).

Moreover, since the grand discovery made in
1859, by the two Heidelberg professors, Bunsen
and Kirchhoff, of the spectroscope and spectrum-
analysis, an instrument and a process of determining the nature and composition of all bodies in
an incandescent or gaseous state from the light
which they emit, we are in a position of ascertaining what materials and elements compose the sun,
stars, comets and unresolved nebulae. The rainbow

colors or spectra appear in them all, just as they
are seen in the morning and evening clouds, or in
the aurora borealis, or the zodiacal light, or in the
phosphorescent glow of certain animals and decayed wood, or in the rich and varied tints of our
autumn foliage, or in diamonds and other precious
stones, or in the more brilliant prismatic sparkle of
frozen snow-crystals and glittering icicles upon the
trees. Dr. Draper's recent discovery of oxygen in
the sun, and Mr. Locyer's scientific experiment,
which seems to point to hydrogen as the one simple
element of all the starry and other bodies, and the
liquefaction and even solidification of these and
other gases in France, recently, all indicate that the
sun and stars, like our own earth, are mere conden-
sations of these gases by the agency of light, and
that other bodies like them are still forming out of
the fire-mists or nebulæ of remote space. Hydrogen being the chief element of water, it is somewhat surprising to be told that the whole chromo-
sphere of the sun is one vast envelope of this gas
red-hot, and that its flames shoot out to the almost
incredible distance of 80,000 or 90,000 miles.
Spectrum-analysis ascertains this and much more
besides, that both sun and stars give out the spectra of iron, salt, nickel, potassium, magnesium,
calcium and other minerals and metals, showing
conclusively that these substances enter into the
composition of these bodies, as they do into the

composition of our own earth; but that under all
circumstances, the hydrogen spectrum is always
present. Water and light then, seem to be the
primary agents of creation, as the old Greek philosopher Thales taught.

The inference from this brief notice of spectrum-
analysis obviously is, that light in the distant places
of the material universe is quite independent of
our own sun; that there are other suns and systems of planets; and that, therefore, light is an
altogether independent thing. Even here there is
other light than that of the sun and stars, as zodiacal light, auroral light, electrical light and phosphorescent light. When, therefore, the book Genesis represents light as existing before the sun,
moon and stars appeared, and before chaotic matter
was reduced to order, and before any life of vegetables and animals existed, we need have no perplexity about the matter; inasmuch as science now
comes to our aid to show us that St. John was right
when he said, that He who was in the beginning
with God and was God, and who made the world
and all things, was Himself the Light who had life,
and that this Light was that of man himself, as a
physical, intellectual and moral being. Cosmic
vapor, meteoric mist or dust, luminous ether,
nebulous cloud, or whatever else worlds, suns,
comets and planetary systems are made of, all have
rainbow hues or spectra of their own; and there-

fore, light existed long before any of them were formed, as itself a motion or life.

Inasmuch as light has chemical and caloric properties, it must be the chief agent in the production of order and life out of the cosmic vapor or matter of the universe. Schelling says that after gravity, light came into this comparatively dead and inert mass, producing movement, form and life; and that by a combination of gravity and light, all organic life came into being. Lavoisier tells us, that all organism, feeling, spontaneous motion, and life only exist upon the surface of the earth and in regions exposed to the light. Without light nature is dead, lifeless and inanimate. A beneficent Being, in providing the earth's surface with light, endowed it with organism, feeling and thought. All vegetation depends upon light, not only as nourishment for man and beast, but also as fuel in wood and coal for our homes, steamships and manufactories. All grass, grain, wood and coal are but the products of light, heat and gases, and without light man himself becomes pale, enervated, decrepid, melancholy, idiotic and lifeless.

In addition to this, I may cite this hypothesis of M. Malet, a distinguished French scientist: " A vapory mass floated and gravitated in space; this mass contained the bases of the present elements; as these elements are susceptible of light now, so were their bases at the beginning; a light from

heaven fell upon this vapory mass, susceptible to
its influence; the action of floating was converted
into rotation on its axis; the action of gravitation
was converted into revolution around its centre,
as I have demonstrated by experiments with the
radiometer; the entire surface of the mass came
slowly under the influence of light; under this
influence the lightest gases of the mass were attracted from the surface to the light; the gases,
which rose highest, became air and formed the atmospheric envelope; the gases, which became condensed into liquids, became the water envelope,
our ocean; and the residue of the vapory mass
formed into solid molecules, which, gravitating to
their own centre, gradually consolidated into the
compact body of this earth, the silicious rocks.   It
will be seen from this that the chief agents in the
formation of the cosmos are precisely the same as
those in the theory of the speculative philosopher,
Schelling, viz., gravity, light and gaseous matter.
This light, says Malet in conclusion, fell in its
wavy streams on the wandering vapor, and reduced
it to obedience, to harmony and to love.   There
are no phenomena upon earth that do not follow on
in their natural course from this beginning.

If our modern science thus explains, as Moses
did, how light was the primal agent in creation,
what shall we think of that venerable tradition of
the Jews preserved in the Talmud, which says the

same thing: "The Divine Being was supposed to have commenced the work of creation by concentrating on certain points the primal universal Light. Within the region of these points was the appointed place of our world. Out of the remaining points or foci, He constructed certain letters—a heavenly alphabet. These characters He again combined into certain creative words, whose secret potency produced the forms of the material world. The great cabalistic creative word –the sum and substance of these celestial letters, with all their inherent virtue and potency in mightiest combination, was SHEMHAMPHORASH, which Moses was forty days in learning of the angel Saxael, on Mt. Sinai; by which Solomon achieved his fiend-compelling wonders; and which Jesus of Nazareth stole from the Temple, as the later Rabbins say, and by its aid was enabled to delude the people."

We read in the first chapter of Genesis that the earth was without form and void; that there was darkness; that the Spirit of God moved upon the face of the waters; and then light was, as a spoken or creative Logos, with the whole order of the world and its life following in its track during the longer or shorter periods of day and night. The only difference here noticeable is that the Spirit of God takes the place of what science calls Gravity, for want of a better name to designate that force of nature which brings matter together or attracts.

20

Both science and Revelation are agreed as to the
chaotic matter being influenced by light as the
agent of life.   And this is as it should be, inasmuch
as nature is just as great a revelation of God as
Holy Scripture is, and God cannot be supposed to
to contradict Himself in one or the other.

Then, again, it is a curious thing to note what a
conspicuous part the light plays, in its seven-fold
effulgence of the rainbow, in the reproduction and
preservation of the life of the earth after it had
been overflowed by a great flood of water.   The
bow was henceforth set apart or designated as a
sign that the moist earth should always be productive under the combined influences of shower and
sun, moisture and light, a state of things only possible in the production of the rainbow.   And
therefore, the rainbow is the most fitting as it is the
natural sign of the life of the earth.   All flesh is
grass—derives its life from the earth's vegetation,
which in turn can only grow and flourish under the
influences of moisture and heat, rain and light, out
of which also comes the rainbow as the assurance
of perpetual sustenance to every living creature
of all flesh that is upon the earth.   It is a fixed
natural order corresponding to the beneficent un-
changing being and word of God Himself.   Whenever, then, the rainbow appears we should hail it
as the sign of a covenant between God and men,
that life, not death, is our normal condition and

perpetual heritage; and that God designs henceforth to fill the world with rainbow-light so that
we may find our way through the drenching storms
of life here to the smiling and peaceful scenes of a
higher and better life elsewhere. Let us give good
heed to the words of Jesus, the son of Sirach,
when he says: "Look upon the rainbow, and praise
Him that made it; very beautiful it is in the brightness thereof. It compasseth the heaven about with
a glorious circle, and the hands of the Most High
have bended it."

This brings us to consider more particularly the
moral and religious uses of the rainbow. This
rainbow around the throne of God came to cheer
and comfort the exiled Apostle in the darkest
period of his life. The clouds were illumined by
the seven-fold splendors of God's symbolized attributes, or rather of His Being as God all love and
justice and mercy and sovereignty and wisdom and
life and holiness or purity, to assure the lonely
exile that all was well and as it should be. The sea
of glass, clear as crystal, was but the symbol of a
new and regenerate life; the beasts, four in number,
personated the four Holy Gospels; the white robed
Elders personated all those prophets of mankind
who have written or spoken for the instruction of
our race, whether as moralists, philosophers, reformers, statesmen, poets or men of science; the
seven lamps make the continuous spectrum of all

Divine illumination as to the nature and will and
ways of God; and all these in combination taught
the Apostle that the dark sorrows of life—its hard
toil and grinding poverty—its sad oppression and
terrible injustice—its banishment from friends and
kindred—its lonely exile on a barren rock surrounded by the sea and from which there was no
escape, were all nothing more than vanishing clouds
on which the sunlight of God's presence fell to
paint the rainbow of His smile and benediction.
The darker the clouds and more drenching the
rainfall, the brighter the bow and more productive
of good, the succeeding state of things in a new
and higher life.

Moreover, the rainbow must have taught St. John
the absolute unity of God—the All in all—one in
essence or substance, with diversity of manifestation and operation. The one white light has a
three-fold nature. It shines or illumines; it has a
chemical property producing accretion; and it has
heat, which is necessary to produce motion or life,
rather which is motion and life itself. So this one
God, or Substance of all things, is Father, as the
Source of all; Son, as the Maker or organizer of
all; and Holy Spirit, as the vital energy, or Lord
and Giver of all life; God as Light—God as Love
—God as Life. Not a correlation of blind forces, but
as an intelligent, ever-active Spiritual Substance, in
whom all things consist. St. Paul teaches that all

things are in God, when he says that in Him we live, and move, and have our being; or as the *Theologia Germanica* explains it : " He hath comprehended and included all things in Himself and His own Substance, and without whom, and beside whom, there is no true substance, and in whom all things have their substance. For He is the Substance of all things, and is in Himself unchangeable and immoveable, and changeth and moveth all things else." Or, as Benedict Spinoza afterwards expressed it in his Ethics : Præter Deum nulla dari neque concipi potest substantia : Besides God no other substance can be admitted or conceived.

Alone of all the New Testament writers, St. John defines God as light; and a distinguished Oriental scholar, Max Müller, tells us that this definition is precisely that of the Vedic Hymns, *deva* or bright. Thousands of years before Homer and St. John, even before a single line of the Vedas was written, there existed in the ancient languages of the world, a word expressive of light, *div*, and from this root *deva* was formed, which afterwards came to mean God, as the source of light and life. (*Hibbert, Lectures*, I.) And this goes to show, that God, who is the true light, enlightened the minds of men in the very dawn of time as He does now ; only now the sun has mounted higher and gives more light.

Again, as the rainbow seems to join heaven and

20*

earth, and to bind the whole universe together into a system of order, life, and beauty, so the mysterious Incarnation of the Logos or Son of God unites the seeming contrarieties of human and Divine, material and spiritual, into one complex being or nature. If in our own nature there is a union of matter and spirit, and if in the world about us there are phenomena and force, it need not seem to us any more strange and mysterious that the Divine and human should be united in Jesus Christ, or as Spinoza says : Nam Christus non tam propheta, quam os Dei fuit : Christ was not only a prophet, He was the presence of God Himself; or as St. Paul expresses it, " the image of the invisible God," —the *icon.* In Him dwells all the fulness of the Godhead bodily ; the brightness of His glory ; the express image or presentment of His Substance. Christ, therefore, is like a prism through whom the one Divine white light comes to us in the seven-fold brightness of the rainbow, uniting heaven and earth, God and man ; and revealing God as loving, wise, good, true, just, merciful and holy. Let us take the prismatic colors in their order, and see how they may possibly symbolize these essentials of the Divine nature.

Red is the first and longest ray. Its numerical value is 620 in length ; 94 in intensity of color ; and 514,000,000,000,000 of vibrations per second. Its color is less intense than some of the others, but deeper, richer, and more attractive to children, birds, animals, and men. It is the favorite color generally; and, therefore, it may represent Divine Love as the first, longest, and most attractive element in God. Red is the strong spectrum of iron.

Orange is the next ray. Its intensity of color is 640; its length is 583; and the number of its vibrations per second is 557,000,000,000,000. In connection with bright yellow, the most intense of all, and because it is the spectrum of salt, we may take the two as representing the Divine Wisdom, forethought and knowledge; salt being that which preserves, flavors and enriches all our food, bodily and mental; and is the symbol of all wisdom and wit in literature and philosophy, in the Senate and in practical life.

Green, so conspicuously designated in St. John's rainbow as that of the emerald, pure and fadeless, is the next and central ray. Its intensity of color is rated at 480; its length at 512; and the number of its vibrations per second at 621,000,000,000,000. It represents the power and perpetuity of life, or all that goodness and grace that first gave life and continues it forever—the life of God in us that shall never fade, like the green of the emerald, and not of the grass,—the eternal goodness and freshness.

Blue is the next ray; in length of wave 475;

in intensity of color 170; in the number of its vibrations per second 670,000,000,000,000. It is almost needless to say that blue represents truth—"true blue" being common the world over: the color of the Virgin Mary and of all true womanhood; the color of the skies, from which truth came to be our guide through this maze of error and perplexity back to heaven again.

Purple or indigo is very much less in intensity of color, being only 31; its wave length 449; its vibrations per second 709,000,000,000,000. In all ages and countries it has been, and still is, the color of royalty, both in Kings and Priests in the exercise of sovereignty—in the combined adminstration of justice and mercy, punishment and pardon. It is the color of the lily of Palestine, greater in glory than the coronation robes of Solomon.

Violet is the last perceptible ray, and the most delicate of all. Its length of wave is 423: its intensity of color is only 6; and the number of its vibrations per second is greatest of all the rest, being 752,000,000,000,000. As it is the most delicate of colors, it is the most easily stained and the least becoming to mortals, and not much worn. It is among the most beautiful of tints in the autumn foliage, and suggests holiness or purity, so little seen among men, as the intensity of its color indicates, but a constituent part of the one white light of the Divine nature, the most energetic and active. The same may be said of purple or indigo.

The chromatic scale in music takes its name from this scale of prismatic colors or rays of light, in length, intensity and vibration, sound being only a vibration, according to the greater or less intensity and length of its wave. And these two, being thus in accord, join to make the fabled music of the spheres. But beyond the red at one extremity of the scale and the violet at the other, there is a still deeper red and a more delicate violet not now perceptible to our imperfect vision, which the rainbow around the throne of God in heaven will doubtless reveal to the improved vision of us mortals, when we come to the high mount of eternal Beatitude to see God face to face, not as now looking through a glass darkly. The tremendous energy and activity of these rays of light, as indicated by the foregoing figures, suggest the ceaseless unrest of our God in giving life and beauty and harmony to the whole universe, of which His creatures shall have their full share of perpetual enjoyment. The glorious Incarnation of the Logos or Son of God, then, is a bridge across the dark chasm that separates earth and heaven, the human and Divine,—a luminous pathway—a bright ladder, such as Jacob saw in his night vision, and such as Christ Jesus claimed Himself to be to the devout Nathanael, by means of which we may safely cross the abyss to the bright realm beyond, and walk forever in the true and full splendor of the Primal Light, encircled by the rainbow round the throne in sight like unto an emerald.

This view of the matter is furthermore sustained by the very term which St. John uses to describe the rainbow. It is *Iris*, the same word which Homer uses to designate one of the most lovely and useful messengers of the Greek Mythology. Mr. Gladstone tells us that Iris was the sole messenger of Jupiter, for the accomplishment of every good purpose on earth and elsewhere, lighter than air itself on her golden wings; swift as lead plunging through the waters of the deep, with incessant labor for some purpose of good and never of ill, and with the total absence of every dark or gross or malicious feature in the sweet delineation; she is a mediatrix between god and god, or between god and man, to effect peace and reconciliation. Iris has no root in the natural phenomenon of the rainbow, although a prevalent tradition in the East, respecting the deluge and its succeeding rainbow, may have suggested to Homer that ethereal creation—that genuine anthropomorphic conception, drawn with infinite grace and tenderness, under the buoyant and brilliant form of Iris. As the rainbow was the token of a covenant between God and man, so Iris, its Homeric impersonation, care-

fully detached from the material sign, is the chosen
and faithful messenger of Zeus.

Or, consider this conception of the rainbow, as
given by Plato in the last book of the *The Republic*,
where he is describing the journey of departed
spirits to new worlds and new occupations, after
having passed the scrutiny and the crisis of judgment. They ascended into the higher parts of
heaven, and came to a place from which they looked
down upon a straight pillar of light, stretching
across the whole heaven and earth, more like the
rainbow than anything else, only brighter and
clearer. Going a day's journey further, and arriv-
ing in the centre of this light or rainbow, they saw
that its extremities were fastened by chains to the
sky. For this light or rainbow binds the sky
together, as a hawser binds and strengthens a
trireme; and *thus it holds together the whole revol-
ving universe.* Here sit the Sirens and the Fates
at their wheels within wheels, all glowing with
rainbow hues, clad in white robes, and spinning
the planets round their courses, at the same time
assigning to the newly-arrived spirits, by lot, their
future occupations, their honors and their destiny.

St. John's vision of the throne of God encircled
by a rainbow and surrounded by white robed Elders, is marvellously like this of Plato, and may
have been suggested by it. And our modern
science is doing little else than verifying the dream

of Plato and the vision of St. John, in discovering
by the aid of the spectroscope, that the whole
boundless universe is filled with rainbow light
which serves to give it order, life, harmony and
beauty, binding it together by seven-fold cords and
ropes of metallic strength around the throne of God.

Then, too, where did the mystic prophet, Ezekiel, find his vision of the Platonic wheels or
spheres irradiated by rainbow hues and animated
by living spirits like the Sirens and the Fates?
Wheels within wheels, and the spirits moving them
round—going straight forward as light travels, and
radiating the colors of brass, beryl, crystal, sapphire, etc.,—as the appearance of the bow in the
cloud in the day of rain. He probably had no
spectroscope; how did he know that the remote
parts of the universe were filled with rainbow
colors, and active agencies of light, described as
spirits.   Ezekiel lived before the time of Plato.
Did Plato borrow from him?   Truth is truth, by
whomsoever announced; and when science, philosophy and religion thus agree in attaching so much
importance to the rainbow, we may not look upon
it as either trivial or fanciful.

Something better than a pot of gold lies at either
end of the rainbow; it is eternal hope—abiding
peace—after the stormy part of life is over.   The
rainbow mounts the highest heavens on the retiring thunder clouds; it descends on both sides to

the lowest depths of this vale of misery and sorrow; it forms a complete circle of cheering promise
on the waters of affliction when their tumult has
ceased; and thus we are everywhere surrounded
by the smile and blessing of God. Call to mind
that profound and soothing utterance of the Psalmist : Whither shall I go from thy Spirit? or whither
shall I go from thy presence? If I climb up into
heaven, thou art there; if I go down to hell, thou
art there also. If I take the wings of the morning
and remain in the uppermost parts of the sea, even
there also shall thy hand lead me, and thy right
hand shall hold me. This is an assurance that
wherever and just as long as the light of God's
countenance shall continue to shine, even in the
depths of *Sheol*, *Hades*, or as the Apostles' Creed
has it. hell, the intermediate place of departed
spirits, there and then, both we and all our kindred
shall have the rainbow as the token of a covenant
between God and men that there shall be no more
destruction,—as the pledge of hope and peace forever. Fire shall come, indeed; but only as a pur-
ifier. Simon Peter the Fisherman assures us that
the flood, which destroyed one of the worst races
of men that ever lived, was no more than a baptism
of the earth to cleanse and purify it for a better
race of men ; and that these wicked antediluvians
themselves, after having suffered on earth, were
visited by Christ in Hades on purpose to preach to

21

them His blessed Gospel of pardon and peace,
which they had never heard; and which same Gospel assures us, that when Christ came out of Hades
at His resurrection, a great company of these souls
came with Him.   Just as Noah and his family went
out of their long confinement in the Ark to greet
the rainbow and worship the God of the covenant,
so these long confined antediluvians went forth
from Hades when Christ, the Light of the world,
opened the prison doors and set them free.

During this stormy winter here at Saranac Lake,
three of the members of our colony, and as many
more of the residents of the place, have gone to
their long sleep with sleeping nature.   This early
return of Spring, with its singing birds, and
brilliant rainbows, is the sign and the promise of
their restored life at the last great Easter.   Some
bright days interjected through the gloom have re-
minded us that our ruined earthly paradise, in which
we suffer so much toil, privation, hardship, sickness and poverty, has nevertheless its glassy prismatic walls through which the light of heaven
streams in seven-fold splendor, shining like rubies
and diamonds and topazes and amethysts at sunrise and sunset, and glittering at their gateways
and basements with solid pools and falls of gold
and of silver, where their rich adornment has run
down molten at their base and crystallized; and
even yet, it is in its splendid ruin, a type of the re-

stored Heavenly Paradise, with its sea of glass clear as crystal—its River of the water of Life—its gates of pearl—its walls of jasper—its streets of gold—its foundations made of all manner of precious stones—its throne of God and the rainbow light—its perpetual peace and plenty. In our weary waiting and watching, let us all draw some comfort from the consideration that the bow appears when the storm is almost over. Our life is short enough at the longest for what we have to do. With some of us it must be nearly at an end. Let us bear its remaining ills as patiently as we can. Let us keep our eyes clear and open for the coming vision of beauty and of peace. It will not tarry much longer. In the dimness and silence of the chamber where we shall all soon go to sleep, there shall come the bright vision, then first and forever realized, of the everlasting hills on which the retiring clouds of life are piled in dissolving masses, out of which arises the throne of God with a rainbow round about it in sight like unto an emerald.

The Chaplain was evidently bent somewhat on cultivating the fancies and affections of his congregation, a very mixed and difficult one to reach. Old Mrs. Runnie was struck with the big word *Shem*—something or other, as so splendid and hifalutin-like, that she could take many a good long

smoke over it without a single twinge of conscience ;
and Peter Cranky, the once ardent Methodist con-
vert, who had fallen from grace into most shocking
profanity and immorality, into atheism and contempt of all religion, said, that if Jesus Christ
went to hell, he was not afraid of going there too,
provided there was such a place. The vanity of
some of the villagers was tickeled by the Latin
quotations from Spinoza, and the smartness of the
Chaplain was so much enhanced in their estimation
that they were moved to give him a permanent
settlement among them on the spot. In this respect they were like the pretentious people of a
vacant church in a little town of Northern Pennsylvania, to whom a Welsh parson came as a candidate for the place, and at once secured it by the
exhibition of his great knowledge of the original
languages of scripture, although he knew not a
single letter of Hebrew, Chaldaic, Greek or Latin,
any more than his hearers did. His rendition of
certain passages in the Old and New Testaments
were made from first to last in his native Welsh,
which passed for Hebrew, Chaldaic, Greek and
Latin with the ignorant congregation. The old
deacons nodded approval, as if to say, " That's the
stuff; that's the thing we want ; " when lo, to the
consternation of the learned preacher, a Welshman
sat in the back part of the church convulsed with
suppressed laughter, to whom the poor candidate

for the vacant pulpit called out in Chaldaic-Welsh,
" For God's sake, my friend, don't say a word about
this till I have a chance to talk with you." The
matter was settled to the satisfaction of both ; and
the congregation, having listened to one of the
most learned of sermons, called the clergyman
soon after for this ability to read the scriptures in
five languages, as just the man for the place.

But, then, Coonscratcher's mud was still sticking
to the surplice of our Chaplain ; and the hell-dances
of The Berkeley were not yet abandoned, but were
denounced more vigorously than ever ; our Chaplain was a rum-guzzler and had never experienced
religion, whatever he might know of Greek or
Latin or Hebrew ; and therefore, he simply followed
the example of his gluttonous and wine-bibbing
Master, when he left Nazareth forever after his bad
treatment there, in the utter hopelessness of over-
coming the narrow prejudices and murderous
designs of the people against him. Our Chaplain
went elsewhere.

But notwithstanding all this, there were some
striken hearts in the congregation of The Berkeley
on the day when the rainbow sermon was delivered,
that listened with no little satisfaction and profit,
notably, those who had lost their husbands, brothers and children. It was a new Gospel of hope and
comfort to them to be assured that these dear departed ones were now in the safe-keeping of a good

21*

God until the general resurrection of the full and
perfect fruition of life, both in body and in soul, in
God's eternal kingdom. Among these were the
still sorrowing friends and kindred of two young
guides who perished on a trapping expedition, a
little more than a year before. Ira Clark and
Henry Newcombe, gone so long on this fatal expedition, were searched for far and near; and their
bodies were found frozen in the ice of Fish Pond.
The matter made a profound impression in the little
community, and was the sucject of tender comment
during our sojourn at Saranac Lake. Newcombe
left a wife and three orphan children, poor and des-
titute. Clark was a young bachelor, whose parents,
brothers and sisters still mourn his loss. Both
were good men, hardy and industrious. How their
boat was capsized, and they were thrown into the
cold water to freeze up in the ice with their packs
on their backs, is still a mystery. It is one of those
sad incidents of Adirondack life deserving of some
special record. Our doggerel poet tried his best,
with this result:

THE TWO TRAPPERS.

Two trappers, tough and strong,
Went forth with hope and song ;
Rough was the winter wind,
Wife, babies left behind ;
Their little all in packs
Bound fast upon their backs :

And loudly rang the crisp frosty air,
With a snatch of song and a trapper's prayer,—
"Good luck, good luck, in our traps to-day,
Beaver, and otter, and fisher, I say,
Sable, and mink, or rat, anyway ;
Good luck, good luck, for the babies to-day,
Wife and sweetheart grieving our long delay."

Two trappers never mind,
The bleak November wind,
Nor driving snow and sleet,
Beneath their busy feet ;
But plodding on less gay,
With nothing much to say,
No bow in the clouds sheds light on their way,
But the traps are baited ere close of day ;
The trappers lie down at a blazing fire,
And shout to the roaring blast in ire—
"Blow on, and burst,—some luck we must find,
For the hungry mouths we have left behind."

Then at the peep of day,
Onward they push their way,
Their little all in packs,
Still bound upon their backs ;
But tearful ones come round,
To hear no greeting sound :
The trappers lay stiff in their cabins bare,
And a wail rose up on the frosty air,—
"Oh, Light of our darkness, dear Lord of our life,
Can this be the end of their struggle and strife ?
Caught fast in the ice-trap, and nobody near,
To go to their rescue and give them good cheer ?"

Then burst upon the sight,
One cold December night, —
As in the time of old,
The vision did unfold
O'er Judah's hill and vale,
Read in the sacred tale,
Of Glory in the Highest--peace—good-will,--
A flood of rosy splendor o'er the hill
Behind the lonely cottage, dark and still,
A rainbow-ladder standing on the sill,
And resting on the Heavenly threshold, far
Beyond the Pleiads and the Northern Star ;
And flaming spirits, darting up and down,
Bore in their hands a richly jewell'd crown,—
A saintly aureole for every head,
Tossing in sorrow on a sleepless bed ;
And with the rest, two trappers did appear,
In glowing love, with message of good cheer :—
Sweetheart and wife stretched out their eager hands,
And mounted with them to the starry lands.

VI

A S T R A Y.

THERE are two kinds of desert places in which
men go astray and get lost. One is a great city
like New York or London; the other is a vast
wilderness like that of the Adirondacks. There is
no need of going astray in either, if one knows
how to use his moral and material compass aright;
but then we all forget ourselves sometimes in the
absorbing pursuit of gain or game, and go astray
before we are well aware of it. This going astray
is very inconvenient to ourselves, and a cause of
anxiety to others. In trying to find our way out
of the woods, all our wit, wisdom, pluck, and
energy must be exercised simply on ourselves;
and then our friends and neighbors are called upon
to organize a great hunt to find us. Besides being
a waste of time, it is very tiresome, disagreeable,
and even dangerous. Suppose your legs get
cramped, or your nervous energy gives out, or you
become bewildered and go round in a circle, or
you have no lunch with you, except a few cigars
and a half-pint flask nearly empty; or suppose
your friends go in the wrong direction to search
for you, ten chances to one the game is all up with

you, and you must lie down alone to die. The bones of a wandering lady were found in the woods at Lake Placid, a year after she had gone into them from the house to take a quiet walk alone. Dear, old Mac. the genial friend and hunter, was lost three days and nights in the woods bordering on the Raquette River, from the accidental breaking of his compass. His subsistence was one partridge, which he shared with his dog. A passing boat found him on the bank of the stream, nearly starved, trying to catch a fish with a hook attached to some yarn which he had ravelled from one of his stockings. He has never entirely recovered from the effects of that exposure, shock and alarm. Our own Chaplain was supposed to have been lost in the woods, during the latter part of October, 1877, and a large party was sent in search of him. Other parsons have gone astray, before and since; but in another sense. As the Chaplain had an appointment in New York, to marry a couple a few days after his tramp in the woods, he was under the necessity of finding his way out. It was not an easy thing to do, inasmuch as he was a stranger to this part of the wilderness, never having been in these wilds before, and never meaning to go into them again alone. His own narrative is herewith given.

THE PARSON ASTRAY.

It was on a fine, bright Saturday, in October, that I set out with my gun and partridge dog to hunt some birds for the invalids at home. I had taken an early breakfast, and intended to return for the afternoon dinner, my object being, the hunting grounds around Colby Pond. My dog was a keen, young Spaniel, not fully broken, of French-Canadian extraction, but with the Irish name of Bridget. My shot gun was a number twelve bore, double barrelled, English breech-loader, light and close shooting. It had served me well on many a hunting expedition for deer as well as birds, and I trusted it now for some much needed small game. For the rifle I have an aversion, as too heavy for carrying and too fine of sighting for dim, weak eyes. The hunting grounds around Colby Pond were reached in about an hour, and the work of the morning began. Bridget was on a trail, and a fine bird rose along the hill side where it had been feeding on fallen beech nuts, booming down like a bomb-shell into the near, thick swamp below, and out of sight in an instant. Of course I went in pursuit with close and careful scrutiny, and soon found myself in Dante's *Inferno*, or the horrible tangle of Doré's Wandering Jew, except that there were no immense serpents dangling from the trees overhead, as in the latter pic-

torial representation, snakes being here unknown.
Axe, tempest, fire, all the furious and destructive
agencies of nature, combined with man's more
awful havoc and greed, had here made about as
good a specimen of a material hell as the most
vigorous imagination could well conceive. I never
realized before that hell, as my Methodist brother
depicted it, was so near Saranac Lake; and as my
toilsome, sweating penance in it had begun in good
earnest, without the remotest idea of the length of
my stay there, my only comfort was, that, like the
other material hell of man's creation, this bore all
the legitimate marks and features of his most energetic agency; and that, inasmuch as it was only
man's awful work, I need not fear any of its ill
effects upon myself, now that it was at an end.
The havoc was complete. Not a single large tree
of any kind was left standing. But as the moist
soil of the swamp could not be burned up, a new
and dense growth of evergreens had sprung up
among the ruins of the primitive forest, making it
almost impossible to advance a single step. The
slimy moss was knee deep, and filled with stagnant
pools of icy-cold water; dead and fallen trees in
most inextricable confusion, breast high, made a
complete *chevaux de frise* to check advance still
more; piles of sharp brush-wood among the low
bushes, and stiff branches of half dead spruce
saplings, scratched the face and eyes and nearly

tore one's clothes off; tangled roots and creeping
vines and horrible witch-hopples caught the feet
and legs, and threw you down headlong; the dense
tangle overhead was like a roof or green canopy,
obscuring the light of day and making a profound
gloom; the felt and oppressive silence was only
interrupted by the distant lowing of hungry cattle
or the crowing of some presumptuous cock; and
worst of all, no partridge could be discovered.
He knew that he was pursued, and was probably
sitting in close concealment over my head, quietly
enjoying my discomfiture. Fortunately, this part
of the swamp was not very wide, and I had pushed
through it, I hardly know how, to another low ridge
where the walking was better. Again the dog put
up more birds; again they flew into the jungle;
and again I went in pursuit, with the same result
as before. It was poor sport.

Late in the afternoon I struck an old moss-grown
wood-road, long since abandoned, but affording
good foothold and leading out of the woods some-
where. Following this road for some distance, I
was more fortunate in bagging some birds. This
gave me heart and hope, inspired me with new
energy and spirit. For of all things in this world,
as an amateur sportsman, next to catching a fine
trout, I love best to bring down a proud and defi-
ant cock partridge. It is even a grander achievement and gives me more pleasure than to shoot a

22

large buck. I have had some of these cock partridges meet me in battle array, with ruff, tail and
feathers puffed out in menacing display, as if about
to fly in my face; and it must therefore, be more
satisfactory to put a stop to such presumption than
to interrupt the flight of a timid, cowardly deer.
This may seem a strange thing to say, but I say it
in good faith. Following the old wood-road still
further, I came at last to a dead halt at one of the
many Fish Creeks in the woods, and the problem
of this road was solved. This was its end, and
Fish Creek was simply the outlet for timber, in
years gone by, to the Lower Saranac. What was
to be done now? I sat down long enough for the
stream to run out and let me pass over; took out
my compass to learn my bearings and lay my
course; had a good long smoke; talked awhile to
Bridget about the matter of getting home as soon
as possible, and then wandered along the muddy
bank of the stream in a thick jungle of bare alder
bushes to find a crossing. After infinite floundering and pushing, and when nearly exhausted with
fatigue, I came to a narrow part of the stream,
across which lay an old log which gave me passage.

But wherefore? On the opposite side rose a
high ridge as steep as the roof of a mansard house.
I wished for a balloon to cross it. The penance of
getting over it to a man of 220 lbs. avoirdupois
weight, was even greater than that of Lenten peni-

tents at Rome, climbing slowly on their knees the
reputed stone stairs of Pilate's Judgment Hall,
now known as *Scala Santa*, in the Basilica of St.
John Lateran. It was a task equal to that of
Sisyphus himself in Tartarus, another evidence that
I must be in hell. Up and at it, I said, even if you
should roll down into the slimy mud of Fish Creek.
I was no stone, but a melting mass of flesh and
blood. I had some birds in my pockets, and they
would help me. A stream of sweat might pour
down, but not I. Flesh or stone; roll down or
climb up, as the case might be, there was the actual
penance of making that difficult ascent on veritable
hands and knees, dragging my gun after me as best
I could. When at length I straddled the narrow
sharp crest of the ridge to take a long rest and
recover breath, it was a far greater satisfaction and
a much prouder achievement than any of the political or ecclesiastical or philosophical straddles of
perplexing questions that I could then call to mind.
But the going down on the other side was a literal
facilis descensus Averni, as all such straddles are
apt to become. Rapid, headlong, breathless, un-
thinking, the plunge is soon made into some horrible slough or fen, as mine was. We go from one
extreme to the other, only to stick fast in the deep
mire, as I did. But if we stay straddled, there is
no help or hope for us in ever reaching any safe and
definite conclusion. The best way is to go on

floundering, sticking fast and pulling loose, until
the way out of the woods is found, and home is at
last reached. In other words, I found at the base
of the other side of the ridge one of the worst
quagmires on this or any other planet. There had
once been a considerable lake or pond here, which
was now, for the most part, overgrown with a thin
crust of roots, mosses and small tamaracks, filled
with holes and shaking under foot like jelly or thin
ice. Macauley pond was all that still remained of
this body of water, and it gleamed in the evening
twilight like an opal. Where and how could this
treacherous bog be crossed? Going far up towards
its furthest extremity from the open water, I ventured the passage. All went well for a while on
the shaking and oozing network of grass, roots and
moss, until, quick as a flash, I went down in one of
the small openings. Had it not been for the instinct of self-preservation which prompted me to
throw my gun across the hole and keep me from
sinking, I might have gone down by a quick passage to the depths of an undiscovered country.
The ooze into which I sank, waist deep, was cold
as ice and slimy as eels or snakes. It was the most
horrible predicament, but one, in which I had ever
been; and that other was when I was nearly
drowned and carried to my poor weeping mother,
insensible, more than fifty years ago. And it still
lingers in my memory like a frightful nightmare

and an event of yesterday. This sinking in the
deep mire was far from all human aid, and my good
gun served me its very best turn. By its aid I
crawled out, shook myself, and ventured on, until
I came to a dense wall of young tamaracks. Against
this living wall I was compelled to throw the whole
weight of my body to force a passage. When this
failed, I searched round everywhere for the slightest opening, poking my gun between the bushes to
see if there was space enough for me to pass. For
the first time in all that day's trying experience,
I yielded to a momentary despondency. Bridget
was gone, my faithful and constant friend; and I
sat down and blew my dog-whistle long and loud;
lit a cigar and smoked it; and waited till the poor
creature came to me, dripping wet and shivering.
Another talk with Bridget about our prospects re-
assured us both, and we forced our way through
the tamarack jungle to another ridge, not so steep
as the one we had lately crossed.

By the light of the moon, now nearly full, I
picked my way over this new ridge among boulders,
stumps and fallen trees, witch-hopples and brush
heaps, until I struck a road, fresh and new. It
was at least a relief to the hard scramble in the
pathless part of the forest. It might lead me out.
Like all other roads it must have two ends, and
one of these ends must be at some settlement, or
in some other way to one. That day's downward

22*

tendency in me combined now with real weariness,
impelled me to follow this road down a gradual and
easy slope in the direction homeward. A little
fresh spring-brook ran along one side of it, gurgling
and singing merrily for the delectation of ears and
parched lips, and keeping up my strength and resolution. I would surely reach home soon, and relieve the anxiety of its waiting inmates. It was
not longer than an hour before I came to the one
end of the road, at a vast body of water, which, as
I then thought, I had never seen before, and which,
in fact, I had but once seen some years ago on one
of my first trips through the lake region. I was at
Shingle Bay on the Lower Saranac, a short distance from Martin's, and about three miles from the
village of Saranac Lake. I was as ignorant of this
fact as a baby in its cradle. There was a revulsion
of feeling which seemed to take the very life out of
me. I was stunned and stupified. My voice was
gone, so that I could not call or shout for help. It
did not even occur to me to fire my gun for a boat
from Martin's. I felt more desolate and woe-
begone than when I stood on the shores of the
Dead Sea, in the far more horrible wilderness of
Judea. I had come to a worse place than Sodom,
from which there seemed no escape possible. Dark
and frowning ridges, stripped of all foliage so
brilliant here in earlier autumn, rose on every hand;
and to find my way along the shore of the lake to

some human habitation might be an affair of more time and wisdom than I had at command. I resolved to retrace my steps, and find the other end of the road. It was a long and weary trudge up and up the slope with frequent intervals of sitting down to rest.

A cluster of new lumber shanties and stables soon came into view. One by one I examined these for a night's lodging. Empty, deserted, and full of dirt and filth, a lodging here was impossible. Besides, I was heated and dripping wet with perspiration, and if I should lie down here without a thick blanket to cover me, a convulsive death-chill might be the result. The night dews were already frozen into a thin crust of ice on my gun barrels, which was admonition enough. I was afraid even to stop long enough to light a fire and cook some of my partridges for Bridget and myself, much as we needed food. It was now past eleven o'clock. I left the lumber shanties behind and continued to mount the ridge until I had reached the crest, when a barred owl set up its familiar hoot in the distant part of the forest. It was the first sound that had broken the silence of that long dreary night. Bard and bird of Minerva as it might be, I resolved to try one of our old camp tricks upon its fabled reputation for wisdom. Besides, I now wanted a guide, and never before felt so much in need of a competent one. So I sat

down upon a log by the way side and listened.
The cry rose again somewhat nearer, "Hoo-hoo-too-
too-this-way-will-do-ah!" Thank you, Sir Oracle;
you were born and brought up in these woods, and
you must surely know the way through them. I
want you as a guide, because you are competent
and without fear. So "Hoo-hoo-too-too-come-here-
to-me-sir," was the simulated echo of my rather
thick and dry voice. In one minute and a half, the
bird and bard of Minerva, light and noiseless as
down, perched on a limb of the tree just opposite
my seat, only detected in the act of lighting by the
slightest stir of the air and the bright effulgence of
the moon high up in the heavens. There was no
time to be lost. My trick would be detected in an
instant, and I should have no guide. Taking deliberate aim without rising, I fired, and the bard
came down gracefully. Bridget leaped from my
side with a bark of delight, and bounded back with
a yelp of terror. The bard had sharp claws, and
like some bards of human kind had the disposition
to use them. Waiting till the fluttering had ceased
and all was still, I went over and picked up the bird,
stretched out its wings which were at least a yard
from tip to tip, and for the first time noticed how
exceedingly light and small the body was under all
this mass of fuss and feathers, just like all the
barred owls or owlish bards, whose occupation is
dark and whose game is silly mice, the bards erotic

and hooters of sensual pleasure, from Sappho down
to Swinburne.

Thus reinforced and in better spirits, I pushed
on and found my road going down the slope on the
other side of the ridge, until it came to an end in
the forest. It had been made for timber purposes
only so far as there was good timber to be had.
Here was a most perplexing problem—a road with
only one terminus into the light of day, and that at
the Lower Saranac. If I kept on down the slope,
I should certainly come to another swamp; and of
swamp I had already found more than enough that
day. What should I do then? Perhaps I had
missed the turn in the road that led out on the
other side of the woods, for teams must come and
go otherwise than by the Lake. I went far back
and found no such turn. I went forward again and
looked in vain for some path or blazed way. Then
setting my teeth and girding up my failing resolution, I plunged into the pathless forest again over
boulders, fallen trees, stumps, brush heaps, and
through tripping, tangled witch-hopples, along the
side of the slope, at right angles to the road, determined now and in utter desperation, to move on
and keep moving until I either found my way out
or perished from exhaustion in the attempt. Had
I not soon found another road; had I found myself
in the vast, horrible fire-slash towards which I was
advancing, there would have been no solemnization

of marriage by me on the next Tuesday or Wednesday, and the poor parson would not only have been far astray but utterly lost, beyond the recovery even of his lifeless body. The road I had now found was a corduroy one laid in low marshy ground, and bore evidences of recent use. It was a slow and tiresome process to pick my way from log to log, and avoid slipping into the ooze beneath. While thus engaged, I suddenly came against a pair of bars across the road. I looked up and saw an enclosed ploughed field. I listened and heard the low tinkling of a cow-bell. What a relief! Thank God, the long agony is over at last. Dog and man sprang forward with equal delight and eagerness to find a group of farm buildings and hay ricks here in this remote and lonely part of the wilderness, miles from any settlement.

The dwelling house was a long, low log-shanty that had once been used by lumbermen. No dog barked as I approached it: there was no light within; it was as silent as a tomb. I went all round it looking and listening, and at last heard the cry of a very young infant and the feeble voice of the mother soothing it. Then I ventured a knock at the door. A sick woman with a little baby was not dangerous. It was not the lonely retreat of robbers and outlaws. A baby is a wellspring of pleasure and good feeling in a house, and I might find hospitality there. No answer to my

knock. I next gave the door a somewhat vigorous
kick with the toe-end of my hob-nail tramping
shoes, which caused some conversation within carried on in tones just above a whisper. Footsteps
approached. A voice tremulous with agitation inquired, "Who's there?" Answer. "A lost man—a
parson astray—a clerical tramp, not at all dangerous or ill-disposed; a partridge hunter from Saranac Lake, who wishes to find his way home. Let
me in, please, to rest awhile; I'm hot, hungry and
tired." A laugh, and an open door; and a great,
tall, gaunt, shock-headed Irishman presents himself, half-dressed. "Come in, and welcome. My
wife is sick, but I'll do my best for you," said the
tall figure, kindly. He lit his kerosene lamp;
made a fire in his old dilapidated cooking stove;
took my wet clothes and hung them up to dry; and
furnished me with drawers, shirt and pants which
only met half way around my body. Another
laugh louder than before, in which I joined till the
rafters overhead creaked and the baby cried out in
a fright. He next filled a great iron kettle with
water and put it on the stove to boil. Then he
spread a coarse clean cloth on the table, a plate,
cup and saucer, knife and fork, bread and butter.
In my heated, thirsty, feverish condition, butter-
milk was best for me, for which I asked. A large
pitcher full was placed before me, then another, and
then a third. It was the very nectar of the gods.

The larger share of that day's churning had gone
to the pigs; how I envied them, when the last drop
of the supply was gone out of the third pitcher.
The bread and butter were ambrosia.

Then a long animated conversation took place,
in which I gave an account of myself, and learned
that my hospitable entertainer was William Mac-
Masters by name, farmer by occupation, hermit by
preference, Wesleyan by profession of religion.
His place is ten miles from Saranac Lake, in the
most dense part of the woods, on the side of the
ridge next to Big Clear Pond. Would William
please tell me how to get home that night—it was
now past twelve o'clock—inasmuch as I wished to
relieve painful anxiety there; hold a Sunday morning service; and start for New York on Monday
morning, to perform a marriage service on Tuesday
or Wednesday? A dry smile and shake of the
head. He could not go with me that night and
leave his wife alone; his hired boy was not there
to go; his wife had no female help in the house.
If I went alone, I might get lost and never reach
home. Would I wait until morning and let him
drive me to Saranac Lake after breakfast. He
must milk the cows and feed the horses, pigs and
oxen. Then he could go; and in his estimation it
would be no violation of the law of the Sabbath,
if he went to meeting to hear Coonscratcher
preach. About this last part of the matter I had

grave doubts, but said nothing, inasmuch as to him who esteemeth a thing right or wrong, to him it is right or wrong. The abstract question of right and wrong was here practically useless, and I yielded to the proposition of a Sunday morning ride to Saranac Lake. Between one and two o'clock I went to bed and slept until eight, a deep, sound, refreshing, dreamless sleep.

What was my surprise to find when I rose that the feeble wife had risen from her recent child-bed to prepare the simple morning meal! It was a kindness and a heroism that went to my heart and rose to my eyes. A great dish of boiled potatoes occupied the centre of the table, flanked by a smaller dish of fat, fried pork swimming in grease, and a bowl of cream gravy, to make the potatoes less dry and more palatable. There was a thin pie of dried apples, dark bread and fresh butter, and something that passed for coffee. This poor woman had done her best; the larder was not amply furnished; and gratitude made a good appetite. A venerable white-heaired patriarch, a friend of the family, had come from Ireland to end his days here, who made one of the group of wife, husband, three children, and the stray parson at breakfast. It was a perfect marvel to me what motive actuated them to come into this lonely place in the woods to live. The wife had been alone in the labor of child-birth; she had no near

23

neighbors to call to her help; she was seemingly contended and happy with her four children, husband and old friend; and with all this before me. I could not help contrasting her condition and prospects in life with the more fortunate, but less happy women of wealth in luxurious city homes, who have far less of her contentment and peace of mind. Well, the stray pastor had found this peaceful and happy fold; and after breakfast he read the 23d Psalm; prayed for the welfare of the little, lonely household; gave thanks for his own deliverance from the peril of death in the wilderness; and rose to take his leave with thanks and some greenbacks for the night's entertainment.

On the way to Saranac, and at the edge of the vast fire-slash, I saw one of the most appalling sights of poverty and utter wretchedness it has ever fallen to my lot to witness; and my calling in Philadelphia and New York, among the poor of the alleys and tenement houses, has given me ample and frequent opportunities to minister to the deep poverty and wretchedness which there abound. Here was a lazy vagabond from Vermont, who had twice married, and now had a family of second wife and fourteen children of all sizes and both sexes, huddled together like swine in a pen, in a small log hut of only one room; having a few dirty rags on their dirtier bodies; with great shocks of albino hair on their heads that had

never been combed, and ranged round the door of
the hovel, gazing timidly and half-ashamed at the
passing team. They were once found in a state of
starvation; the man had gone to Vermont on a
visit, to get something to eat for himself, leaving
his sick wife and numerous progeny to perish of
hunger and cold; the town had to take charge of
them; the poor, sick woman's hair was so tangled
and matted that it had to be cut off; the eldest
child, a girl of sixteen or seventeen, was put to
service, but soon ran away and returned to the
nasty sty; and their only food was potatoes and
salt, not always certain on this barren fire-slash.
Dickens never saw a worse scene of poverty and
degradation in London, nor Thackeray in Ireland.

Passing on to the main road, scattering groups
of men with guns and dogs were encountered—
hunting parties—who eyed us closely and with
grim smiles. Suspecting their object, I ventured
to ask one of the men whom I knew, whether they
were looking for me. A nod in the affirmative
was given, and then three shots, the signal that
the lost man and stray parson was found, and the
hunt was over. At Colby Pond a larger group
was gathered, and a boat or two crossing it in
search. Pausing a moment to make another
inquiry, a tall gentlemen in gold spectacles came
rushing at us, exclaiming with trembling voice and
moist eyes: "My God! is this Dr. L.? Fifty or

a hundred men have been looking for you all night, and are yet out." Touched to the quick, and controlling my deep emotion as much as possible, I replied: "Sir, it is very kind and thoughtful; I fully appreciate it; but allow me to say that this is the first time in my life that I ever realized my importance, or felt that a stray parson was of enough consequence to excite such a kind interest in his welfare. Poor, stray parsons are apt to be hounded to death by the newspapers, or consigned to infamy and prison, while their rich neighbors escape such degradation." Good Mr. Milford, for it was he, smiled, blew his nose, wiped his eyes; and then told me how Mr. Colvin had taken the measure of my shoes so that I might be tracked; organized hunting parties to go in all directions to look for me; and was now sending dispatches and fleet couriers on horses to rouse the whole surrounding country. For which great interest and kindness, Mr. Colvin has my eternal gratitude.

The Berkeley gentlemen were coming in great long boots for the day's hunt, when the signal guns again announced that the game was brought to bay. One of them dryly asked me, "why I did not send them word that I had spent the night at Mac-Masters'?" "This is the first and only chance," I replied; and we all formed a glad triumphal procession into Saranac Lake. Arrived at home,

there was a shower of sunny tears, and a little
breeze of osculatory greetings and congratulations.
A hunting party had been on the mountain east of
the village all night, and must now be called in. I
fired three shots over Coonscratcher's house, just
across the street from the cottage in which we were
then living while our Berkeley rooms were in preparation; and for this alleged violation of the
peace and quietness and sacredness of the Sabbath,
I received a broadside from the schoolhouse that
night; and have survived to tell my story of the
parson astray.

Well; what is life but a tramp like this? We
start from home—our home afar—in the morning
of existence, full of hope; soon get bewildered and
entangled in swamps and bogs; overcome difficulties steep and high only to plunge down into
greater ones; take wrong roads that lead nowhere;
and never get out of scrapes until we follow the
compass and the Pole Star of truth, and find lodging and rest for the night in our graves. It will
be well if the eternal Sunday morning brings us
home again.

Our poet read the following verses on the next
Sunday evening to the inmates of The Berkeley.

23*

ASTRAY. *October* 20-1, 1877.

Astray, alone ; in the forest wide,
   And the night-chill creeping near ;
My gun at rest, and dog at my side,
   I listen in hope and fear.

Astray, alone ; far from human aid,
   Not a sound in the frosty air ;
The muffled pulses scarcely made
   A sign of the heart's despair.

Astray, alone ; where the darkling pines
   Contend with the sun's strong light ;
All compassed round by their serried lines,
   No rescue, escape or flight.

Astray, alone ; where steep ridges frown,
   Like walls of some prison grim ;
I crawl like an insect up and down,
   Exhausted, with vision dim.

Astray, alone ; amid thickets dense,
   I strive with all might and main ;
Hope folds her wings in silent suspense,
   Shall I reach my home again?

Astray, alone ; I sink through the fen,
   A Slough of Despond to me ;
My soul cries out in an agony then,
   Dear Lord, come, and set me free.

THE SARANAC EXILES.

Astray, alone ; in the night profound
   Its silence so dread and great ;
The Frost-King going his quiet round,
   And Death, his treacherous mate.

Astray, alone ; I have sat me down
   On a log in the tangled gloom ;
To catch my breath, and relax the frown
   That knits up the coming doom.

Astray, alone ; the poor shivering dog
   Lays her head upon my knee ;
Shall we both lie down beside this log,
   And the Frost-King set us free?

Astray, alone ; there is grief, I fear,
   In the home I have left behind ;
And sleepless men search far and near,
   The wandering man to find.

Astray, alone ; 'tis the owl's loud hoot,
   Rising far on the midnight air ;
I mock his cry, and grimly shoot
   This scoffer of my despair.

Astray, alone ; I start up in my wrath,
   And plunge through the dismal shade,
To do or die in search of a path,
   That some human hands have made.

Astray, alone ; lo, the way appears,
   And a mead bell tinkles nigh,—
Sweeter than music of fabled spheres,
   Or pæan of victory.

Astray, alone ; I am found again,
  In a woodman's lowly place ;
A blissful rest, ~~release from~~ aching pain, *surcease*
  All bounteous good and grace.

Astray, alone ; from our Home afar,
  And the night fast closing round ;
Our earthly tramp by the Polar Star,
  Shall end in the Peace profound.

Astray, alone ; no more we shall be,
  From that House of light and love ;
The morning breaks ; and we all shall see
  The glory and bliss above.

VII

C A M P.

HAVING tried both for purposes of health and recreation, I much prefer tent-life in Palestine and Syria to tent-life in the Adirondacks, on the score of greater comfort and economy, and because I could have my wife with me. Ladies do, indeed, go into camp in the Adirondacks to visit their husbands and brothers for a few days at a time, or for a jollification or a picnic; but they seldom spend a month or two there for any purpose. It is too inconvenient, tedious, and rough. There is too much exposure, and too little to do. But ladies travel in Palestine and Syria from Hebron to Damascus, and thence to Baalbec across the Lebanon mountains to Beyrout, with less exposure and inconvenience, though, perhaps, with a little more fatigue. The reason is that the greater number of tourists there through a long course of years, has had the effect of making tent-life perfect in its niceties and conveniences, and amazingly cheap. The skies are just as bright as our own; the air is pure and sweet, though not so bracing or full of ozone as in the Adirondacks; riding in it all day long and sleeping in it soundly all night improves the appe-

tite and invigorates health and spirits there just as
much as here; and the sacred and historical asso-
ciations rouse the mind and swell the heart far
more. No such dreadful sights of poverty and
wretchedness, except the few cases of leprosy that
you meet, rouse your disgust and sympathy there
as in the Adirondacks; the population is sparse
and live together in the towns and villages, not
scattered in lonely wilds and farm houses as here;
and as a consequence, we could always obtain a
good supply for the table, horses and donkeys.
The forests are gone, indeed, which is the chief
drawback; but the green shrubbery of Carmel and
the vast paradise around Damascus seem all the
more lovely and attractive by contrast with the
universal barrenness and desolation elsewhere.

Your outfit is furnished by the Dragoman, who
acts as your guide and interpreter; and who also
obtains all the supplies on the trip, say of thirty-
five or forty days; hires the horses and donkeys;
furnishes cook, waiter, and muleteers at his own
cost; gives you large circular tents with double
canvass roof; iron bedsteads, clean and comfort-
ably furnished; good table, neatly and attractively
spread at each meal; wholesome and abundant
food, well cooked and palatable; polite and faithful service; and all this for the insignificant sum of
six dollars per day, each person of the party.
These Orientals are early risers; you are never

obliged to call them up in the morning so as to get
a good start for the day's journey from village to
village, or from town to town ; they call themselves
and call you to breakfast by six o'clock ; send the
muleteers in advance so as to have the tents pitched
and dinner ready late in the day upon your arrival
at the next halting place ; are civil, quiet and
obliging ; never get drunk or use profane and obscene language ; do not quarrel or dispute angrily
over cards : and are altogether the best of guides
and servants. All this at six dollars per day, and
no extras or tips.

Camping in the Adirondacks is another affair.
You furnish your own tents, beds and blankets,
table supplies and outfit ; have guides that love to
sleep late in the morning and must be called ;
guides inert, profane, obscene, and always on the
lookout for presents and extras beyond their wages
of $2.50 or $3.00 per day and found : claim every
deer skin ; are disputatious, often sullen and
drunken ; guides sometimes thievish and insolent ;
putting every possible obstacle in the way of other
hunting parties than their own ; claiming every
stray dog that comes into neighboring camps ;
shooting in advance of your boat in pursuit of your
own game ; securing every " carry " in advance of
you and putting you back as much as possible ;
guides doing their utmost to vex and annoy you if
you do not employ them ; and making a sojourn in

the woods anything but desirable and improving
to the temper or manners; and all this, including
your own outfit of tents and supplies, at the modest
sum of $8 or $10 per day, each person of the party.
In the one case, you are among mere semi-savage
Turks, who know no better; in the other, you are
among free and enlightened Americans, who know
a hawk from a hand-saw. In this view of the matter and the difference, I am, perhaps, somewhat justified in my preference for tent-life in the East.

An Adirondack camp is often nothing more than
a place for a long drunken debauch, or a retreat in
which to get rid of some loathsome disease. The
pretext is recreation in hunting and fishing—rest
from business cares and anxieties. The reality is
a prolonged drunken sleep and a hiding from
shameful exposure at home. This is its worst
feature; and happily it is becoming less frequent
every year, now that reputable persons, invalids, of
both sexes, are sent here for the improvement of
health, and are making permanent camps for each
entire summer season. One improves more rapidly
and certainly in camp than in a noisy, crowded
hotel. The cost is greater, and must be borne. A
cheap inconvenient camp is worse than none for
an invalid, and only a vexation to one in health. I
prefer the bivouac among the balsams and thick
moss, with a great fire blazing at my feet all night long.

There is a philosophy of camp-life most whole-

some and improving to the student of nature, and
to every contemplative mind. There is a poetry,
too, most delightful and refreshing. And there is
a practice or activity most invigorating and en-
during in its good effects on both soul and body.
This philosophy is simply a return to the first
principles of nature and of human existence. This
poetry is the romantic sympathy of the mind and
soul, with nature as the exponent of all the higher
inner spiritual forces of the material universe,
brought into prominence by the dappled play of
light in the woods—the sweet aromatic air—the
deep soothing silence—the songs of birds by day
and the noises of wild animals and owls and loons
at night—the splendors of sunset and sunrise—the
violence of the wind in tornadoes crashing down
the great forest trees—the deep roll of thunder and
vivid flashes of lightning—and, above all, the midnight vastness and impressiveness of your forest
cathedral lit up by the great camp-fire. The practice or activity of camp-life is nothing more or less
than the hereditary exercise and occupation of your
remote ancestors in hunting, fishing and trapping
for food and clothing. The life by day is innocent,
the sleep at night is sound and refreshing. There
are no temptations, no idle callers, no vexations,
no disturbers of the peace. You are a happy boy
again. You experience with that philosophical
angler, Sir H. Davy, a peculiar effect from this

24

kind of life—a bringing back of early times and
feelings—a new creation of the hopes and happiness of youthful days; freedom from all conven-
tional restraint—freshness of mind and body—
innocence and simplicity.   Even Walton's intimate
friend and adopted son, Charles Cotton, Esq., of
Beresford Hall, Suffolk, that gay lark of a spend-
thrift and of smutty song, whose only redeeming
trait of character and title to any posterior consideration was his fondness for fly-fishing and his
master, Walton, seems to have been impressed with
the innocence and simplicity of rural scenes, as
this better outburst of poetical feeling indicates :—

> Good God ! how sweet are all things here !
> How beautiful the *woods* appear !
>   How cleanly do we feed and lie !
> Lord ! what good hours do we keep !
> How quietly we sleep !
>   What peace ! what unanimity !
> How innocent from the lewd fashion,
> Is all our business, all our recreation !
>
> Dear Solitude, the soul's best friend,
>   That man acquainted with himself dost make,
> And, all his Maker's wonders to entend,
> With thee I here converse at will,
> And would be glad to do so still,
>   For, it is thou alone, that keep'st the soul awake.
>
> How calm and quiet a delight,
>   Is it, alone,
> To read and meditate, and write ;
>   By none offended, and offending none ?

Oh, my beloved rocks ! that rise
To awe the earth and brave the skies :
From some aspiring mountain's crown,
   How dearly do I love,
Giddy with pleasure, to look down,
   And from the vales, to view the noble heights above !
Oh, my beloved caves ! from Dog Star's heat,
And all anxieties, my safe retreat ;
What safety, privacy, what true delight,
In th' artificial night,
Your gloomy entrails make,.
Have I taken, do I take !
How oft when grief has made me fly
To hide me from society,
Ev'n of my desert friends, have I
    In your recesses friendly shade,
    All my sorrows open laid,
And my most secret woes, entrusted to your privacy !

Lord ! would men let me alone ;
What an over-happy one
   Should I think myself to be,
Might I, in this desert place,
Which most men in discourse disgrace,
   Live but undisturb'd and free !
Here, in this despis'd recess,
   Would I, maugre winter's cold,
And the summer's worst excess,
   Try to live out to sixty full years old !
And, all the while,
   Without an envious eye
On any thriving under Fortune's smile,
   Contented live, and then—contented die.

No doubt poor Cotton's peace of mind was often disturbed by debts and duns, which boon companions and gay society failed to restore; and, therefore, it is no wonder that he should prefer the wild solitudes of nature in which to recover his equanimity of spirit and get rid of all annoyances. Greater ones than he have gone to the wilderness and to the mountains to be alone for awhile, hunted and pursued by their persecutors like wild beasts, as Moses and Elijah were by Pharoah and Ahab; or they have gone there to meditate and to develop some grand scheme of reformation, like the Prophet of Nazareth, Christ, or like the later Arabian prophet, Mohammed.

This return to nature through an instinctive yearning of the soul gives the better opportunity for converse with the God of nature. We can there see the Light of life and of the world, as Moses did at Horeb in the Burning Bush; or we can there hear the still small voice or Logos of God in our own inner consciousness, as Elijah did in the same desert place and mountain; or some revelation of the spiritual powers of the universe will there be made to the earnest seeker, as to Mohammed. For, nature is the visible sign or symbol of the invisible God, just as the Bread and Wine of the Eucharistic Sacrifice are signs or symbols of the spiritual Presence and Person of the Son of God. Nature and man are but prisms

through which God as Light can be known; or
they are telephones through which the voice of the
Invisible can alone be heard. The highest philosophy and the purest religion are herein in perfect
accord.

Camp-life in a secluded part of the Adirondacks
for two months, under the towering ridge of St.
Regis and on the edge of one of the most beautiful
lakes in the woods, gave me abundant opportunity
for reading and reflection. On looking over my
record, I find one bright September Sunday credited
with the following citations: 1. Emerson's remark,
in a *North American Review* article, on *Perpetual
Forces:* " The laws of material nature run up into
the invisible world of mind, and hereby we acquire
a key to those sublimities which skulk and hide in
the caverns of human consciousness. Things are
saturated with the moral law. There is no escape
from it. Violets and grass preach it; rain and
snow, wind and tides, every change, every cause in
Nature, is nothing but a disguised missionary.
Where is the source of power? The soul of God is
poured into the world through the thoughts of
men." 2. A similar observation of the Emperor
Marcus Aurelius: " All things are bound up with
one another, and the bond is holy; and there is
hardly anything unconnected with any other thing.
For things have been co-ordinated, and they com-
bine to form the same universe or order. For there

24*

is one universe made up of all things, and one God
who pervades all things, and one Substance, and
one Law, one common reason in all intelligent
animals, and one Truth; if indeed there is one perfection for all animals which are of the same stock
and participate in the same reason. To those who
ask, Where hast thou seen the gods, or how dost
thou comprehend that they exist and so worshippest
them? I answer, in the first place, they may be
seen even with the eyes; in the second place,
neither have I seen my own soul, and yet I honor
it. Thus, then, with respect to the gods, from
what I constantly experience of their power, from
this I comprehend that they exist, and I venerate
them." 3. Epictetus more expressly and clearly:
"Are plants and animals also the works of God?
They are; but they are not superior things, nor yet
parts of the gods. But you are a superior thing;
you are a portion separated from the Deity; you
have in yourself a certain portion of Him. Why
then are you ignorant of your own noble descent?
Do you think that I mean some god of silver or of
gold, and external? You carry Him within yourself, and you perceive not that you are polluting
Him by impure thoughts and foul deeds." 4. Benedict Spinoza, later and more emphatic: "All
things are in God, and in God they live, move, and
are, as St. Paul affirmed to the Athenians. All
things, I say, are in God and move in Him, because

God and Nature are by no means one and the same
thing. (*Quod Deus et natura unum et idem sint,
tota errant via.*) They are altogether astray who
say that God and Nature are one and the same.
Whatever is, is in God, and nothing can be conceived to exist without God. All things, I repeat,
are in God; and all things that come into existence
do so through the laws of the infinite nature of
God alone, and are the necessary results of His
nature or essence." 5. St. Paul, who was neither
atheist nor pantheist : " The unknown God ; Maker
of all things ; not dwelling in earthly temples ; not
worshipped by images and costly sacrifices ; Giver
of life ; Father of all men ; in whom we live, and
move, and have our being ; it is the same God
which worketh all in all ; ye are the temple of the
living God ; the invisible things of God are clearly
seen from the creation of the world, being understood by the things that are made, even His eternal
power and Godhead ; the Son of man and of God
who is the image of the invisible God ; Moses for-
saking Egypt, endured, as seeing Him who is invisible ; beholding the glory of the Lord we are
changed into the same image from glory to glory ;
partakers of the Divine Nature, and partakers of
His holiness ; sons of God, like Him at His appearing ; Christ in you, the hope of glory ; the kingdom of God is within you."

The sour and severe Calvin was philosopher

enough to say of nature as the visible outcome and
revealer of the invisible God, as the Stoics did:
" God by creating the universe, being Himself invisible, has presented Himself to our eyes conspicuously in a certain visible form. He fills all
His work, as Seneca says; and wherever you turn
your eyes, there you shall see Him." Then turning to my *Theologia Germanica*, written long before Spinoza's day, I read this: " Behold ! even as
God is the one Good and Light and Reason, so is
He also Will and Love and Justice and Truth, and
in short, all virtues. But all these are in God as
one Substance, and none of them can be put in
exercise and wrought out into deeds without the
creature, for in God, without the creature, they are
only as a Substance or well-spring, not as a work.
But where the One, who is yet all these, layeth
hold of a creature, and taketh possession of it, and
directeth and maketh use of it, so that He may perceive in it somewhat of Himself, behold, in so far
as He is Will and Love, He is taught of Himself,
seeing that He is also Light and Reason, and He
willeth nothing but that One thing which He is.
In such a creature there is nothing willed or loved
but that which is good, because it is good, and for
the sake of goodness; and this goodness in a God-
like man makes him truly a partaker of the Divine
nature."

All religion, then, starts from God's visibility in

nature and in human consciousness,—God in all,
through all, and for all. Max Müller, in his ex-
position of the *Origin and Growth of Religion*,
clearly and forcibly states the doctrine, when he
says, that although the ancient Aryans sought God
in nature and in human consciousness, the Divine,
if it is to reveal itself at all to us, will best reveal
itself in our own human form. All distinct revela-
tions from God and of God have been through
human agency in philosophy, science, poetry, art,
legislation and religion, or State and Church. The
Christian religion is the best of all ;—our love of
God, call Him what you like, the infinite, the invisible, the immortal, the Father, the Highest Self,
above all, and through all, and in all,—manifested
in our love of man, our love of the living, our love
of the dead, our living and undying love, culmin-
ates in the Man Christ Jesus as the special manifestation of God as Love. The highest which man
can comprehend is man ; and that much decried
philosophy of evolution, if it teaches us anything,
teaches us a firm belief in a better future, and in a
higher perfection which man is destined to reach.

Now, it is upon this deep and abiding conviction
that God is in external nature as His creature, and
in the human mind and soul as His image or likeness, that the best and noblest of our race have
ever acted, when they have retired to the deep
solitudes of forests and mountains to see God

more plainly, and gain ideas, courage and resolution in maturing their plans for human welfare.
Abram did it when he left Ur of the Chaldeans to
be a wanderer in Palestine ; Moses did it when he
left the court of Pharoah for the desert of Horeb
to see the Light of the world, and mature his plan
for the liberation of his oppressed people and
found the Hebrew Commonwealth ; Elijah did it
when the Voice or Eternal Logos commanded him
to carry out the reformation of Israel in the days
of Ahab and Jezebel ; Christ did it, when He
meditated the plan of human salvation in the wilderness of Judea. Zoroaster, Buddha, and Mohammed did it ; and the Apostle Paul did it in the
solitudes of Arabia before he entered upon his
great work. Marcus Aurelius, in order to fit himself for study and the grave duties of state, often
retired to the little village of Lorium, to fish and
hunt and mingle with the simple rustics in their
sports and vintage merry-makings. Pliny, the
younger, did the same. And ever since, great
thinkers, reformers, statesmen, theologians, poets,
and philosophers, have gone to the solitudes of
nature for their best inspirations.

Far back in the dim twilight of prehistoric
times, we discern other creatures than wild beats
moving in dignity among the trees of the primeval
forests—the pious, white-robed Brahman reciting
the sacrificial hymns of the Veda to God, known

to him as *deva* or light, whether material or spiritual,—that awful and all-pervading brightness filling
the sky and the forest with His presence. Even
in later times, when the Brahman had reared his
family and discharged all his social duties, he considered it his rare privilege and pleasure to retire
at fifty, to end his days in the quiet rest and enjoyment of the forest, where in meditation and prayer
he might fit himself for the higher and better life.
It was to him a place for the enjoyment of perfect
freedom of thought and action; here he hummed
over his sacrificial hymns, for the forest was the
abode of the gods; solitude, silence, repose, peace
of mind and virtue were the things he sought.
But when Buddhism arose this old Brahman forest-
life was superceded; and Buddhist pilgrimages
and monasteries took its place. Says M. Müller:
"To us this forest-life is interesting, chiefly as a
new conception of man's existence on earth. No
doubt it offers some points of resemblance with
the life of Christian hermits in the fourth century,
only that the Indian hermitages seem to be pervaded by a much fresher air, both in an intellectual
and bodily sense, than the caves and places of
refuge chosen by Christian sages. How far the
idea of retirement from the world and living in
the desert may first have been suggested to Christian hermits by Buddhist pilgrims, who were themselves lineal descendants of Indian forest-sages;

whether some of these extraordinary similarities which exist between the Buddhist customs and ceremonials and the customs and ceremonials of the Roman Catholic Church (I will only mention tonsure, rosaries, cloisters, nunneries, confession, and clerical celibacy) could have arisen at the same time—these are questions that cannot as yet be satisfactorily answered. But with the exception of these Christian hermits, the Indians seem to have been the only civilized people who perceived that there was a time in man's life when it is well for him to make room for younger men, and by an undisturbed contemplation of the great problems of our existence here and hereafter, to prepare himself for death. In India the struggle of life was a very easy one. The earth, without much labor, supplied all that was wanted, and the climate was such that life in the forest was not only possible, but delightful. Several of the names given to the forest by the Aryans meant originally delight or bliss." (*Hibbert, Lectures*, c, vii.) In Persia the name of paradise was applied to a park.

This suggests the fitting and timely consideration of the poetry of camp-life, apart from its philosophical aspect. I hope that I am not crazy or too enthusiastic about this view of tent-life in the woods. If poetry is the sublimated essence of all thought and feeling—the very soul of man crystallized into lustrous and priceless gems of

song, then the deep, dark solitudes of nature are
the fitting places where the spiritual chemistry can
best accomplish its purposes. There is a freedom,
an exaltation, an elasticity, and a freshness of mind
and heart here which nowhere else exist so well.
The imagination has no restraints; the whole
boundless universe is before it in all its grand and
lovely garniture; and there is a profound mystery
pervading all things which invites the boldest
flights and the deepest plunges of investigation, of
which the fancy and wit of man are capable.
Nature is all poetry here, save where the cupidity
of man has turned it into dull, flat prose, or his
bad taste has attempted insipid elegance. Its
dithyrambics roll along the mountain-sides and
resound through the forest in great, wild thunder-
storms that make a dance of earth and water, and
loud shouts from peak to peak, compared with
which the noisy orgies of the Bacchanalian Mys-
teries were mere children's rattles and trumpets.
Its lyrics are bird songs; its dirges are nightly
sung by owls and loons; its dramas are the con-
tending elements; its grand epics march along
with the sun and the signs of the Zodiac and the
equinoxes and the change of seasons in the orderly
course of nature; and the *denouement* is an earthquake. The human being, in whom no poetry or
music can be roused into vigorous activity by all
these agencies, must have no poetry or music in

25

him: and is fit for nothing but treasons, strata-
gems, and spoils.

But not to ride the Pegasus too far, lest the
wings melt and precipitate a fall, I simply affirm
that there were some things in our camp-life of two
months at St. Regis Pond that inspired a feeling
akin to poetry. It was the feeling of color. What
there is in color to awaken the attention and admiration of birds and animals as well as human
beings, it would not be easy to say. A whole
octavo volume of nearly 300 pages has lately been
written and published on *The Color-Sense*, by
Grant Allen, B. A.; in which he attempts to trace
the modifications of insects, animals and birds, and
our own derived fondness of color from them. His
theory is this, stated in his own language: " The
taste for bright colors has been derived by man
from his frugivorous ancestors, who acquired it by
exercise of their sense of vision upon bright colored food-stuffs; that the same taste was shared by
all flower-feeding or fruit-eating animals; and that
it was manifested in the sexual selection of brilliant
mates, as well as in other secondary modes, such as
the various human arts. The color-sense is one and
continuous throughout, in origin and in result.
The highest taste of color in human art is only the
last link in the chain whose first link began with
the insect's selection of bright-hued blossoms.
The long series may be briefly summed up in this

formula : Insects produce flowers. Flowers produce the color-sense in insects. The color-sense
produces a taste for color. The taste for color produces butterflies and brilliant beetles. Birds and
mammals produce fruits. Fruits produce a taste
for color in birds and mammals. The taste for
color produces the external hues of humming-
birds, parrots, and monkeys. Man's frugivorous
ancestry produces in him a similar taste; and that
taste produces the various final results of human
chromatic arts." It seems to me that this is the
doctrine of evolution run mad. It is all very fine
as a speculation; but can it be established as true?
Before insects, birds and animals can exist at all,
there must be vegetation for them. Vegetation depends for its existence on light and moisture. And
all color is inherent in light. The seven prismatic
colors, therefore, must be the source of the color-
sense in all living beings possessing it, as well as in
leaves, flowers, fruits and brilliant gems. If the
simple absorption of light is sufficient to develop
color in all these latter things, why is not light
alone sufficient of itself to awaken and develop the
color-sense in all insects, birds, animals and man
alike, or in proportion to the appreciative intelligence of each? Why this long, intricate, round-
about, incomprehensible process of transmitting the
taste for color from insect to man, when the sim-
pler and more direct process of prismatic light

acting on all alike is sufficient to account for all the
facts? Without light there can be no color in anything, and consequently no taste for it. A child is
attracted and stimulated by light before it is by
color; but use a prism or show it the rainbow, and
instantly the little creature crows with delight.
Does a dog or a cat show any such feeling? Color
is the poetic adornment of nature; and if it can be
shown that the mere instinct of self-preservation in
seeking food from bright colored flowers and fruits
is of the nature of poetical taste and feeling that
rejoice in color for its own sake, the argument is at
an end. The Bower Bird of Australia is made
much of as an illustration of incipient poetic feeling in adorning its love-making house; but, then,
this bower is a long way behind a cathedral, and
the bird is an exception to all other birds. It
loves bright pebbles and bits of glass, as other
birds love insects and fruits; and that seems to be
all. It simply prefers bright colors more than the
rest. Bees extract honey from putrid carcasses as
from bright blossoms; but that does not prove that
man's love of long-kept game is an inherited taste.

The first color that attracts a child is the very
first color of the spectrum,—red; and orange is
the next. And it is precisely these two colors that
primitive man first used in decoration, and that yet
conspicuously appear in Egypt, China and India.
Red, too, is pre-eminently the poetical color, and is

made the symbol of love. It is the most universally pleasing of all colors. Or, as Mr Allen
points out the probable reason, when he says:
"The great red sun sinks nightly, amid red clouds,
into the red waters of the sea. Rosy-fingered
dawn spreads crimson glories over the empyrean;
the scarlet flush of eventide encarnadines the fiery
sky." Red and gold are the colors most employed
by the poets, ancient and modern; and no doubt
the reason is because they are the prevailing colors
of the sky at the pleasantest parts of the day,—
morning and evening.

The mixture of deciduous trees, especially maples, in the Adirondack pine forest, gives it a peculiar charm and glory in September. These maples
blaze like fire among the evergreens. The color is
intensely bright and clear,—red as the first ray of
the spectrum. Then the yellow of the beeches,
and the purple of the black-ash and cherry, and the
various shades of mode color in other trees, inter-
spersed with the lighter or darker masses of green,
present a study for the artist and the decorator. I
have sat for hours trying to take it all in, with infinite pleasure, feeling how impotent were all human
imitations on the canvass, or in churches, halls of
music, and dwellings of the more pretentious class.
When I assured my guides that these colors were
not the effect of frost, but of the sun ripening the
leaves into glory, they smiled incredulously and

25*

knew better. And when these leaves thus changed their colors and began to fall off the trees before any frost came, these same guides, convinced against their will, were of the same opinion still.

Poor Ben, so ignorant as not to know a single letter of the alphabet, came to my tent on the Sunday when I was reading about God and the universe in some of my favorite books, and asked me to read to him that finely illustrated article in *Scribner's Monthly*, for August, 1877, on "North American Grouse," by Charles E. Whitehead. The poor fellow had been looking at the pictures, especially the one representing the drummer on his log and the shy demure mate in front of him, admiring their naturalness; and when I came to the statement that the bird beat the log with his wings, Ben cried out excitedly, " That's not so; I've watched 'em often, and they jest flop their wings on the air like a rooster when he's goin' to crow, only slower at first, an' then much faster." As this experience of an old hunter agrees with John Burroughs' account of the matter, as given in a previous chapter, as well as with my own careful observation, I went on and finished the article; and then entered into some conversation with Ben about his family, which I understood to be large and illy provided for. His only occupation was that of fishing, hunting and trapping; and his family consisted of a wife and ten children, with prospective increase.

All were healthy. The only time Ben ever had a doctor in the house was during the prevalence of small-pox in the neighborhood. " Then I had to send for the doctor," he said, " to come an' mater-lize the children; but he naterlized them so bad, an' charged so much for the job, that I shifted the doctor out of the house, an' have never had one sence." Vaccinate was not in Ben's vocabulary; and his shifting process was the very poetry of sarcasm on the medical profession.

The sun was near his setting, and I proposed to Ben that we should take a turn on the lake to enjoy the air and the scene. We entered the boat and glided out into the vestibule of Heaven. Space and time had vanished. There was no appreciable distance between visible objects, great or small. The air was a sparkle and a glory of prismatic light. All the feeling and poetry of form lent their additional fascinations to the feeling and poetry of color. The great towering Whiteface range of mountains, in beautiful outline, seemed to be light, graceful clouds floating near us, at whose base we might land and walk aloft in mid-air, although they were more than twenty miles distant. The towering ridge of St. Regis was not a mass of solid rocks clothed with forest trees, but an aerial body of rainbows and flaming spiritual fires, set up majestically between earth and heaven. It was, indeed, the great King in his coronation robes.

All nature was afloat, like ourselves, in a sea of
fine brilliant ether. Mountain, lake and forest were
now turned into a transparent veil of light through
which the stately steps of the Divine Majesty could
be seen, as in the Burning Bush of Horeb, the
Shekinah of the Wilderness, and the Transfigura-
tion of the Son of Man on Mt. Hermon. The real
essence of things was here; and I exclaimed with
the Psalmist of Israel: "O Lord my God, thou
art become exceeding glorious; thou art clothed
with majesty and honor. Thou deckest thyself
with light as it were with a garment, and spreadest
out the heavens like a curtain or tent. In the beginning thou hast laid the foundation of the earth,
and the heavens are the work of thy hands. They
shall perish, but thou shalt endure; they all shall
wax old as doth a garment; and as a vesture shalt
thou change them, and they shall be changed; but
thou art the same, and thy years shall not fail."
Then I remembered how well my *Theologia Germanica* expressed the same thought: "God will
have His own Self or Substance or Well-Spring exercised and clothed in form, for it is there only to
be wrought out and executed; and this cannot
come to pass without the creature. If there were
not a world full of real things, what were God
Himself, and what had He to do, and whose God
would He be?" A changing universe, and an unchangeable God; a varied vesture of light and

beauty, and the same King of Glory ; a transient
world passing into other cloudy shapes, and a permanent Being abiding always in the midst of it,
giving it order, life and motion,—this is the lesson
taught to every lover of nature with a poet's eye
and heart, in such scenes as these. All over the
monarch mountains, fold on fold, lay the rich robes
of state—clouds of ermine-white overlaid and inter-
laced with gold and purple ; above them, a canopy
of purest blue lit up with richest crimson hangings
and ruby adornments : in the midst, St. Regis like
a vast throne encircled by rainbow hues ; below,
the green glad earth and crystal waters reflecting
the scene above. A voice, low and soft, like that
which Elijah heard at Horeb, floats on all the upper
air, and seems now to say : " Lift up your heads, O
ye gates ; and be ye lift up, ye everlasting doors ;
and the King of Glory shall come in." And if we
be wise and good, we shall one day join His triumphant train as it passes up and onward to the
Heavenly City—the New Jerusalem.

That night I lay awake for hours under a strange
nervous excitement, to which I have been lately
subject on the approach of a storm. At intervals,
I heard the loons, not laughing now, but uttering
mournful cries like human beings in distress and
calling for help. This was another sure presage of
storm. My nervous barometer of a weak body,
and these sensitive, quick-witted loons must now be

tested as to their accuracy in predicting a storm,
as Gilbert White tested his pet tortoise or land-
turtle. It was so slow and deliberate in its movements, as " to be a whole month in performing one
feat of copulation, and so sensitive to damp and
wet weather as to retire from every shower, and not
move at all in rainy days. It has a shell that would
secure it against the wheel of a loaded cart, and
yet it discovers as much solicitude about rain as a
lady dressed in all her best attire, shuffling away on
the first sprinklings, and running its head up in a
corner. If attended to, it becomes an excellent
weather-glass; for as sure as it walks elate, and as
it were on tip-toe, feeding with great earnestness in
the morning, so sure will it rain before night."
(*Selborne*. Jardine's Ed. pp. 112, 178.) If such a
slow and stupid creature as this felt the approach
of a storm, why not loons and a nervous loony like
myself?

Monday morning, October 13th, 1877, was one of
the very many bright and pleasant ones we had
long enjoyed in camp, with no sign of a storm
anywhere; and yet so confident was I in my double
barometrical signs, that I ordered the camp to be
dismantled, packed up, and removed to Paul
Smith's, about six miles distant. We reached that
comfortable hostelry late in the evening, and not
an hour too soon. A cold wind and a pouring rain
set in next morning, and continued without inter-

ruption, during the remainder of the week,—an
old-fashioned Adirondack storm; after which we
removed to Saranac Lake for the winter.

The practical part of our camp-life is easily
summed up in fishing and hunting. In two months
we captured four deer ; about forty trout ; as many
grayling as we could use; and shot a fair amount
of ducks and partridges. The place had long since
been hunted and fished to death ; but it was the
best camping ground we could find within hailing
distance of our friends, mail-matter, and supplies.
A log shanty, two large wall tents, a cooking shed,
and a large spring of deliciously cool clear water,
made up our encampment; together with two invalids, three guides, and six dogs.

Of course, to most Adirondack campers the hunt
or chase is the favorite occupation, although I confess to a weakness and preference for fly-fishing.
Floating for deer at night has its weird fascinations, but it is rather an ignoble way of taking undue advantage of the poor creatures in the act of
feeding. Stalking deer in the woods after the first
slight fall of snow, is for those who hunt for the
market as an occupation. But to slaughter deer
by the score merely for their hides is the infamous
act of such miscreants as destroy thousands of
forest trees for the bark to tan them. The chase
with dogs is the most primitive, and the only historical, classical, poetical, civilized, noble and

princely diversion of the true gentleman, the
mawkish sentimentality of *The Atlantic Monthly*
to the contrary notwithstanding Some Boston
parson, not Murray, affects great horror at the
slaughter of hundreds of deer, every season, in the
Adirondacks, by means of the chase on the part of
gentlemen sportsmen from New York and Brooklyn, which fiction of his sickly imagination was
rudely demolished by a resident of Long Lake,
whose truthful account of the matter is this : " At
the approach of autumn the farm hands, the guides,
the village idlers, and the vagabonds go in from
the settlements with packs of deer dogs and boats.

The deer are run into the lakes, where they are
easily overtaken and clubbed to death. In the late
fall and in the winter they are hunted in the snow.
After a crust has formed the deer is unable to run,
for his sharp hoofs cut through it, and he flounders.
Men on snow-shoes easily come up with him and
kill him. In a recent article it was computed that
30,000 deer are annually killed in the northern part
of the State. Yet they are so plenty that in a recent ten days' sojourn near Oswegatchie Lake, no
less than fourteen deer were seen by one member of
the party. But the circle is growing smaller and
smaller every season."

In Mr. Colvin's recent Report to the Legislature
of New York, he speaks of retired places where
whole herds of deer may be seen in yards, and of

unfrequented lakes and ponds, out of which fish
may be scooped with the hands. In May some
such herds of deer may be seen feeding along the
Bog River, near Hitching's Pond. The most I
have ever known to be killed in the hunting season
proper and legal, by gentlemen from New York,
during an encampment of two or three weeks, did
not exceed twenty. Our own camp at Mud Lake,
in the fall of 1879, took just nine. And yet the
guides were jealous, and freely expressed their
indignation at this slaughter and waste, when little
or none of the meat was wasted at all.

Geology discloses the fact, that in the Post-
Pliocene period of the earth's condition, long
anterior to the present races of men and animals,
our pre-Adamite ancestors hunted the gigantic elk,
cave-lion and bear, and the woolly rhinoceros with
spears and arrows; for their remains are intermingled and brought to the light of day. Sir
Charles Lyell, a competent authority, says, respecting the Aurignac cavern of France, especially:
" If the fossil memorials have been correctly inter-
preted ; if we have here before us at the northern
base of the Pyrenees a sepulchral vault with skeletons of human beings consigned by friends and
relatives to their last resting place; if we have
also at the portal of the tomb the relics of funeral
feasts, and within it indications of viands destined
for the use of the departed on their way to a land

26

of spirits; while among the funeral gifts are
weapons, wherewith in other fields to chase the
gigantic deer, the cave-lion, the cave-bear, and
woolly rhinoceros,—we have at last succeeded in
tracing back the sacred rites of burial, and, more
interesting still, a belief in a future state, to times
long anterior to those of history and tradition."
More recent discoveries, in this direction, confirm
the statement that these pre-Adamite races of men
were contemporaneous with these extinct races of
animals, and that they subsisted on hunting and
fishing alone. Strange, that with the chase should
have been associated, in that remote era as now
with our own red Indians, ideas of immortality
and a happy future.

If we examine the monuments of ancient Assyria
and of Egypt, we shall find them full of represen-
tations of the chase on the part of kings, princes
and nobles,—a pastime still kept up in the East
and in Europe by the same classes. Wilkinson
and Rosellini give us good drawings of lion-hunts,
wild goats, gazelles and other game; and assure
us that field sports were much favored by the
kings of Egypt and their nobles. Not only dogs,
but wild animals, such as leopards and lions, were
trained to the chase, as the cheeta now is in India.
Layard, too, gives us drawings to the same effect
of the monuments of Assyria. These kings and
nobles could forget the cares of state in the chase,

and preserve health and spirit in its animating
pursuit, as Victor Emmanuel did, and Bismarck
still does, or that princess of Austria, so fine a
horsewoman, lately did in coming to Great Britain,
at so great a cost, to indulge herself in a stag hunt
or running foxes. The education of the sons of
nobles, in ancient Persia, consisted in speaking the
truth, in being courageous, obedient, and to rever-
ence the gods; to hunt, ride, plant trees and discern between herbs; literature belonged to the
Magi.

Royal Charlie of England is to be forever held
in grateful memory, if for nothing else than this,
that he gave his Bishops, Earls and Barons the
privilege of hunting in the parks of the Realm, on
their way to and from Parliament, at his summons.
The law, yet unrepealed, is this: "Whatsoever
archbishop, bishop, earl or baron, coming to us at
our commandment, passing by our forest, it shall
be lawful for him to take and kill one or two of
our deer by view of our forester, if he be present;
or else he shall cause a horn to be blown for him,
that he may not seem to steal our deer; and likewise they shall do returning from us." That's a
game-law to some purpose, protecting the deer and
the reputation of the hunter at the same time;
and above all, recognizing the great dignitaries of
the Church as men, whose oppressive load of lawn,
logomachy, respectabilty, and sanctity, might make

them dull and dyspeptic. That is a good story which is told of Abbot, Archbishop of Canterbury, in the time of James. Bishop Williams was intriguing for the place, but Laud was too much for him. Nevertheless, when Abbot was hunting one day in Lord Zouch's park, and shot a deer, he became by that act "a man of blood," and fell under canonical disabilities. James, who enjoyed a theme of canonical disputation, instituted with promptness a Commission, composed of bishops, judges, and doctors of laws, to sit on the offender; and while the unfortunate criminal retired to melancholy solitude in his native town, Guilford, a variety of opinions was given. Sir Edward Coke looked on the matter with a lawyer's eye. On the question being propounded, "Whether a bishop might lawfully hunt in his own, or any other park?" (in which point lay the greatest pinch of the present difficulty), that most profound lawyer returned this answer thereunto, viz.: "That by the law a bishop at his death was to leave his pack of dogs to be disposed of by the King at his will and pleasure. And if the King was to have the dogs when the bishop died, there was no question to be made, but that the bishop might make use of them when he was alive." Williams most characteristically wished to be lenient, but also wished for the Primacy, to which he looked forward on the first vacancy; and his letter was a model of significant

ambiguity : " I wish with all my heart his Majesty
would be as merciful as ever he was in his life ;
but yet I hold it my duty to let his Majesty know,
that his Majesty is fallen upon a matter of great
advice and deliberation. To add affliction unto
the afflicted is against the King's nature : to leave
virum sanguinem, a man of blood, primate and
patriarch of all his churches, is a thing that sounds
very harsh in the old councils and canons of the
Church. The Papists will not spare to descant
upon the one and the other. I leave the knot for
his Majesty's deep wisdom to advise and resolve
upon." Laud and Bishop Andrews thought Williams the more formidable person of the two, and
kept Abbot in his see to prevent Williams getting
it. (Mozley's *Essays*, I, p. 136.)

In view of this unrepealed law and this example
of the Lord Archbishop of Canterbury, what a
gracious and glorious spectacle it would have been
to have seen the late Lambeth Conference of a
hundred bishops going forth to the chase, with his
present Grace of Canterbury at their head, respon-
sively chanting Sir Walter Scott's merry hunting
song :—

> Waken, lords and ladies gay,
> The mist has left the mountain grey,
>   Springlets in the dawn are streaming,
>   Diamonds in the brake are gleaming,

26*

And foresters have busy been
To track the buck in thickest green ;
  Now we come to chaunt our lay,
  Waken, lords and ladies gay.

Waken, lords and ladies gay,
On the mountain dawns the day ;
  All the jolly chase is here :
    *   *   *   *   *   *
To the green wood haste away,
  We can show you where he lies,
  Fleet of foot and tall of size ;
We can show the marks he made,
When 'gainst the oaks his antlers frayed ;
  You shall see him brought to bay ;
  Waken, lords and ladies gay.

Louder, louder, chaunt the lay,
Waken, lords and ladies gay !
  Tell them youth and mirth and glee
  Run a race as well as we ;
Time, stern huntsman ! who can balk,
Stanch as hound and fleet as hawk ?
  Think of this, and rise with day,
  Gentle lords and ladies gay.

Unfortunately, no report of such a manly pro-
ceeding as this has yet appeared from the sacred
precincts of Lambeth Palace and its secret conclave
of bishops.

The chase in the Adirondacks is a very simple
affair. Its chief charm to me is the deep interest
which the dogs take in it. To see dumb creatures

like these supremely happy, is next to the pleasure
of seeing a lot of happy children together. On a
fine frosty morning, when the air is still and crisp,
and the bushes are moist so as to retain the scent
before the sun evaporates it, there is something
more than delight in the spectacle of these dogs
grinning, capering, wagging their tails, twisting
themselves into all possible shapes as if they would
go out of their skins, almost speaking and laughing
with joy, their eyes sparkling, leaping up and down
around and upon you so as almost to upset you;
and this something is your own strong feeling of
sympathy with them, as though they were your
own cousins or half-brothers. When Cuvier said
that "the dog is the most complete, the most
singular, and the most useful conquest ever made
by man over any part of the animal creation," he
was only speaking half the truth. So sagacious, so
affectionate, so courageous, and so faithful is he,
that some of the old mythologies of the world
absolutely deified him; and from the time of Homer,
who celebrates so pathetically the dying dog's
pleased recognition of his long absent master,
down to our own day, what volumes have been
written in praise of his many virtues as man's best
friend and companion, often dying of a broken
heart on his master's grave. At Chantilly, France,
the dog's fine nature is duly appreciated in that the
chase is inaugurated by a religious ceremony. The

huntsmen, beaters, *piquers* and grooms all in gala
costume, take the impatient and noisy pack as far
as the entrance to the choir of the church ; the
service is then celebrated, and, after the benediction. the oldest dog in the pack is decorated with
the colors of the Duc d'Aumale, and the exit is
made from the church to the cover-side to the
sound of the fanfare or flourish of trumpets. It is
called the Ceremony of Benediction of the Hounds,
usually celebrated on St. Hubert's Day. Here is a
subject for Warner's fine humor and sentiment to
make a gush in the pages of *The Atlantic Monthly*,
as in the article of " A-Hunting of the Deer."

This article is not half so pathetic as Mr. Tait's
fine picture of the dead fawn and the poor mother
doe trying to lick it back into life, and a great
black raven standing by to get his morning meal.
A June snowstorm had killed the poor little creature newly born ; and He who feedeth the young
ravens when they cry. had provided this feast. Is
the more noble dog to have no share of game captured in the chase? If Esau does not go out with
his hounds, how can good old Jacob have any venison? If the Lamb of God is not slain, how can
there be a feast in our Father's house above? If
the fatted calf is not killed, what of the prodigal's
welcome on his return home? Deer and dog were
made for each other ; and both deer and dog were
made for man's welfare and happiness in the chase.

whatever mere sentimentalists may have to say
about it. The chase is too old an institution to be
sniffled out of existence, or to be put down by
absurd game laws. Dogs are no worse to frighten
deer away than wolves and panthers; and far more
deer are killed by night-floating, still-hunters,
trappers and snow-shoe crusters, than are ever captured in the chase.

An Adirondack chase is without horses, gay attire, lords and ladies, and flourish of trumpets.
Whether it take place in some remote and unfrequented solitude or near a hotel, it has its interest
and excitement. All the arrangements must be
made on the preceding evening. Runways and
stations must be chosen or drawn by lot. The
dogs must be examined and fed. An early breakfast before daylight is necessary. You must be on
your watch before the dogs are let loose. In a remote and secluded camp, the game will soon appear; and by nine o'clock you may have two fine
young bucks hung up to cool. Near a hotel, you
may watch all day and get nothing. And yet, it
sometimes happens even now that a hotel hunt is
successful. Having once sunk a noble spike-horn
buck in water too deep for recovery, I resolved
henceforth to take my chances on the runways or
stationed on the shore of lake or pond, and capture
my game on the jump or let it go. I have never

had any reason to regret that resolution. My luck has been as good as the average.

One such hunt I well remember at the outlet of St. Regis Pond. The morning mists had rolled away, and the King-fisher was busy near me, diving and chattering and eating his breakfast, while a great bald-headed eagle came swooping down in front of me to catch a fish. I was smoking my pipe to keep away the flies and mosquitos, and looking over Shakespeare's *As You Like It.* Fred was watching and scraping his throat as usual, smoking and chewing tobacco by turns. I imagined myself in the Forest of Arden. I was vain enough to personate the Duke, and generous enough to substitute Warner in place of the melancholy Jaques. I had arranged this hunt with the fine flourish of the speech :

Now, my co-mates, and brothers in exile,
Hath not old custom made this life more sweet
Than that of painted pomp? Are not these woods
More free from peril than the envious court?
  *   *   *   *   *   *   *
Sweet are the uses of adversity ;
Which, like a toad, ugly and venemous,
Wears yet a precious jewel in his head ;
And this our life, exempt from public haunt,
Finds tongues in trees, books in the running brooks,
Sermons in stones, and good in everything.
  *   *   *   *   *   *   *
Come, shall we go and kill us venison?

And yet it irks me, the poor dappled fools,—
Being native burghers of this desert city,—
Should in their own confines, with forked heads
Have their round haunches gor'd.

Jaques has gone apart in the sentimental mood
of a mere observer; and as the frightened herd
sweeps past him, he notices one poor creature, no
doubt a doe separated from her fawn and listening
for the dogs, standing at the stream weeping;
whereupon Jaques philosophises:

Poor deer, thou mak'st a testament
As worldlings do, giving the sum of more
To that which has too much.
'Tis right ; this misery doth part
The flux of company.
Sweep on, you fat and greasy citizens ;
'Tis just the fashion : Wherefore do you look
Upon that poor and broken bankrupt there?

After the hunt is over, and the buck is brought
in, Jaques is suddenly inspired with another feeling, asking like tender-hearted ladies still do after
every successful hunt:

Who is he that killed the deer?
1st. Lord.—Sir, it was I.
Jaques.—Let's present him to the Duke, like a Roman
conqueror ; and it would do well to set the deer's horns
upon his head for a branch of victory. Have you no song,
forester, for this purpose? Yes, sir. Sing it ; 'tis no
matter how it be in tune, so it make noise enough :

What shall he have that kill'd the deer?
His leather skin, and horns to wear.
　　Then sing him home :
Take thou no scorn, to wear the horn ;
It was a crest ere thou wast born, etc., etc.

Or, as Jaques-Warner puts it about his doe:
" The poor thing worked her way along painfully,
with sinking heart and unsteady limbs, spurred on
by the cry of the remorseless dogs, until, late in
the afternoon, she staggered down and stood upon
the shore of the lake. She plunged in. A boat
with two men in it pursues. She turns to the shore
where the dogs are lapping the water. And again
she makes for the centre of the lake. The brave,
pretty creature was quite exhausted now. She is
caught by the tail, and the guide shouts, ' Knock
her on the head.' The gentleman *was* a gentleman,
with a kind, smooth-shaven face, and might have
been a minister of some sort of everlasting gospel,
who took the paddle, but could not use it,—exclaiming, ' I can't do it ; let her go.' The guide's knife
was used without remonstrance ; and the gentleman
ate that night of the venison." Of the two accounts, I prefer Shakespeare's.

And now, far away in the direction of Osgood
and Mountain Pond, rifle shots are heard in quick
sharp succession ; and presently the inspiring music
of the ringing trumpet tones of the approaching
dogs. It was all as we liked it ; and the time for

action had come. Other guns, and the dogs nearer,
along the ridge of St. Regis. A crashing noise in
the thick undergrowth of young balsams and
spruces, and a Pegasus leaps out in the very poetry
of all graceful motion and spirit to gain the narrow
outlet, when our two guns suddenly stop all noise
and motion. A great fat buck, with beautiful antlers, lay prostrate in a thick bed of moss among the
bushes; and the dogs came in smiling and happy.
We were satisfied. It was the celebration of a
Roman victory on our way home that evening, especially as another boat followed in our wake from
another lake, having a dead doe and her live fawn
aboard. We had captured the whole family; and
our invalid friends could now share the spoils of
victory with us and the sacrificial feast for at least a
week. The noble antlers are hung up in the temple
of a cheerful Philadelphia home with other trophies
of the chase; but from which that one accomplished
son, whose this hunt was, has gone to the higher
pursuits of Paradise.

The hunt over, a fishing expedition is next in
order. It was in the last days of August, 1872,
after a steady rain of nearly two weeks. Hank
Tenk or Tank had just returned from Meacham
Lake with the welcome intelligence that the trout
were biting like fun on the Stillwater. The Tank
was rolling round Paul Smith's piazza more than
half full of whisky, with external indications of

27

having been in the mud; but it was yet capable of
a sound answer to my pointed interrogatories as to
the fact and its evidence. A merry twinkle of the
eyes cast a bright beam on the dark tide of tobacco-
juice rolling out of each side of the Tank's bung-
hole of a mouth, and the gurgling response came
forth : " Take my carcass for fish-bait, if I did'nt
see old Crandall stumpin' past our camp with a string
of fifty or sixty trout, each a pound and more in
weight, which he ketched on the Stillwater, yister-
day. I lost old Moscow, the best hound in these
woods, and had to look for him ; and when I got
home, the old woman twitched me round the house
with a broomstick, 'cause I come back with no
game, fish, dog and nothin."

Quietly communicating this information to my
friend H., of Providence, R. I., we soon made our
preparations and were on our way to the Stillwater, a dozen miles distant, early the next
morning. My good boy, Fred, had been brought
up at Meacham, and had frequently urged me
to go there and camp. He was now all smiles
and attention to business. Arrived at the bridge
which crosses the Meacham outlet, we were about
to joint our fly-rods for an experimental trial,
when the guides set up a derisive remonstrance to
this effect: " That the trout here could not be
caught in that way ; nobody had ever used flies
here before ; we must use tamarack poles and bait."

But we had no bait, and I ventured to catch a min-
now with my flies, when lo, a great rush of a half-
dozen fine large trout was made at the first cast.
That settled the question as to the mode of our
fishing. The guides stared in stupid wonder, but
said nothing. They had never seen anything of the
kind before on these waters. My cast consisted of
a brown hackle, a royal charlie, and a red ibis,—all
large flies on stout hooks, and new strong gut and
oiled silk line. On a dark day and in turbid water,
I hold with Charles Kingsley, that late lamented
prince of anglers and good fellows, that large flies
are the best. The larger the fly, the larger the
fish. When you see a small trout, hardly six inches
long, jump far out of water at a great dragon fly
or darning needle, or catch one of the same size
with three young mice in his stomach, or have a
rush made, in a turbulent pool below a waterfall, at
bass flies, it is useless to talk about gnats and other
small flies. Besides, a small hook will not hold a
large strong fish; and the mouth of a small trout
is large enough to take in a salmon fly itself. In
still, clear water small dark flies have the advantage
of not splashing and scaring the fish. But in rapids
or any troubled water, large flies are the most
easily seen and taken.

Satisfied with catch enough for supper and breakfast, we soon reached the Stillwater and floated
down the full rapid stream to our camping ground·

A deer is seen and captured on the way. Our
tent was pitched on a high bluff, in the midst of a
thick second growth of young spruces and balsams,
a wild, lonely place, fit haunt of wolf, wild-cat, bear
or panther. The camp-fire was kept blazing all
night to absorb some of the intense damp night-
chill. But the dreadful snores of some of the
party were more alarming than those which frightened Duncan's murderers, and louder than any
howl of wolf or scream of wild-cat and panther.
Nobody else could sleep. A bear's heavy tread
near us could not have been heard. No owl ventured to hoot. Providence was asleep, and Fred
was there in his native element.

At four o'clock the war-whoop was sounded, and
the camp was startled into yawning activity.
Breakfast was not long in preparation; and then a
careful, anxious scrutiny was made into the state
of the weather. Cloudy, warm, and the breeze
south-west. Perfect. Providence went down the
stream; I went up to the meeting of the waters,
where good signs appeared the evening before.
About eight o'clock I began operations, at a deep
pool under a bank overgrown with dense alder-
bushes, and at the outlet of a mountain brook
joining the main stream. For three hours the
work, rather than sport, went on to the detriment
of three rods and a pair of worn-out arms. Always
one, sometimes two, and occasionally three great

trout at a cast, until the boat was full. At eleven
o'clock we dropped down the stream to a little
spring rivulet for repairs, rest, lunch, and to dress
our fish. All this done, signs and sounds of a
thunder-storm admonished us to make our way to
camp as soon as possible. It burst upon us on the
way, and was nearly over when we reached the
landing at the foot of the bluff on which our tent
was pitched. Providence and myself both tried
the experiment of fishing, when " the lightnings
shone upon the ground, and the earth was moved,
and shook withal; " and at the first terrific outburst of the storm, not a fish rose to the flies; but
after a few moments, while the thunder and lightning were still shaking the earth, a few of the
bolder sort readily rose and were captured. This
settled another vexed question about angling in a
thunder-storm; and our conclusion was, that after
the first scare is over, trout will come to the flies
just as readily then as at any other time. At least,
so we found it on this occasion. Providence came
into camp with his boat just as full of trout as
mine was, caught, as they were, two and three at a
cast. We had a jollification that night; and louder
snores succeeded shouts of laughter and snatches
of old songs.

Our ambition was more than satisfied. We
broke camp next morning and started for Paul
Smith's. Our trout were strung upon green withes,

27*

twenty-five each: and these withes were hung over
a long, stout pole, after the manner of the great
grape-clusters of Eschol: and two men, now as then,
bore it in triumph through the woods to our team
in waiting at the bridge. Our teamster, Theodore,
when he saw the men approaching, stood up on
tiptoe, with bulging eyes and open mouth, exclaiming: " Golly, what a lot o' suckers! " But when
the trout were laid in the wagon, he changed his
tune and asked where this new fishing place was.
After giving away about sixty fine trout to some
of the Meacham guides for their families, we carried
away *one hundred and twenty pounds* of the most
beautiful and uniformly sized trout it has ever been
my privilege to see together, and laid them on the
grass in front of the St. Regis Lake House. Of
course, there was a commotion. The guests gathered round with surprise and congratulations; the
guides looked for marks of the gill-net in vain.
The fame of this unusual catch spread over the
whole region, and is still spoken of as the best of
recent years. Under the same unusual combination of favorable circumstances, I am inclined to
think it could be repeated, but not otherwise. I
have repeatedly tried it since, when the water was
low and the season dry and warm, and considered
myself fortunate if I could catch enough trout to
supply a small camp. My Providence friend, being
a collector of all American poetry that has ever

been written, as well as a collector of fine engrav-
ings and rare books, is surely entitled to the following effusion, recently discovered in manuscript
among the papers of the Saranac Colony of Exiles,
the authorship being, like that of this ended Winter's Tale, anonymous.

ADIRONDACK CAMP-SONG.

A life in the woods for me,
　A camp by the crystal stream,
Where all is fresh and free,
　And pure as a maiden's dream ;
Where the birds their revels keep,
　And the deer go bounding by ;
Where the night-breeze rocks to sleep,
　With its sweetest lullaby.

The morning is good for sport,
　Then, up, boys, and away,
The beauties shy to court,
　And catch them, if we may ;
They heed not the thunder's roar,
　They lie in the deep, dark pool ;
And, like rainbows, leap and soar
　Through the sparkling waters cool.

"Come, tell me, Angler Bill,
　Where I shall cast a fly ;
How I my creel may fill,
　And yet keep nice and dry ;"
Then Bill, with a quiet smile,
　My feet on a boulder set,
But I was caught the while,
　And landed dripping wet.

ERRATA.

On p. 58, line 6, for "truthful," read "truthfully."
On p. 141, line 20, strike out the word "dollars."
On p. 145, line 1, for "largest," read "largess of."
On p. 218, line 5, for "sounds," read "sound."
On p. 290, line 15, for "Epictelus," read "Epictetus."

www.ingramcontent.com/pod-product-compliance
Lightning Source LLC
Chambersburg PA
CBHW060519030726

47498CB00004B/1001